Questions piled up inside her mind faster than she could process them

What would it be like to see Ronan naked? To have his bare skin against her own?

"Cassie, sweetheart." Ronan's voice was a ragged plea. "You have to stop thinking whatever it is you're thinking, because otherwise I won't be held responsible for my actions." He sucked in a breath. "I'm trying so hard to do the right thing here."

Surely the right thing couldn't be denying this energy that thrummed between them, the desperation to hold him again that seemed to pour from her every nerve. Even if it was the very last thing in the world she should be thinking, let alone doing. He was exactly the wrong kind of man for her. She wanted safe, he offered reckless. She wanted stable and settled, he traveled the world for his work, no doubt had a girl in every port.

And yet...

Dear Reader,

While unlike Cassie, I'm not afraid of flying, I am very familiar with frequent travel for business. I've always entertained a fantasy that one day, I'd board a plane and sitting next to me would be Bradley Cooper or Alex O'Loughlin. (I seem to conveniently forget those guys aren't likely to fly coach!) I have a definite weakness for broad-shouldered men in crisply tailored suits, white shirts and silk ties. Especially when they're a little crumpled after a day's work. Unfortunately, also unlike Cassie, I've yet to find a consultant quite like Ronan on one of my plane trips.

While Cassie might be about to go through the audit/job interview from hell, at least the scenery's good! And like many people who've experienced this kind of review, for Cassie it turns out to be a watershed moment, a critical turning point for her to review her life and reassess what she wants from it. It's a big upheaval for her, because the one thing she's not good at is *change*. But she's boarded the ride now—it's too late to turn back.

Writing Cassie and Ronan's story was a roller-coaster ride for me, just like the Scenic Railway they ride at Luna Park—although with perhaps more extreme highs and lows. Thankfully the ride ended with the greatest high of all: this, my first published book. There are lots of people who went along with me for the ride—too many to thank individually. I just hope they're not too worn-out from all the squealing!

I'd love to hear from you. Visit me at www.emmiedark.com.

Cheers,

Emmie Dark

Cassie's Grand Plan
Emmie Dark

TORONTO NEW YORK LONDON
AMSTERDAM PARIS SYDNEY HAMBURG
STOCKHOLM ATHENS TOKYO MILAN MADRID
PRAGUE WARSAW BUDAPEST AUCKLAND

Recycling programs
for this product may
not exist in your area.

ISBN-13: 978-0-373-71769-9

CASSIE'S GRAND PLAN

This edition published by arrangement with Harlequin Books S.A.

For questions and comments about the quality of this book
please contact us at Customer_eCare@Harlequin.ca.

® and TM are trademarks of the publisher. Trademarks indicated with
® are registered in the United States Patent and Trademark Office, the
Canadian Trade Marks Office and in other countries.

www.Harlequin.com

Printed in U.S.A.

ABOUT THE AUTHOR

After years of writing press releases, employee news-letters and speeches for CEOs and politicians—none of which included any kind of kissing—Emmie Dark finally took to her laptop to write what she wanted to write. She was both amazed and delighted to discover that what came out were sexy, noble heroes who found themselves crossing paths with strong, but perhaps slightly damaged, heroines. And plenty of kissing.

Emmie lives in Melbourne, Australia, and she likes red lipstick, chardonnay, sunshine, driving fast, rose-scented soap and a really good cup of tea.

For my sister, Georgina.

CHAPTER ONE

SWEAT PRICKLED THE BACK of his neck. It was too hot for a suit, but professional pride insisted he drag his Hugo Boss jacket from the backseat and shrug it on anyway.

Funny, he hadn't thought he had any pride left.

Ronan Conroy surveyed the scene from inside the car a bit longer, delaying the moment he'd need to turn off the engine and lose the blast of cool air from the vents—little as it was doing to assuage the heat.

Two women stood outside the Country Style furniture warehouse in the grimy, industrial outskirts of Melbourne. Heat shimmered in air that smelled of dust and smoke, perceptible even inside the car. Concrete buildings and asphalt roads only magnified the temperature. It was hot as hell and that was probably fitting—this was, after all, supposed to be a punishment.

The women were talking animatedly. Stacks of furniture—chairs, tables, cabinets, bed frames—were haphazardly arranged around them. Guys dripping sweat emerged from inside the warehouse, grabbed an item and disappeared back into the darkness with it.

As jet lag pulled at his eyelids, Ronan watched the women continue to talk, each of them occasionally pointing at a clipboard one of them was holding.

The one closest to where Ronan had parked was

short, blonde and dressed in a light green skirt and matching short-sleeved suit jacket. Her hair was cut in a neat bob, shiny and precise. Even from a distance he could see her lips were outlined in bright lipstick.

The other was taller. She wore dark trousers and a pale blue shirt with the Country Style logo emblazoned over one breast, the sleeves rolled up. A streak of dust marred one pant leg, and her cheeks were flushed. But her hair…long, dark, wavy. It was barely constrained by a clip at her nape and hung down to midway between her shoulder blades. As he watched, she tucked a stray lock behind one ear. If that beautiful mane was out, allowed free, it would swing forward, over her shoulders. Would it cover her breasts? Maybe. Maybe not quite. Maybe just—

Ronan gave himself a mental shake. It was just this sort of thing that had got him into trouble before.

It was why he was here, on the other side of the world, while his disapproving father was back in San Francisco waiting to see if he could prove himself. Again.

He grabbed his briefcase and turned off the engine, stepping out of the car. This one was going to be strictly business. There was too much riding on it for it to be anything but. His chance to finally prove that he was good enough for the partnership in Conroy Corporation that should have been his long ago—even if it was by completing a job that barely matched his skill level. It was going to be a walk in the park.

He'd been sent here to work with Cassidy Hartman, the head of operations for Country Style. He straightened his shoulders and headed toward the women. He'd bet she was the one in the suit.

CASSIE NOTICED SOMEONE approaching out of the corner of her eye, but she was too absorbed by the figures on her assistant's clipboard to pay much attention. The delivery was short—*very* short—and they were going to have a problem meeting customer orders, never mind having floor stock for display in the fifty-seven Country Style stores around Australia. The tedious task ahead of them now was to match the consignment note with every item that had been delivered and then she'd be on the phone to the manufacturer, making her displeasure clear. This was the third time this company had short-delivered and Cassie's patience was running out.

"I'm not standing for this, Mel," Cassie said, one hand going back to play with her hastily gathered-up ponytail. Her other hand grasped her paper coffee cup dangerously tightly.

"I know, I know," Melanie said soothingly. "They've tried this on us before. But don't worry, we'll get on to it and it will be sorted."

"As if we didn't have enough to deal with today," Cassie said under her breath. Being caught in the middle of an argument with a supplier was the last thing she needed.

A surprise phone call from her boss the previous afternoon had informed her that some high-flying international business analyst would be arriving this morning to begin a review of the entirety of Country

Style's operations. Graham Taylor, the owner of Country Style, hadn't needed to spell out that Cassie's own performance was what was really under the microscope here.

Cassie checked her watch. It was only just before eight, so she figured she had at least another hour or so to prepare. She did a mental run-through of her to-do list, checking off priorities on her fingers. "I still have to confirm the travel arrangements for the store visits, finalize the contracts for the new ad campaign and iron out the problems with the signage on the new Hawthorn store before the opening next Monday."

"I know," Melanie repeated sympathetically. "I'll deal with this and I can work on the travel stuff. You just focus on Hawthorn and do what you need to do."

Cassie was grateful for her assistant's encouraging smile and composed demeanor. Normally a very cool, calm and collected businesswoman herself, today's inspection had Cassie feeling jittery, doubting herself and her management abilities. She'd barely slept last night after staying up late to prepare herself for the inquisition. She'd worked through every possible scenario, rehearsing her responses to any question she could think of. It hadn't helped. Now she was just nervous *and* sleep deprived. She took a long sip of her coffee, hoping that the caffeine would give her a jolt, get her back to her normal, take-charge self.

Still caught up in self-analysis, Cassie was just taking another sip of coffee when a tall, suited man suddenly appeared next to them, making her gasp in shock.

He held his hand out to Melanie.

"Hello, you must be Cassidy Hartman." Smiling broadly, his American accent rang out as if someone had just turned on a TV. "I'm Ronan C—McGuire from the Conroy Corporation. I understand Graham called to let you know to expect me."

Cassie's world slowed for a moment.

This was the pencil-pushing number-cruncher Graham had sent to check up on her?

But there wasn't a bow tie, pocket protector or pair of horn-rimmed glasses in sight. Instead, everything about this man screamed money and sophistication, from the tailored shoulders of his fine wool suit all the way down to the shiny, no doubt Italian, leather lace-ups. His dark hair was artfully tousled, just enough to look as though care had been taken, but not so much that it would look fussy.

If this *was* a sitcom, then the star had just walked in—straight out of central casting, with "tall, dark and handsome" written in script under his name. Cassie half expected to hear whoops and mad applause in the background.

Melanie, flustered, looked from the man who held his hand out toward her to Cassie and back again, her pretty face creased with confusion and anxiety.

Cassie, for her part, remembered to breathe at the same time as she also remembered to swallow her mouthful of lukewarm coffee. Bad idea.

Choking and spluttering, she struggled to draw breath.

"Um, I'm..." Melanie stuttered, clearly unsure

whether to introduce herself, deal with Cassie's coughing fit, or maybe just run away.

Ronan looked over at Cassie and patted her on the back firmly a few times. "Are you okay?"

His eyes sent a ribbon of heat through her that had nothing to do with the oppressive northerly wind whipping around them. Blue. Perfect reflections of the summer sky above them. Sultry and flirtatious, his gaze made Cassie's heart skip, even as she tried to swallow and breathe normally.

She fought to restore her composure. "I'm fine," she said hoarsely. She blinked back the tears threatening to stream down her cheeks from the coughing fit.

"Good." Ronan nodded and turned back to Melanie. "So, Ms. Hartman, I know Graham probably told you to expect me at nine, but I like to arrive a little early so we have a chance to get to know—"

Finally Melanie recovered enough to speak. "Sorry, but my name's Melanie. Cassie is—"

"I'm Cassidy Hartman." Cassie drew herself up straight and held out her hand. She knew her face was red and not just from the coughing. This was Graham's consultant, and he'd mistaken Melanie for her. Who could blame him? She was filthy from crawling through the recently arrived stock trying to do a rough estimate on quantities. She'd barely slept so she knew her eyes were baggy and her hair was in its usual messy ponytail. Whereas Melanie—well, she was Melanie. Cool, crisp and utterly perfect.

The mistake was understandable, but no less embarrassing. And, much as she didn't want to admit it, it hurt. Part Two of her recently drawn up Plan-with-a-capital-*P* was all about making sure this kind of misunderstanding didn't happen, but she had to get Part One bedded down first—and that meant making her position at Country Style rock solid. She just hadn't considered that the report she'd spent her nights and weekends researching and writing would prompt her boss to call in professional analysts instead of simply granting her the CEO position as she'd recommended.

The smarmy-but-gorgeous Ronan turned to Cassie and gave a slight bow, extending his hand to grasp hers. His eyes flashed with a moment of regret at his misstep, but he covered it quickly. "My apologies, ma'am." He cocked his head to one side as she stifled another cough. "I admire your new caffeine delivery system, but perhaps it still needs some work?"

Cassie had been about to apologize for her appearance, explain about the short-delivered order, but his condescending expression stopped her in her tracks. She wanted more than anything to slap that grin off his face and send him packing back to his big glass office in America. Instead, she forced herself to smile, as much to stop herself insulting him out loud as anything else.

She shook his hand and released it quickly when a jolt ran through her body, as if she were holding hands with the devil.

"Can I get you a coffee, Mr.…uh," Melanie stuttered.

Cassie looked over at Melanie and was surprised to find her unflappable assistant looking at a loss.

He hesitated just a split second before answering smoothly. "Mr. McGuire," he reminded her, "but please, call me Ronan. And I'd love a coffee. Black, no sugar— I'm sweet enough," he added with a wink and Cassie was staggered by Melanie's response. She gave a shy giggle and a telltale blush marched across her face. Melanie was the target of flirting from just about every man she met. This was the first time Cassie had ever seen it *work*.

She guessed any woman would fall weak at the knees faced with this perfect specimen of the male sex. Objectively, Cassie could see why. He wasn't her type, though. Too polished. Too worldly. Too good-looking. Too overwhelming. It'd be too easy to lose yourself— lose control—with someone like him. It wasn't something she would ever allow to happen.

Besides which, it was pointless even thinking those kinds of thoughts. He was here to assess her performance—at work, not in the bedroom. Thank goodness. At least at work Cassie knew what she was doing.

Well, she'd thought she did up until Graham had called for this review.

Her stomach twisted into ever-tighter knots.

"Sure, *Ronan*." Melanie lowered her voice to say his name, as if it were sacred. Her eyes didn't leave the man's face as she asked, "Cassie, can I get you another one?"

Cassie could only nod, even as the coffee she'd already consumed that morning curdled in her belly. She figured she was going to need every bit of help she could muster to get through this day and more caffeine was a good start.

The fragile balloon of self-confidence she'd tried to pump up last night was rapidly deflating. In all the scenarios she'd pictured, she'd been imagining herself answering to a bow tie–wearing nerd. She honestly had been expecting some gray-haired, button-down bore. Not the kind of man who'd make most women think of beds instead of budgets. Of sex instead of stock levels.

And she'd expected to have more time to prepare. Not get caught out in the middle of a delivery blunder, dusty and hot and annoyed. She swallowed again, resisting her tickly throat that still urged her to cough.

"I'll be back in a moment." Melanie seemed to have recovered from her little swoon and was back to her normal efficient self. "I've set up the conference room for you both. All the documents you requested are in there, Cassie, and I even found an adaptor so you can plug your laptop in, too, Ronan." Again, that sexy tone when she said his name.

"Why, thank you, Melanie."

No. Oh, God. Had he winked *again*?

When he turned back to Cassie, his face was all business. Cassie refused to feel disappointed. "After you, ma'am."

Without another word, Cassie led him into the warehouse and through the side doorway that led into the office area and the conference room.

"Conference room" was a grand title for the space that they used for staff meetings and big client pitches, but it was the most presentable part of the building. It had also allowed Cassie to exercise her passion for interior design—a passion that had played no small part in her success. Predicting trends and designing merchandising schemes were her favorite parts of the job.

Cassie had furnished the space as if it were a provincial dining room; instead of the typical imposing boardroom table surrounded by black leather swivel chairs, she'd brought in a large, whitewashed-timber dining table, plush dining chairs and a kitchen sideboard for storage. Audiovisual equipment was stored away in a large wooden trunk and dresser, while a kitchenette gave the impression of a family space ready to prepare an evening meal. The view of the loading dock from the window was the only thing that broke the illusion that the visitor had stepped into a country home.

It was one of Cassie's favorite hideaways and she managed to take her first deep breath of the morning as she walked in. A measure of calm settled over her jangled nerves. Whether it was the fact that she had designed it herself, or that it was just the kind of room she dreamed of having in her own home one day, she didn't know. She just knew that on those frequent late nights at work, she often left her office and came in here to soak up the comfort the room offered. Then she could pretend that she was finishing up her work at home, her family tucked up safe in bed, a lovely, soft, gentle man offering her a nightcap.

Soft and gentle was what she wanted, not sculpted and swoon worthy, she reminded herself as she took another sideways glance at Ronan McGuire. He was looking at her, an openly appraising expression on his face. Cassie swallowed hard. If she didn't know better, she'd think he liked what he saw.

She quickly looked away. "We're all set up in here," she said needlessly, gesturing to the table.

"Interesting choice of furnishings, ma'am," he said as he pulled out a chair and opened his briefcase. A hint of Southern twang to his accent stopped his "ma'am" from being smarmy—but only just. Cassie wanted to say something witty and cutting, but reminded herself of what was at risk. Besides, witty and cutting— especially in front of a hot guy who had apparently just been checking her out—had never been her forte.

Cassie sucked in another deep breath before answering. "It's used for commercial clients and supplier meetings," she said crisply. "It allows us to show off the Country Style look and range. Why should we buy boring gray office furniture when we have these beautiful pieces at our fingertips?"

She could hear the defensiveness in her own voice and scolded herself. It was crucial to get control of her nerves! If she was going to gain this guy's confidence and win him over to the idea of her as CEO of Country Style, sounding bitter and defensive wasn't the way to go about it. She had to sound like a leader. Calm. Absolutely in control.

"I understand why you'd use your own furniture range, ma'am," he said, his tone betraying no hint of a reaction to her aggression. "Makes perfect sense."

Cassie's frayed nerves shredded. "Stop calling me 'ma'am'!" Oops. She was pretty sure snapping at him didn't count as either calm or controlled.

"Okay, I just—"

"I'm not a ma'am, I'm a miss. But don't call me that, either," Cassie added, flustered. How had she managed to get off on the wrong foot so quickly? She sucked in a breath and let it out slowly before continuing. "I don't know if it's different in America, but in Australia we're quite informal, even in business. So Cassie will do. Just plain Cassie."

Those sky-blue eyes of his swept over her, and the hardness melted away, just for a moment. A lazy seductiveness took over as his eyes did a slow sweep of her body. "Oh, I don't think there's anything plain about you, Cassie Hartman." One corner of his mouth crooked up in a ghost of a smile before his eyes shuttered with the professional reserve she'd noticed earlier. "Now, shall we get to work?"

Cassie felt her stomach clench, not sure if she was furious, pleased or simply confused by his approach. Perhaps this was what he did—he got people unsettled, all the better to manipulate them so he could find what he wanted.

All she knew was that she had to be on her guard every moment he was around.

He got under her skin.

CHAPTER TWO

CASSIE WAS BARELY AWARE of the time passing until Melanie knocked on the door and walked in, interrupting them with lunch.

After that initial flirty comment, something in Ronan McGuire's demeanor seemed to change, as though he'd flicked a switch, and from then on it had been strictly business. He delved straight into the work in front of them, polite, friendly, but entirely business-like. It was as if the spreadsheets in front of him called to him like sirens, more attractive than any real woman. Especially plain old Cassie.

Which was fine by her. It was a relief, actually. Gave her time to pull herself together after the deep unease she'd felt at his arrival. It wasn't just nerves about the ordeal ahead of her—something about him resonated deep within her. Was it his eyes? His accent? His smell? She put it down to the potential impact he could have on her life and tried to remember her little internal pep talk. *Behave like a true leader. Calm. In control.*

Once they got down to business, things were easier. When she was talking about Country Style, Cassie was in her element, and her agitation slipped away. Country Style was her baby, her home, her life. She loved her work; it was the only place that had offered her stability, security and a chance to prove herself. As she'd worked these past weeks on her proposal for Graham, she'd felt a new sense of motivation, imagined a new picture of what her life might be like. Shoring up her job at Country Style was Part One of her Plan-with-a-capital-*P*.

The idea that Graham might not simply rubber-stamp her pitch to become CEO had never occurred to her. Pretty much every success Country Style had had over the past four years had been her doing. Graham had moved on to his next business endeavor—another chain of retail stores, this time selling luggage—and left Cassie more or less in charge, in action if not in title. She'd worked so hard for him. And the reward was the job interview from hell.

Clearly she'd overestimated his trust in her. Perhaps because he was the nearest thing she had to a father, she'd taken for granted that he'd be as eager for her to succeed as she was herself. Instead, Graham had shown her that despite their relationship, his primary concern had to be his company. *Nothing personal,* he'd said. They might be close, Cassie told herself, but when it came down to it, business was always going to be business for Graham. She knew that. It shouldn't have been a surprise.

She turned her attention back to the man in front of her. They'd spent the morning combing through Country Style's financial reports, Cassie explaining her decisions and pointing out particular gains and losses. She was proud of her truthful, matter-of-fact answers and thought she'd shown just the right amount of passion and enthusiasm for the business.

For his part, Ronan McGuire asked pertinent questions that evidenced his knowledge of budgeting and management. To the point that she had to grudgingly admit his input and advice might just be very useful for planning the business's future success.

His insightful questions had prompted new ideas, and she'd taken pages of notes. Even in just a few hours, he'd brought fresh thinking and original concepts to her future plans for running Country Style.

It was both depressing and exhilarating, Cassie thought, watching as Ronan politely—but still somehow flirtatiously—accepted a sandwich and coffee from Melanie.

Exhilarating because she could see how all the ideas could be implemented to create a dramatically better business.

Depressing because she hadn't thought of them herself.

Perhaps Graham was right to doubt her management abilities.

"Thank you, Miss Mel," Ronan drawled, bringing Cassie out of her reflection. He was so confident, she thought, so arrogant and sure of himself. But perhaps she was just seeing things that way because she was suddenly feeling so very *un*sure of herself.

"Thank you, Mel," Cassie said. She wasn't thrilled to see that Ronan's thanks had elicited yet another little giggle and a blush, while Melanie barely acknowledged Cassie's words. And she absolutely was *not* jealous of the low, sexy tone Ronan used when talking to her assistant rather than the practical, no-nonsense tone he used with her. Men didn't talk to her that way—they never had—and she couldn't miss what she'd never had, could she?

"Is there anything else you need, Mr. McGuire?" Mel asked.

Before Ronan could say anything—like encourage Melanie to use his first name again in that breathy Marilyn Monroe voice she seemed to have suddenly developed—Cassie interrupted. "Mel, could you please bring in the schedule for the site visits? Including the travel arrangements?" After Graham's call yesterday, Cassie had immediately started work preparing a tour of the largest and most successful Country Style stores across Australia. She figured it was the best way to show off her success. Spreadsheets were all well and good, but nothing beat seeing the real thing in person.

"No worries. And just so you know, Cassie, I've cleared up the signage issues for the Hawthorn opening. The sign writers are redoing the car-park notices and the painters will be in later today to fix up the front fascia."

"Thanks, Mel, that's great news." Cassie breathed a sigh of relief. She couldn't believe it, but for the whole morning she'd not once given a thought to the store opening that had dominated her workload for the past several weeks. Thank goodness Melanie was still on the ball. Cassie had opened new stores before—dozens of them—but this would be the largest store in the Country Style group. Located in one of Melbourne's most affluent suburbs, it was going to be a showcase of Country Style design and flair. With only a week to go until the opening, the major work was done—stock ordered, staff hired, store layout confirmed—it was all the little details that now needed attending to.

Melanie vanished out the door, but not before bestowing a hundred-watt smile on Ronan.

"Hawthorn signage?" Ronan asked.

"We have a new store opening next Monday," Cassie explained.

"Ah." He pushed the plate of sandwiches toward Cassie. "Melanie seems very efficient," he said.

"She's great, very organized and resourceful," Cassie said, reaching for a salad sandwich triangle. "She's been with us for almost five years now, and is a very important member of our team."

He gave Cassie a considered look. "And how long have you been with the company?"

"Eleven years," she replied, even though she was sure he already knew the answer. It was impossible someone as obviously prepared as he was wouldn't have scoped her out—although she was reasonably sure his background check would start and finish with her career. Maybe, if he dug deep enough, he might find out about her family and what had happened to her parents—that was a matter of public record. But that would be it. No one knew *how* she'd come to join the company when she was seventeen except Graham, and he'd given her his word of honor that he'd never tell. She didn't always trust Graham—and Ronan's presence was clear evidence as to why—but on that one topic he'd never given her cause to doubt him.

Her career with Country Style since then, on the other hand, was likely to have been an open book to Ronan McGuire, especially the last four years she'd spent as operations manager and second in charge to Graham. He probably knew what she had for breakfast, Cassie thought grimly. The answer of course was nothing, and remembering that, she took a bite of her sandwich.

"That's a long time to be with one organization," he commented, one eyebrow raised in a way that caused a corresponding spike in Cassie's blood pressure—much as she tried to ignore it. "Especially these days."

Cassie chewed and swallowed. "How long have you been with the Conroy Corporation?" she asked, keen to dodge the spotlight while she considered how to respond. She wasn't sure if he was trying to gauge her passion for the business or hinting that she had limited herself by not broadening her experience. Cassie had the strong feeling that every question he asked had an ulterior motive, no matter how innocent it might seem on the surface.

One side of his mouth cocked up in a crooked smile. "Ah, you have me there. I joined the company right after college and I'm about to become a partner." His eyes grew harder with something Cassie couldn't quite identify and she wondered why. Shouldn't he be proud? The emotion, whatever it was, was gone again in a flash.

"Where are you based?" she asked.

"San Francisco," he replied in clipped tones, letting her know that the subject was effectively closed. "So, what's kept you at Country Style for eleven years?"

He was persistent, she'd give him that. "I love it here," she said simply. It was far, far more than that, but there was no way she was going into it all with a stranger.

Besides, it was none of his business.

"You've arranged a site tour?" he asked, pointing at the documents Mel had left behind, and Cassie was thankful he changed the subject back to the matter at hand.

He took a large bite of his sandwich and chewed without breaking their shared gaze. For some reason, watching his jaw move was incredibly distracting. It started Cassie thinking about his mouth, his lips and then his tongue; she hurriedly looked down and took another bite of her own sandwich before he could read the blush she knew was stealing across her face.

What on earth was wrong with her? Thinking about this man as anything other than her judge and jury— her potential executioner—was a recipe for disaster. Developing a crush on him was the stupidest idea from Stupidtown. Cassie had to stay on guard. Besides, anything like those belonged to Part Three of the Plan, and she was a long way from that.

The Plan-with-a-capital-*P* was simple enough. She'd come up with it when she'd found herself at home, alone, on New Year's Eve. Sitting there by herself had felt as if the rest of the world had learned some lesson that she'd somehow skipped. How could she have got to twenty-eight years old and have such a narrow life? All she did was work, eat and sleep. She was friendly with people from work, but rarely socialized. And when everyone else was occupied with their family, or away with their real friends, Cassie was by herself. Suddenly feeling very alone.

Clearly, something needed to be done, and for that she needed a plan.

Part One—secure her future with Country Style. That was most important. It was her life, her home, her family. Her foundation in the world. It came first. That's why she'd spent two weeks researching and writing a report for Graham—analyzing the marketplace, proposing expansion options, showing him how much she cared for this company and what she could do for it—if he'd just give her the chance. It was exciting—Cassie felt a thrill of anticipation whenever she thought about the business's future with her leading it—but it was only Part One. When Ronan's analysis ratified her proposal to become CEO, and Graham adopted it, she'd be able to relax. She'd be able to take her eye off the ball just for a moment, and get some other areas of her life sorted out.

Part Two was to do something about herself—address her admittedly plain appearance. She'd planned to call on Mel's help for that. Some new clothes, maybe a new haircut. Perhaps learn how to use eyeliner so she didn't end up looking like a panda. Nothing too dramatic—this wasn't *Pygmalion*—but just make the best of what she had. She knew she was okay looking, and if she could learn to tame her unruly locks, her hair could become an asset instead of a nuisance. Her hour-glass figure wasn't what most fashion designers had in mind when they made clothes, it seemed, but she'd put a little money aside and that could be used to buy some new clothes that flattered—instead of swamped—her curves.

Part Three was to get herself a love life—see if she could meet a guy who would finally be The One. She wasn't entirely sure how to go about that as yet, but she did have a reasonably good picture of what The One looked like for her. Not in terms of looks—that wasn't so important. But he'd be the kind of guy who'd support her career. The kind of guy who took out the rubbish without being asked. Most important, the kind of guy who'd make her feel safe.

Part Four—well, Part Four of the plan was still murky. But basically it was take Parts One, Two and Three, mix well, and hopefully create a family. A nice, neat little family of her own—they would always be there for her, and she'd always be there for them.

A nice home, a caring partner, a rewarding job and a couple of kids.

Was it really too much to ask?

Cassie didn't think so.

But right now, Part One had to be her focus. She shouldn't be sitting here dreaming about Part Three, let alone Part Four.

Not to mention the fact that Ronan McGuire was absolutely the last person for her, regardless of how arousing she found his sandwich eating. She needed someone soft and gentle. Someone who made her feel secure in herself, not poised on a knife-edge the way she'd felt ever since he'd turned up.

Suddenly the tour of stores she'd arranged seemed like a special kind of torture. Cassie was signing herself up to spend almost a week in close quarters with a man who made her all kinds of hot and bothered. A man who reminded her of physical reactions she had gone a long time without. A man who at the same time threatened the very foundations of her life's work.

"So, are you going to share the details with me or is it a surprise? A magical mystery tour?"

His mocking tone made Cassie wonder if he had somehow read her mind.

What had they been talking about again? Oh, yeah, the site tour. She took a deep breath to lend strength to her voice. "I thought the best way for you to get a handle on the scope of the business would be to visit some of our stores. You can meet our staff, look at the merchandising and the layout and get a better understanding of our customer base."

He nodded. "Sounds like a good idea."

Melanie returned and placed a small pile of documents in front of Cassie. She tucked her hair behind her ear as she leaned low over the table. Subtle as a brick. Cassie could just imagine the view Ronan had down Melanie's silk blouse.

"If you'd like, Cassie," Melanie purred, "I can take you and Ronan through this, explain how I've organized the flights and—"

"Thanks, Mel, but I'm pretty sure I've got it," Cassie interrupted, giving Melanie a firm smile that clearly communicated "go away." Melanie's foolish and obvious flirting was just the push Cassie needed to get serious.

All the thoughts that had kept her awake the night before flooded back as Mel gave another flirty smile and flounced from the room.

Despite the loyalty Cassie had shown, Graham was a businessman and his decisions were always impersonal when it came to making money. Cassie knew she'd worked hard, she knew that Conroy Corporation would find no evidence of mismanagement or incompetence in her record. But Ronan was right—she'd never been employed anywhere else. What if putting her in charge cost Country Style the opportunity to grow? What if that was more important to Graham than the loyalty she'd shown him for eleven years?

What if Graham decided it was in *her* best interests to move on? What if he asked her to leave?

Cassie could have sworn the ground shifted underfoot at the very thought. In reality she knew it wasn't an earthquake, just her own hard-earned sense of security being shaken, but her stomach swooped anyway.

It would be the end of her dreams of becoming CEO and Part One of her plan would come crashing down around her head.

Really, it meant the end of everything—because, quite frankly, what else did she have?

"Flights? So we'll be going further afield than Melbourne?" Ronan asked, bringing Cassie back to the issue at hand. Site visits.

She willed her voice to come out steady. "Yes. Although our headquarters is based here, we actually have more stores in New South Wales right now. And Fremantle is one of our newest stores—we've been able to benefit from the real estate peak in Western Australia, and business there is booming," Cassie explained.

"Western Australia," he mused, "isn't that on the other side of the country?"

"Yes, but it only takes four hours to fly there." Cassie pointed at the documents, where their flight schedules were detailed. "Graham said you'd be here for a week, so I thought this would be the best approach. You'll get to see our stores in operation, and still be back here for the opening next Monday. Traveling will take up quite a bit of time, but you can read the reports and go over our financials during the flights. I think it will be worth the investment—there's no better way to understand the business."

"And what if I have questions I need to ask you?"

Cassie was confused by the question for a moment, but then she realized he didn't understand. "Then you can ask them. I'm coming with you."

He straightened in his chair and another of those hard, emotionless looks that Cassie couldn't quite identify came into his eyes.

"Thanks, but that won't be necessary." In contrast to the pleasant, if occasionally condescending, manner he'd been using all morning, his tone was cold. "I don't need to talk to you in detail again until next week. I prefer to work alone."

No, sir, Cassie thought. No way was she letting the

man who'd be deciding her future out of her sight for a minute.

Except for maybe when he slept.

And then her brain supplied an image of Ronan McGuire lying in bed, a crisp white sheet gathered at his waist, his chest bare and those dark eyelashes fanned on his cheeks.

Was the air conditioning working?

Get a grip! Cassie scolded herself. *What happened to getting serious?*

She straightened her shoulders and screwed up her courage. Her entire life was riding on these next few days and she was going to do everything in her power to get the outcome she wanted.

"I'm afraid that's nonnegotiable, Mr. McGuire," she said, pleased with the firm tone of her voice. "I can't allow you free rein of our stores without supervision. You understand—I have to prioritize customer service and operations above the needs of Graham's *little investigation.*" Did she sound bitter? Cassie inwardly winced. Yes, probably, but then it didn't hurt for this guy to understand the relative importance of this exercise. They might be deciding the company's future— Cassie's future—but on a day-to-day level, customers still had to be served, furniture still had to be sold, operations still had to continue. Otherwise there'd be no future to plan for.

"But shouldn't you be around to manage the store opening?" he tried again.

Yes, she should, but Cassie wasn't about to admit that she wasn't capable of being a retail superwoman.

She gave what she hoped looked like a carefree shrug when in reality her mind was filled with a list of the seemingly unending tasks that had to be completed between now and next Monday. "It's mostly all bedded down now. I can handle any last-minute things from the road. Our flight leaves Wednesday, *tomorrow,* for Perth. We'll stay overnight and then catch an early flight to Sydney on Thursday. We'll spend two nights in Sydney and come back to Melbourne on Saturday morning. Monday is a soft opening for the store—the advertising and marketing doesn't start until later in the week with the official grand opening on Saturday."

He gave her a considered look and nodded. "So there's the weekend to finalize things, too, if need be."

"Exactly."

He studied her for a while, his eyes searching her face, and Cassie steeled herself not to look away. Eventually his mouth curved into an almost smile and his eyes softened. With a nod of his head, he let Cassie know she'd won. This round.

"Of course," he said.

"I assure you, we will make our visits as effective and efficient as possible."

"Effective and efficient works for me." That teasing tone was back. If she hadn't just spent the morning with him, going through the financials, and seen his expertise firsthand, she'd wonder if the man ever took anything seriously.

"We have the rest of today here, then we leave first thing in the morning for Perth. It's an early flight, I'm afraid."

"Fine with me. I'm an early riser."

She'd just bet he was. He looked like the type that rose at dawn to go for a run—always one step ahead of the world.

"Would there be a soda in the fridge?" Ronan stood up and stretched subtly, like a panther that had been crouching in the bushes, watching its prey for too long.

"Sure, help yourself."

He was still wearing his suit, including jacket, and while the office part of the building was air-conditioned, it was definitely warm. Too warm for more than shirtsleeves. Cassie's own shirt felt suspiciously damp under her arms, but that could be explained by the combination of nerves and heat. It was the weather, the situation, the man. She must remember not to lift her arms too high, just in case her shirt betrayed her.

"Want one?"

Cassie shook her head. She'd stick with water. The caffeine from the morning's extra coffees was still zinging around in her bloodstream. Any more and she'd start to shake.

He sat down next to her, unscrewing the bottle he'd selected. She expected him to drink straight from it, but he poured the dark liquid into a glass.

She had to remember not to expect anything when it came to Ronan McGuire.

"Have you had enough lunch?" she asked. Much as Cassie loved this room, it was starting to feel a little stifling. Having watched Ronan do something as in-nocently domestic as get something from the fridge, she was on the verge of reclining and enjoying a little

Part Four fantasy about being at home with him—her husband—sitting at their kitchen table, going over the business that they ran together. Two dark-haired little angels—because any children they had would have to be brunette—were tucked up in bed upstairs.

And Cassie was in no position to become CEO of Country Style because she was certifiably insane.

"I'm good," he said, beaming another of those toothpaste-ad smiles her way.

Did all Americans have teeth like that or just the Californians?

Cassie stood up and managed to plaster what she hoped was a neutral smile on her face. "I thought I'd take you through the warehouse before we move on to looking at our inventory. It might make it easier to visualize the reports."

"Good thinking." Ronan stood, as well. "I'd also like to speak to the staff. With your permission, of course."

"Fine," she said, because she couldn't think of a reason to say no. Cassie could just imagine how those conversations might go, though. Her burly, tattooed, hearts-of-gold but gutter-mouthed warehouse guys were going to be less than respectful to a shiny American in a posh suit and tie. The man had product in his hair, for goodness' sake.

"Just so you know," she said, "I've distributed a memo to staff to let them know only that you're visiting at the request of Graham to learn more about our business. I didn't want to cause uncertainty or anxiety for anyone about any potential…*changes*. No point getting everyone worried over nothing. So I'd appreciate it if you could keep the purpose of your enquiries discreet."

Ronan nodded. "Of course. And you weren't lying— I *am* here to learn more about the business."

You're here to determine whether or not I can step up to the top job and we both know it, Cassie wanted to blurt. But now wasn't the time. Now was the time to play nice, to be a leader in the truest sense of the word, and—for now, anyway—helping Ronan to realize that Country Style was a strong, successful business was in her best interests.

He gestured for her to lead the way.

Cassie paused and looked him up and down. When her eyes returned to his face, the expression in his eyes told her he'd been very aware of her unsubtle review. He wasn't pleased. Or even teasing. No, his eyes had gone hard again, masking whatever he was thinking. She was reminded of her initial impression—this man was like a bright, beautiful tropical fish with a poisoned spike that could kill its prey in less than a minute. She had a sudden, visceral sense that Ronan McGuire would make a potent enemy. "Uh, the warehouse isn't air-conditioned," Cassie said, gesturing to his suit, wincing at her uncertain tone. "You might want to…uh…"

"Lose the jacket?" He visibly relaxed. He was relieved she hadn't been checking him out, Cassie realized.

He found her *that* unattractive?

It was ridiculous to be disappointed. And it was just lucky he couldn't read her mind.

Cassie nodded. "Yeah. It can get pretty steamy out

there. It's supposed to get to thirty-six degrees today, and inside our tin shed it can be even hotter."

"I assume you have health and safety regulations in place to look after the welfare of the employees?"

It was a simple question with a simple answer. But Cassie's mouth went dry as she watched him shrug out of his jacket and drape it on the back of his chair. His white shirt was still pristine, a heavy cotton that had no visible logos and screamed "more expensive than you can imagine in your wildest dreams, Cassie Hartman."

But he didn't stop there.

"If I'm talking to warehouse guys, I should lose the tie, too," he said, almost to himself.

It was a good idea, on so many levels.

His fingers loosened the knot of his burgundy tie and the luscious silk slipped through his collar with an illicit whisper. He undid the top two buttons of the shirt and revealed the beginnings of a light dusting of dark hair against smooth, tanned skin. Then his hands worked at his cuffs and a moment later, the shirt was rolled up at the sleeves, exposing muscled forearms sprinkled with that same dark hair.

It was only the burn in her lungs that reminded Cassie to breathe.

This was not a strip show on King Street. But Cassie had a sudden urge to order a cosmopolitan, sit back and watch as he continued. Button. Another button.

She shook her head and sucked in a breath. To give herself recovery time, she looked down at the table and shuffled some papers around. But as soon as she'd managed to tear her eyes away from his delectable body, another element hit her senses—his scent.

He wasn't as unaffected by the heat as she'd thought—there was a whiff of sweat there, but it was the good kind, the kind that made her want to inhale deeply. It was only just discernable under his expensively discreet aftershave, musky and woody, a smell that reinforced the conflicting impressions Cassie was trying to assimilate. On the one hand, he was all coolly professional sophistication, on the other, he radiated earthy, primal masculinity.

Cassie's eyes lit on the cuff links from his French-cuffed shirt that were sitting on the table—quirky little enameled blocks decorated to look like dice.

It was an effective reminder of the reality of the situation. They probably cost more than every item of jewelry Cassie owned combined.

And for Ronan, this little exercise was a game. A roll of the dice and Cassie won or lost. It didn't matter to him. He'd go back to America and his waiting partnership and never think about Country Style or Cassidy Hartman again.

Now was not the time for Cassie's underdeveloped sex drive to suddenly come to life. Part Three had to wait until Parts One and Two were in place.

She stopped fiddling with the papers and set her eyes directly on his face, bypassing those arms, that chest. "Yes, of course we do." It came out a little more direct than Cassie had planned.

He frowned.

"Have a health and safety policy," she clarified,

moderating her tone. "The foreman has an ambient-temperature monitor. As soon as it gets over a certain level, we send everyone home. And we try to plan our shifts around the weather report during summer. For example, today we started at dawn to ensure we could receive and store the stock before the heat really hit."

He nodded, seeming to take Cassie's undisguised defensiveness in stride.

"Good to hear. Shall we?"

He raised that single eyebrow again, but this time Cassie was prepared; she'd fortified herself and the expression didn't melt her into a messy puddle.

"Absolutely. Follow me."

CHAPTER THREE

RONAN WAS READY TO FALL into bed by the time he got back to the hotel after a full day at Country Style. But, determined not to let the jet lag win, he changed his clothes, ran a couple of miles on the hotel gym's treadmill and then swam a few laps. A quick meal from room service and he was feeling better—still tired, but now in a physical sense, not just a blurred, fuzzy, jet-lagged sense.

He cracked open his laptop and crawled into bed with it, sitting a nightcap of substandard Scotch from the minibar on the side table. A quick review of his emails and then the whisky and he'd be guaranteed a decent night's sleep before he had to get up at dawn to catch the plane to Perth.

Two hundred and fourteen emails.

Not bad, considering it had been a full day since he'd last checked.

Only one of them from his father. Requesting a progress report according to the subject line—no surprises there. Ronan's finger hovered over the delete key, but then remembered how much was riding on this job. Instead, he clicked on the message, and his father's brusque words filled the screen.

Ronan

Report back on progress with Taylor job ASAP—client expects interim recommendations by end of week. You know what outcomes are sought. Keep your nose clean. Keep your pecker cleaner!

    Patrick Conroy

    President and CEO, Conroy Corporation

Didn't even bother to sign it "Dad," just his full name and company signature, which was as effective a reminder that Ronan was in the doghouse as anything else.

Ronan bristled at the warning in the email. As if he were a child. As if the point hadn't been made loud and clear before he'd left San Francisco.

It was why he'd made a last-minute decision to use his grandmother's maiden name for this job. He didn't want the CEO-son stigma following him around the world. "Ronan Conroy" brought too much baggage with it, whereas "Ronan McGuire" was nice and anonymous. It gave him space and time to think through what had happened—which was exactly what his father had hoped for by sending him to Australia in the first place.

The past month had been a mess. Everything had been going so well up until then, or so he'd thought. Now that he looked back on it, he wondered just how long the storm had been brewing.

An image of Sarah Forsythe swam up in his mind's eye and made him shudder.

Ronan didn't like to think of himself as the kind of

man who spent time tying himself up in knots over regrets, but he couldn't let this one go.

How had he not predicted what would happen? How had he been so wrong? Probably because he'd been concentrating on the long blond hair and the swimsuit-model body hidden within prim business suits, he reflected ruefully.

It wasn't as though he'd never slept with a client before. It was a line he'd crossed, but always carefully. This time he hadn't been so careful. He'd simply seen what he wanted and he'd taken it.

He'd been groomed his entire life to take over the leadership of Conroy Corporation one day. And until recently, he'd thought that was what he wanted. The last job he'd managed—a complex M&A in New York—had been a goldmine. A runaway success for the client had resulted in a tidy packet of consulting fees—and a newly polished reputation for Conroy Corporation on Wall Street. Ronan had been full of his own success.

He and Sarah, an accountant with one of the companies, had worked long hours together. When, toward the end of the job, a late night turned into drinks after work, they'd both had one too many. And when the night had ended with them sharing her bed, he'd been reasonably sure they were on the same page. It had been mutual; two consenting adults seeking pleasure in each other. These things happened in high-pressure environments. It was a release valve for both of them.

The next morning Ronan had tried to let her down easy. Given her a bit of the patented Ronan Conroy charm. She'd smiled, walked away, and Ronan had thought things were fine as he focused on tying up the loose ends as the job came to a close.

Two days later, he was on a plane, summoned back to his father's office where a lawyer's letter threatening a sexual harassment lawsuit was waved in his face.

Ronan had been incensed. His father had been so livid Ronan had actually feared for his health, watching him go puce with rage.

The words of their fight still echoed in his mind. His father had accused him of coasting, of not taking things seriously, of having a sense of entitlement over his career at Conroy Corporation, of being immature and shortsighted. Ronan had argued the exact opposite: he'd never been granted the slightest advantage, always had to work twice as hard as everyone else, never taken a shortcut, never once ridden on his father's coattails.

Patrick Conroy had made Ronan work his way up the ranks just like any other employee.

No, not like any other employee.

Ronan had had to work harder, longer and more diligently than anyone to get even half the recognition.

And it stung. Not that Ronan wanted to be given a free ride, but once, just once, it would have been nice to know that his father considered him a worthy successor. He wasn't looking for special treatment—just acknowledgment that his hard work had been worth it, that his natural talent for the business made him stand out.

But no.

Always conscious of the optics, Patrick Conroy had practiced reverse discrimination, putting more complex and difficult hurdles in front of his son than anyone else.

The partnership should have been his as soon as he'd got back from New York.

Unlike his father, Ronan knew that it didn't matter what the reality was; there'd be plenty of people at Conroy Corporation who would greet the news of his partnership with a sneer and a joke about nepotism. But anyone who'd ever worked with him knew that Ronan not only deserved that partnership, he'd worked harder than anyone else in order to win it.

And then one stupid move, one wrong decision…

He was angry—with his father, with Sarah, with the world.

Also, even if he wasn't quite ready to admit it aloud, with himself.

Ronan made his living from analyzing situations and predicting outcomes—and he was damn good at it. But he'd screwed this one up, big-time. How had he not seen that Sarah wasn't just looking for one night of mutual fun? He'd been high on success, full of himself and his New York triumph, the partnership he'd had to bust his ass to achieve finally within his grasp.

Only to have it jerked away after one little mistake.

He blew out a breath and shook his head, trying to focus. All he had to do was make a decent job of this Country Style project and he'd be back on track. Simple.

Ronan scanned the subject lines of all his other emails and decided there was nothing desperately urgent. He could deal with the rest of them on the plane tomorrow.

He closed the laptop, drained the Scotch, switched off the light and lay back and stared up at the ceiling. Alert and awake, despite his physical and mental exhaustion.

"Damn." He swore again, more savagely, punched the pillow and rolled on his side. His mind was racing and wouldn't shut down. His thoughts still tumbled over each other, churning over his current predicament.

His entire future was riding on this Taylor job. He'd been sent to Australia as a punishment, just like the British convicts that had settled the country. But it was also his last chance of redemption. His chance to prove to his father—and to himself—that he really did care about some things. Like his future.

Like not becoming a laughingstock.

Did you hear the one about the CEO's son who got demoted?

Oh, yeah, that was a good one.

Unless you were the CEO's son.

The payout Patrick Conroy had had to make to Sarah to ensure her silence was now held as ransom over Ronan's head.

You've lost sight of what this business is all about. His father's words rang in his ears. *How can I put you in front of the board as the future leader of this organization when you still behave like you're twenty-five and sowing your wild oats? Go to Australia and get this right. Do you good to get back to basics and remember why you're in this business in the first place.*

Patrick Conroy had offered an opportunity for redemption—in reality, a demeaning punishment. His old
friend, Graham Taylor, needed a favor. One of his busi-
nesses in Australia was at a turning point; Graham had
courted a multinational conglomerate interested in expanding in Australia—starting with purchasing his top-
performing chain of fifty-seven retail furniture stores.
All the stores would be rebranded, global purchasing
power would provide a more competitive edge and the
local management would no longer be required. They
were prepared to pay Taylor a bucket load of money, so
as far as Ronan could see, it was a no-brainer. But for
some reason, he wanted a Conroy Corporation report
on the state of the business before he signed on the
dotted line.

Ronan had been given a careful brief by his father.
He was to do a thorough investigation, without revealing his true purpose to any of the local management.
Along with confirming Taylor's decision to sell as the
correct one, Ronan had to prove that he didn't need an
army of business analysts and auditors to do a proper
scoping exercise. Prove that he was worthy of Conroy
Corporation. Prove that his error of judgment in New
York was just a blip, not a symptom of a more serious
problem.

Ronan twisted in bed and punched the pillow again.
The whisky burned in his gut.

Of course, the staff of Country Style had no idea
why Ronan was really there, no suspicion of the possible merger. It wasn't the first time Ronan knew more
about people's future than they did and it wouldn't be

the last. It was part of the job—part of the challenge of being a management consultant. Sometimes the recommendations he had to make affected people's jobs. Sometimes he had to conceal that from them until the time was right.

Cassie Hartman, for example, thought he was there to review a document she'd created proposing a restructure of the business. Putting herself in charge, as CEO. The irony was, her report was probably what had prompted Taylor to think about selling in the first place. Her document was competent, and she clearly had a thorough understanding of the business she ran, but if things went as Taylor hoped, she'd not only *not* be CEO, she'd be out of a job.

Ronan checked the clock, the red numbers burning brightly in the darkness of the room. Only ten minutes had passed since he'd switched off the light. This was going to be a slow and torturous night if he couldn't somehow make himself sleep.

There was *one* thing he hadn't tried yet.

Grasping himself, Ronan cast around in his mind for images to accompany this last shot at overcoming his sleeplessness. He wasn't proud, but it would only be a few hours before his alarm clock would go off and he'd be heading for the airport to catch a plane with Cassie Hartman.

Cassie Hartman.

He wasn't surprised when his body responded to the thought. She possessed an intriguing combination of control and vulnerability, one moment smoothly professional, the next delightfully awkward. But it was the brunette curls she tried hard to restrain that spurred his physical response. Even the boring tortoiseshell clip that held the mane at the back of her neck wasn't enough to fully hide the thick, shiny strands. He remembered his first thought when he'd seen her—what would her hair look like loose, swinging over her shoulders? He wondered how long it was—would it cover her breasts when she was naked? Maybe it would just reach the tips, letting her nipples peak out from between the curled ends.

He groaned.

That uniform she wore was utilitarian, another of her intriguing contrasts. All buttoned-up and proper on the outside, all lush curves and full breasts underneath. He wondered what she wore under her uniform. White cotton or white lace…

Ronan's pulse picked up and he stroked himself more firmly.

Her breasts were large; they'd fill each hand and maybe then some. She had a sweet smile, too. She'd been nervous today, he could see that, but also determined to stand her ground and exceptionally proud of her achievements. He got the impression she was shy and not very confident around men—unlike that assistant of hers, she'd not once even attempted to flirt with him. And when he'd taken off his jacket and tie, he'd been sure she had blushed.

He could just imagine the blush on her face, that sweet smile, looking up at him as he touched her, as he moved over her, as he took her body, when she—

Ronan swore, released himself and flopped back on the pillows in disgust.

Hadn't the experience with Sarah Forsythe taught him anything? Was his father's impression of him right? Was he a player who could never take anything seriously?

Fantasizing about Cassie Hartman was about as wrong as it was possible to get. The very last thing he could afford on this job was another romantic entanglement with the client.

She probably had a boyfriend, he told himself. That was why she didn't flirt. It didn't matter anyway—she was so far off-limits she might as well be a nun.

Thinking about Sarah and the situation he was in was enough to kill any arousal. He'd just have to lie there until the alarm sounded. If necessary, he'd sleep on the plane.

He yawned.

This was going to be one damned long week.

CASSIE'S INSTINCTIVE RESPONSE to flying was filed under *T* for *torture*. But a career that often demanded her presence interstate meant she'd had to reconcile herself to filing it under *N* for *necessary evil* instead. If there was any way she could avoid stepping on another plane in her life, she'd take it.

It wasn't that she was scared, exactly. No, *terrified* would probably be a more apt description. A shame, since she was sure her enthusiastic amateur-pilot father was looking down at her and shaking his head sadly at her phobia. He'd done his best to instill his own love of flying in her and she'd adored pretending to be his copilot—until the accident that had given her a fear of anything that went faster than her zippy, if dated, little hatchback.

It was mainly the takeoff and landing that were the problem. Once she was up in the air, she was better. As long as there were no bumps. Or strange noises. And God forbid that the cabin crew look nervous in any way.

But she couldn't afford to let Ronan McGuire see it. It wasn't a weakness that affected her ability to manage Country Style, but it was still a weakness. Cassie was determined not to let him see anything other than the person who was the obvious choice for leading the business into a new realm of success.

Calm. Control. The words had become her mantra.

"Are you a nervous flyer?"

Damn. Those blue eyes peered at her as they fastened their seat belts. Since they'd met in the airport, conversation had been restrained and polite. He'd seemed distracted and had opened up his laptop as soon as they'd been settled in the lounge. Cassie had done the same—she had plenty to keep her busy, anyway. There was still a great deal of work to do to finalize the details for the store opening on Monday.

"No, I'm…fine," Cassie replied, trying for a relaxed smile.

Ronan nodded, the ghost of a smile playing on his lips.

He was laughing at her! *Get a grip, Cassie.* She peeled her fingers from the armrest and folded them neatly in her lap, wishing she'd thought to bring a book with her so she could sit there and pretend to read. Even better would have been a set of those massive, noise-canceling headphones, so she could block out the plane and Ronan's annoyingly seductive voice. Leaning forward, she scrambled in the seat pocket in front of her for the airline magazine and stared blankly at a random page, figuring it was better than nothing.

She heard a low chuckle beside her.

With a blush heating her cheeks, Cassie turned the magazine the right way up and studied the article about resorts in Bali as if her life depended on it. The safety demonstration started and she half watched from behind the magazine—usually she paid rapt attention, but again, she didn't want to give away her nerves to her seatmate.

As the plane's engines fired up for takeoff, Cassie couldn't help the panic that rose inside her. Memories threatened to overwhelm her, of the time when flying had been exciting, the little tilts and loops of a plane thrilling, her father at the wheel, turning to grin at her in shared exhilaration. That had been before. Before life had changed permanently.

She closed her eyes as the wheels left the ground, her teeth gritted as the plane dipped and righted itself. Then the wind caught them. The plane veered sideways, leaving her stomach somewhere near her throat. Cassie's hand shot out, reaching for the armrest, and she twisted her feet around the seat in front of her as makeshift anchors. The magazine fell with a rustle of pages to the floor.

"Hey, it's okay."

Instead of cold metal, her hand met warm flesh. Fingers that interlaced with hers and held on tightly. Reassuringly.

"It's just a little turbulence."

Yeah, that's probably what they said before every plane fell out of the sky.

"It'll even out as soon as we get higher." Ronan's voice was low and gentle, that accent of his reassuring.

The plane dipped again. Cassie screwed her eyes shut even tighter and squeezed his hand hard enough to make her knuckles ache. Blood pounded in her ears and her calves began to cramp from her ankles' awkward grip.

"Breathe. In and out."

She made an effort to take in some air.

"That's better. See? We're smoothing out now. Nothing to worry about."

Nothing to worry about? This was the worst flight she'd ever been on. Surely when she opened her eyes there'd be chaos, people screaming, children crying, panicked flight attendants running down the aisles.

She cracked an eye. Everything looked...*normal.*

The businessman across the aisle nonchalantly turned the page of his newspaper. The child in the seat in front of her yawned and dropped his half-chewed apple on the floor. The women behind them continued to talk about the shoe and handbag shopping they'd done in Melbourne's famous laneways.

Cassie sucked in a deep breath and opened both eyes.

The breath froze in her lungs.

Ronan McGuire was twisted in his seat, his face just

inches from hers. He clasped her hand in both of his, stroking the inside of her wrist with one thumb, seemingly unconcerned by the death grip she had on him. He was peering at her, and those calculating blue eyes of his were filled with concern and compassion and—around the edges—amusement.

As her eyes met his, a slow smile spread across his face. "So you don't like flying much, huh?"

Cassie swallowed hard and had to force her voice not to waver. "It's…it's not my favorite activity." His research clearly hadn't covered her family background.

"And you've signed us up for a week of travel?"

That devastating single arched eyebrow again. Thankfully this time Cassie was too wound up to let it affect her. Much.

"I've never let my little problem interfere with my job." Cassie bristled at the insinuation and it helped to dampen her fear. The plane had leveled out and a loud ding sounded as the seat-belt sign went off.

Ronan's thumb was still stroking the inside of her wrist. It had been comforting before, now it was…now it was…

She loosened her fingers from around his and gave him a tight smile, tugging her hand free of his grasp.

It took him a moment to release her. His thumb paused against her pulse point, his eyes still locked with hers. Something flashed there, an awareness, and Cassie hoped like hell he couldn't read her mind. Not only was she grateful for his calm support, but more than anything she wanted him to hold her hand for the next four hours. Forever, if possible. And that stroking thumb of his? She was absolutely not thinking about what it might be like if it explored her arm, her shoulder, her breast, lower…

"I'm sure you haven't," he drawled as he settled back in his seat by her side. "You're far too professional for that."

Cassie drew in a breath, not sure whether to be thankful or disappointed that he'd let her go. To cover her confusion, she was about to launch into a review of all the work-related travel she'd done for Country Style, when he leaned forward, pulled out the laptop he'd slid under the seat in front before they'd taken off, opened it and appeared to get to work.

Cassie closed her mouth with an audible snap.

He didn't so much as look up from the screen, and Cassie had the strange feeling she'd been dismissed. Fine. It was for the best. There was no point entertaining thoughts about Ronan McGuire, his strong fingers and lush mouth. It had been enough that ideas like that had kept her awake most of the night before.

Besides every other logical reason she had not to encourage this crush she seemed to have developed, guys like him didn't go for girls like her. He was suave, sophisticated, experienced. And she was…the opposite. Plain. Inexperienced. Nervous.

She didn't want a guy like him, anyway, she told herself for the billionth time. A jet-setting playboy, he probably had a girl in every port and his closest relationship was with the air hostesses he met as he flew between them. He would think Cassie's ideas of stability, work, home and family old-fashioned and boring.

God forbid he ever hear about her Plan-with-a-capital-*P*. He'd laugh until his sides split.

Cassie pulled out her own laptop, ignoring Ronan's dismissal. It wasn't as if she didn't have enough to do—there were still the hundred or so things to be done before the Hawthorn store opened and then there were the notes she needed to make for each of the store managers they'd be visiting.

The rest of the flight passed without incident. Occasionally, Ronan had popped his head up to ask Cassie something and a couple of times those questions had led into discussions about the operations of Country Style.

They talked briefly and politely when the flight attendants brought around a morning snack and they had to momentarily each put their computers away, but otherwise he paid her little attention—peering at his laptop and typing furiously right up until the plane was about to land.

As the flight attendants made preparations for landing, Cassie could feel the familiar panic begin to build. She knew it was irrational, and she wasn't proud of her fear. It was just something she couldn't control. Crashes happened, as she knew all too well. And although the odds weren't high—especially on a large passenger jet—it was still *possible.*

She screwed her eyes shut again in an attempt to block everything out. Hopefully Ronan would think she was taking a nap.

"Cassie?"

She silently cursed her traitorous responses as a

shiver went through her at the sound of her name on his lips. Would he hold her hand again?

"Yes?" she answered. It was too late to try to hide her terror from him, but she still tried her best to sound calm. She opened one eye.

He gestured to a hard copy spreadsheet he'd pulled out when he'd been forced to pack away his laptop. "I've noticed an anomaly with this supplier, Brentons. They seem to deliver late, almost every time."

Cassie blew out a breath. Of course he'd noticed that. She opened both eyes to look at the report he referred to.

"Yes," she said, nodding slowly. "They are unreliable. But the cabinets they make are one of our top sellers." Beautiful timbers, handcrafted and hand painted, Brentons made mini works of art, not just furniture.

He frowned. "But not one of your most profitable."

"No. But they pull in traffic—all our managers know if they're having a slow week, put a Brentons cabinet in the window and they can double the passing trade."

"So they're a loss leader for you?"

"We don't make a loss, but you're right, they're not especially profitable. And when they're late with deliveries, it does make our lives difficult."

His lips tightened in thought. "So why not pull them into line? They're a boutique supplier—Country Style must be their biggest customer. Have threats not worked?"

Threats? Cassie shook her head in disbelief and a mounting sense of anger. "No, it's not like that." She shifted to face him, memories of her last conversation with the owners of Brentons fresh in her mind. "Brentons is run by a couple—it's a family business, like ours. They've had a rough year—their daughter was diagnosed with leukemia. She's only seven and understandably her treatment has interrupted their time with the business. They've worked very hard to fill our orders, but I've let it slide when they've occasionally delivered late."

"Occasionally?" An eyebrow quirked as he ran a finger down a column that Cassie knew was showing him that the Brentons had consistently run late—very late—for the past year.

"Okay, so more than occasionally. But I decided to cut them some slack, given the circumstances."

"Can Country Style afford for such personal concerns to take precedence over efficiency and reliability? Surely you can find another supplier who'd make something comparable? And probably cheaper. What about sourcing a similar product overseas, say in China?"

Yesterday Ronan's questions had been gentle, probing; more like suggestions, really. Apparently he'd just been letting her in easy, preparing her for the onslaught. Once again, Cassie had to tell herself to be on guard at all times, no matter how charming and good-looking he was. Despite the lack of pocket protector or bow tie, he clearly had a heart made of spreadsheets and calculators instead of flesh and blood.

"Yes, we probably could get a cheaper product overseas," she answered, her tone betraying her outrage at his callousness. She couldn't help it. "Although I doubt we would find the dedication to quality and craftsmanship that Brentons pride themselves in. But more important the Brentons have been valuable partners to Country Style for a number of years—as our business has grown so has theirs. I felt that given what was happening to Molly—that's their little girl—they deserved some compassion and leeway."

His eyes met hers and he nodded. "Fair enough. I probably would have made the same call." And then he smiled, something Cassie didn't understand until the announcement came over the PA.

"Ladies and gentlemen, welcome to Perth. Please remain seated until we have come to a full stop at the gate and the captain has turned off the fasten-seat-belts sign."

Comprehension dawned.

"Did you do that to distract me?" A wave of irritation flooded through her, although she wasn't sure why. She should probably be thankful—but that idea grated.

The slight smile tipped into a cocky grin. "Not entirely. I did want to find out the official story."

"Official story?"

"In the warehouse yesterday I commented on one of the Brentons cabinets. Beautiful pieces of furniture, by the way—you're right about the craftsmanship. The warehouse manager told me all about the late deliveries, and about Molly, and even some of the fundraising Country Style has done for children's leukemia charities."

"That *is* the official story."

"Indeed. And now I know." He cocked his head on

one side and gave a short nod, as if that concluded the conversation. She watched as he gathered his laptop and belongings, preparing to disembark.

Cassie's frayed nerves tingled. She wasn't sure which was worse: a plane landing or an inquisition from Ronan McGuire. At least the plane landing was uncomplicated, pure, clean fear. Cassie's feelings about Ronan were far muddier. There was an element of fear, for sure. So much was riding on this; she'd be an idiot if she didn't recognize that. But he unsettled her in so many other ways, many of which she was still struggling to pin down.

Like why, for example, did she always seem to notice how good he smelled? And why was she fascinated by those blue eyes of his—hard as arctic glaciers one moment, sparkling with amusement the next? He'd held her hand to help calm her, that was all. And yet the touch of his thumb on her wrist had woken feelings all through her body. In places that had never been disturbed before—places Cassie had long thought must be defective. That was why Part Two of the plan was so important, and she only hoped it would help with achieving Part Three, the part of her plan that felt like the most impossible. Surely if she *looked* the part of a sexy woman, the rest would follow naturally?

She stood up and crowded into the aisle. Ronan stood next to her, twisting around to reach the jacket he'd laid out in the overhead compartment to stop it from creasing. He shrugged it on and Cassie told herself not to notice his expensive cologne or the way the tailored jacket emphasized his broad shoulders and narrow waist.

He noticed her look and gave her a quick smile that reached all the way to his eyes before he busied himself with zipping up his laptop case.

He did that a lot, Cassie noted. Did something flirty—a look, a smile, a touch—and then pulled himself back. It was probably his nature. He flirted with all women, but when he remembered he was flirting with *her,* he stopped. She really must be *that* unattractive to him. The idea hurt more than it should.

She shook her head. At least in an hour or so they'd be in the store, and there'd be other people around. Dealing with him one-on-one was far too stressful.

CHAPTER FOUR

THE HEAT WAS UNRELENTING and so, it seemed, was Cassie Hartman. Ronan could feel his shirt sticking to his back—he'd given up on his jacket hours ago— as they climbed into their rental car after the last store visit of the day.

The sun was beginning to move toward the horizon but the temperature didn't feel as if it had dropped a single degree since midafternoon. The air itself was oven-hot, and he gratefully gulped in lungfuls of the air-conditioning inside the car.

Cassie seemed oblivious, powering her way through the stores, greeting the staff like a long-lost older sister, praising good work done, gently chiding when she saw things requiring improvement. Ronan noticed that she couldn't help tweaking things when they needed it— without doubt every store they'd been to had looked better, more inviting, more stylish, by the time they left. It was only a matter of a lamp here, or a vase there, but clearly Cassie had a knack for interior design.

He wondered what she'd make of his apartment back in San Francisco. The entire top floor of an old Victorian-style mansion, he'd always known it had the potential to be a showpiece—he'd just never got around to doing anything about it. A window in the kitchen was permanently open to let an old cat that seemed to have adopted him come and go as she pleased—leaving mess and paw prints as she went. The whole place never failed to produce comments from visitors. He lived like he was still in college—crates for shelves, movie posters tacked up on the walls, secondhand mismatched furniture—and not in a good, bohemian kind of way. More in a "Is that sofa safe?" kind of way.

He'd just never been all that concerned about it. His focus had always been on Conroy Corporation and, as long as he had a bed, a fridge and somewhere to park his car, he didn't care so much about what his home looked like. Besides, he was too restless to settle in one place for long. It was why he was always the first to volunteer for projects that involved travel—although usually that meant within North America or, occasionally, Europe. When he was away from headquarters, away from his father's all-pervasive influence, it felt easier to breathe, somehow. Not that he didn't love his family. Just sometimes the pressure of being Ronan Conroy and heir to Conroy Corporation—and all the seemingly impossible-to-fulfill expectations that accompanied that—was a heavy burden.

No amount of pretty furnishings in his apartment was going to help cure those feelings, he knew. But his mind went back to Country Style's boardroom—that incongruous room in a warehouse that Cassie had decorated as a family-style kitchen. He'd been comfortable there. It made him wonder whether proper decor in his own apartment might help him feel more settled. It also made him think that it might be a good gesture to demonstrate his commitment to his father—show that he *was* the mature leader Conroy Corporation needed. Perhaps his college-student-style approach to furnishings reflected his approach to life.

The more he thought about it, the more the idea appealed. He could imagine getting the place redone and then inviting his father and the board over for a dinner party. That would show his maturity and readiness for leadership, surely. He made a resolution to investigate that as soon as he got home. Maybe Cassie could help refer someone—she clearly had links to the interior design industry, although he knew she'd never done any formal study.

From her résumé, he knew that Cassie had begun her career with Country Style at seventeen, working her way up from junior salesperson to her current role. A couple of times he'd found himself standing back and watching, smiling to himself as she fixed a display or chatted to a staff member. Then he'd shake himself and give a stern internal lecture about why he was there. As much as he might want to let down her hair and get rid of those unflattering clothes—he expected she'd look like a brunette Botticelli's Venus when he did—flirting with Cassie Hartman was off the table.

Watching her through the day, Ronan felt the faint stirrings of guilt about the true purpose of his investigation. He knew it was almost certain that Cassie would lose her job as part of the buyout. It wasn't anything to do with her skills or knowledge—simply a matter of economies of scale. The other company already had head-office management in Australia—they didn't need more managers. Likely, that was another reason Taylor had called in Conroy Corporation—because he wanted to be able to place the blame for it all on someone else. Ronan could just imagine how Taylor's conversation with her would go: *I'm sorry Cassie, but Conroy's made it clear this was the right decision.*

It was a pity, because she was very good at what she did. He didn't understand why she'd spent so many years with Country Style—with her talent and experience, she could easily have moved into a more senior, higher-paying role somewhere else. He made a mental note to ask her about that when the time was right. Perhaps with a little push from him, she might start to see her potential beyond Country Style, which would make her termination seem not quite as serious as it otherwise might. She could certainly look at a lucrative career in merchandising, if she didn't want to work for a Country Style rival.

Ronan adjusted the car's air-conditioning vents and sent a welcome blast of cool air over his face.

"Heat getting to you?" Cassie asked, pulling the car out onto a wide, empty road. She'd insisted on driving and given that she knew where they were going and was familiar with driving on the left-hand side of the road, Ronan had been happy to acquiesce. Still, their bland, white rental sedan had given him a surge of longing for the sports car he'd hired in Melbourne and been forced to return early once he'd found out about the travel plans. Hopefully it would still be available over the weekend when they returned.

"I could use a beer," Ronan said, conceding that San

Francisco's comparatively chilly summers had in no way prepared him for Australia's scorching temperatures.

She gave a little laugh. "Yeah, that sounds good. Our hotel isn't far. I knew the Fremantle store would be our last stop of the day, so I had Mel book our accommodation down here—it's really pretty. It will take us a bit longer to get to the airport tomorrow, but it's worth it."

There was a glow about her as she spoke, Ronan noted. It had been there all day. Well, once they'd left the airport and the green tinge to her skin had disappeared. There was no doubting that Cassie loved her job. *Really* loved it. Even the heat hadn't dampened her enthusiasm. She wore that unremarkable Country Style uniform, but despite the long, hot day, looked fresh and alert. The only sign that the heat had affected her was the wispy curls that had formed around her face. Her mane was tied back and tucked up and away somehow, but perspiration and enthusiasm had loosened some of it, creating ringlets around her ears.

Ronan itched to unfasten the clip and run his fingers through her hair. He clasped his hands firmly in his lap.

Cassie pulled up in front of a colonial-style building that turned out to be their hotel. They climbed out and were efficiently checked in by a cheerful young man who filled Ronan's hand with tourist brochures when he heard the American accent.

Cassie grabbed her bag and gave him a smile. She was satisfied with how the day had gone, he could tell, and it had lessened the nerves she seemed to have when she was around him. He couldn't blame her.

"Well, thanks for today." She jangled the key in her hand. "You know, I really appreciate the way you've been talking to the staff we've met. You've been friendly and engaging, but still discreet. I…I appreciate it."

Ronan shrugged. "Of course." He hadn't done anything out of the ordinary, but he was pleased with the compliment.

"We have to leave here about seven tomorrow morning to catch our flight to Sydney."

"Sounds good." He fixed her with his most winning smile as he grabbed his own bag. "So, see you down here in about half an hour?"

Her confident expression faltered. "Half an hour?"

"Is that enough time to freshen up? You're not going to make me find my own dinner in a strange city all alone are you?"

Spending any time outside of work with this woman was a dumb idea, but the riot of responses that flooded her face at his request was too much fun to resist. Besides, he was a big boy. He could have dinner with a colleague and behave himself.

"Uh…I was planning to get room service…catch up on some work."

Her stammering excuse betrayed the lie.

"But that's what flying time is for. Come on. One beer and a quick dinner. I insist."

Insisting was probably the wrong move, but for the moment he knew she thought it was in her interests to keep him happy. He wondered if she realized just how open her face was, how easy she was to read. She was torn, knowing it would be unwise to refuse him, at the same time scared to accept. Scared? Yes, he was sure it was fear that flashed in her eyes. Hmm, that was interesting. He wondered why.

She was attracted to him—he knew that. It wasn't vanity on his part; life had taught him that most women were. But unlike most women, Cassie had been prickly from the start, not just coolly professional, but actively keeping her distance. Part of him—his pride, mostly, he had to admit—wanted to know why.

Eventually she gave a short nod. "Half an hour."

Ronan ran the shower as cold as it would go and dressed in tan chinos and a pale blue cotton shirt—untucked, collar open and sleeves rolled up. The corporate wardrobe he'd packed for this trip wasn't especially well suited to this weather and if it kept up, he'd be forced to shop for new clothes.

He'd been waiting in the foyer for a few minutes when Cassie appeared. She kept her eyes averted from his, looking all sweet and shy. And for a moment Ronan was glad, because he wasn't sure how well he hid his reaction.

Her summery floral dress swirled around her knees, revealing shapely calves and strappy sandals. Intriguingly, her toenails were painted orange—not red, not even a strange coral shade of red—but definitely, absolutely, orange. The dress had a little belt at the waist, showing off the hourglass figure that he'd just known lurked under that stuffy uniform. Buttons down the front were fastened demurely, but showed enough for Ronan to glimpse the creamy swells of full breasts. A fine gold chain hung around her neck and her hair was…tied back. As always. Damn.

She was stunning.

If she'd taken bold, confident strides through the foyer, head held high, that mane of hair flowing behind her, she'd have had the jaws of every guy in the place on the floor. Hell, she'd cause accidents in the street.

The contrast puzzled him. When she'd walked into the stores that day, she'd had exactly that air about her: confident, in charge, charming. People's eyes had naturally been drawn to her.

Now, she seemed wallflowerish. Still attractive enough to garner admiring glances from the other men in the foyer, but not the showstopper she should have been.

Part of him was glad that he was the only one who'd noticed that about her.

"Good evening," he said. Yeah, so he was using his sexy voice. It wouldn't hurt.

She smiled and her glance skated up to his. There was a moment of shared recognition, of acknowledgment of the less-than-businesslike charge in the air, before she quickly looked away again.

Two competing desires warred inside him, a little angel and a little devil perched on each shoulder as if he were a cartoon character in the midst of a moral dilemma. The angel told him to behave, to be a gentleman and remember what was riding on the successful, nonscandalous completion of this job. Annoyingly, the angel's voice sounded very much like his father.

On his other shoulder, the devil reminded him of Cassie's figure, her hair, and taunted him with graphic images of what it might be like to make love to her.

Cassie's hands were clasped together and her fingers twisted around each other, betraying her nerves.

The angel and devil warred again. She was nervous about spending time with him without the careful boundaries of work. He'd bet she didn't have much experience with men—she certainly didn't seem to be aware of the effect she was having on him. He'd be doing the men of Australia a favor by getting this gorgeous woman to loosen up, to recognize her own simmering sensuality.

"It's only dinner," he said, trying to calm her down and remind himself of the limitations at the same time. "You don't need to be nervous. I promise I've left all my toughest questions in my briefcase."

She gave a weak laugh and a look that told him instantly that his toughest questions for her would have nothing to do with work. But her shoulders straightened and a mask settled over her face. "Shall we go?" she asked simply.

"Lead the way."

She nodded, then headed for the doors. "There's a place a little way down the street, a pub. They have decent food and cold beer."

"Sounds good."

She fell silent and they walked side by side. A hazy dusk had fallen, but the street was busy, crowded with people in restaurants and sitting at outdoor tables. The temperature had thankfully fallen a little with the sun's disappearance, but warmth still surrounded them—in the air and radiating from the pavement and buildings around them.

It was a beautiful evening, warm and languid. Although the pavement was packed, no one was moving fast, as though the heat of day had made everyone lethargic and unhurried. The only person who broke that pattern was Cassie. He could almost feel the waves of agitation flowing from her as she walked beside him. Her movements were stiff and brisk, as if she were facing a chore that she wanted to get over with.

"In here," she said after a couple of minutes, gesturing to a large stone building. The pub's windows were all thrown open wide to the breeze and, once they stepped inside, Ronan could see the place had been renovated to create a single large, open-air dining room. It was busy, but not full, and Cassie led the way to a table in the middle. There were plenty of other, more private tables in darkened corners that Ronan would have preferred, but he went with her selection and pulled out her chair for her.

"Uh…thanks." Cassie gave him a surprised look, but allowed him to seat her.

"My mother is from the South—I spent a lot of time visiting with her family in Louisiana during vacations. Manners are big with them," he explained as he took his own seat. "No such thing as the feminist revolution when it comes to gentlemanly manners as far as my mother's concerned."

Cassie didn't seem to know what to say to that, so she picked up the menu that stood in the middle of the table wedged between salt and pepper shakers. It wavered slightly in her hands.

A waitress appeared and they both ordered beers which were quickly delivered to their table. Ronan picked up the icy glass with a real sense of gratitude.

"To Country Style," he toasted, raising his glass to Cassie's.

"To Country Style," she echoed, meeting his gaze.

Ronan's mouth went dry. Her velvet-brown eyes were wide, bright with nerves and arousal. He'd never seen such a naked display of vulnerability and sensuality in a single glance. A similarly conflicted wave of protectiveness and desire washed over him, making him want to simultaneously seduce her and protect her from himself.

Devil and angel indeed.

The beer slid down his throat like the elixir of life. He was quite sure he'd never had a better beer, ever, and it was nothing to do with the hops or malt.

He resisted the temptation to wipe his mouth with the back of his hand, but put the half-empty glass down on the table with a satisfying clunk. "God, that's good."

Cassie laughed. "I thought for a moment there you were going to down the whole lot."

"It was a near thing," he said, giving her his best friendly, open smile. He needed to get her to relax, to unwind, to lower her guard a bit. Just to see if he could.

He glanced around the room. It had been decorated with old newspaper pages, sepia photographs and posters that looked as if they belonged in the Old West, pro-claiming who was "most wanted."

"It's nice here," he said casually. "I was sure we needed somewhere air-conditioned. But it's quite comfortable."

"You get the breeze from the ocean," Cassie explained. "It's more comfortable than air-conditioning."

"The ocean's that way, right?" He pointed toward the front windows.

She nodded. "Yep. Just across the strip of parkland. It's a nice walk."

He'd just bet it was. What could be better than walking along the foreshore with a beautiful woman on a balmy evening? "Maybe after dinner then."

"Uh…" Her forehead creased, but whatever she'd been about to say was interrupted when the waitress came to take their orders.

Their food arrived almost as quickly as their beers, and while it wasn't exceptional, it was perfectly acceptable. Ronan kept the conversation light, resisting the temptation to talk about work. He wanted to see if he could get Cassie to relax without resorting to her favorite topic—Country Style. Eventually she did seem to loosen up a little. Her shoulders dropped, she sat more comfortably in the chair, didn't jump out of her skin when Ronan accidentally-on-purpose crossed his legs and brushed her calf with his foot.

When their meals and a second round of beers were done, Ronan sat back in his chair and studied her. "So, shall we take a walk?" he suggested.

All the stiffness that had gradually leached out of

her over dinner suddenly returned. "Um...I think I'm ready to head back to my room," she said hesitantly.

Ronan jumped up and grabbed her hand. "Come on. It's dangerous to walk alone at night. I need your protection." He gave her a wink. "And it'll help you sleep better. A little exercise, a little sea air. What's not to like?"

She hesitated, but then let him drag her from her seat. When they were outside in the street, heading for the grass that led across to the beach, Cassie tried to pull her hand from his grasp, but he held it tighter.

"Ronan," she said, her voice heavy with warning.

He ignored her and kept walking, even though she was dragging behind him. At first he'd taken her hand as encouragement. But it was too pleasant a sensation to let go—yet. Oh, his self-destructive streak was running hot tonight. "Come on, lazy bones," he urged, ignoring the saner parts of him that were telling him to get back to the hotel and say good-night. *Now.* "You said you'd arranged this so I'd get to do some sightseeing. Don't wimp out on me."

She sighed but her pace picked up until she was walking alongside him. Her hand was loose in his, but her fingers curled around enough to make it comfortable.

They walked in silence for a while, the gentle shushing of the waves and occasional call from a seagull the only sounds around them.

"So, tell me about your family," Ronan said, determined to continue to see how far he could get her to relax.

"Wha—what?"

It was as if her whole body stuttered. Her hand clenched his and her feet tripped over nothing.

"Tell me about your family," he repeated gently.

"Why?" Her tone dripped with suspicion and defensiveness.

"No particular reason." He'd meant it to be an easy conversation starter, a way to find out more about Cassie outside of her work. Seemed he'd stepped on a personal land mine instead. Damn. "You don't have to tell me. I just thought seeing as we're spending a week together it might be nice to know a little about each other."

"Right."

Silence stretched between them and Ronan wondered if he'd just undone any progress he might have made that evening. Then her voice came out, halting and quiet, in a way that told him there was a lot more to the story than she was prepared to admit.

"My parents died when I was fifteen. I have an older brother. He lives in London now."

There was so much emotion behind her simple statements, Ronan didn't know where to begin. He squeezed her hand and drew closer to her. "That must have been tough." Understatement of the century, he was sure.

He felt her shoulder shrug against his arm.

"What about you?" she asked.

It was a deflection, but Ronan went with it. "No brother, a sister, younger than me. She's a doctor—a resident now—at a hospital back home in San Francisco. She's into orthopedic surgery. Smart as a tack.

My mom is a Southern belle who insists on manners, is stronger than a mule and just as stubborn. She lets my father think he's in charge, but we all know she's the one who really pulls the strings."

"And your father?"

"Very driven, very successful. He came to America from Ireland with my grandparents when he was only a small child. He has that special drive to carve out a niche in the world that lots of immigrants seem to share. A leader in the community. A fine, upstanding gentleman." He wondered if she caught the hint of bitterness in his tone.

If she had, she didn't let on. "You sound like you're very fond of your sister," she said diplomatically.

"Siobhan? She drives me nuts. She's reckless and irresponsible and always getting herself into trouble. I love her to pieces."

"You look out for her."

"Yeah, I do."

"That's nice."

Her wistful tone made him want to ask about her relationship with her brother, but before he could, she stopped suddenly. He halted and turned to face her.

"What's up, Cassie?"

"This is starting to feel like…"

"Like what?"

"Like a *date*."

"Yeah. It would be a nice date. But it's not."

"It's not?"

Ronan resisted the temptation to smile at the combination of disappointment and relief etched on her face. "No, it's not a date."

He stepped toward her, near enough to smell her fresh, floral perfume, to feel the heat of her body. Any closer and her breasts would touch his chest. "It's not a date unless we kiss." He took her other hand in his. She didn't resist.

"Well, we wouldn't…"

Her voice trailed off as he brought his lips closer to hers. Closer, closer. Her breath tickled his lips. Those bronzed eyes looked up at him, and he could see the moment she gave in. But he was too distracted to pay attention to his triumph, too aroused to recognize the challenge he'd set himself had been won. Far too focused on the woman in front of him to hear the warning bells that should have been clanging loud enough to wake the dead.

He concentrated on her lips, full and pouty and just crying out to be kissed. They parted slightly as she sighed and her eyes fluttered closed in the ultimate surrender.

CHAPTER FIVE

RONAN'S LIPS BRUSHED hers in the lightest of touches. Until he did it again, Cassie wasn't entirely sure she hadn't imagined it.

So soft and gentle, he eased her into it. An aggressive kiss would have been easy to reject. But this subtle brushing of his mouth against hers was impossibly compelling.

Their breath mingled in the salty air.

His lips met hers again, a little longer this time, a little firmer.

Without her conscious permission, her lips parted in a sigh that was answered by a groan rumbling through Ronan's chest.

His tongue dipped inside to taste her, his lips slanting over hers to take her more fully, and Cassie lost all awareness of herself and her surroundings. The pool of yellow light from the overhead streetlamp faded, the sound of the beach and calling of gulls disappeared, awareness of other people enjoying the cooler breeze along the shore vanished.

All she knew was his taste, the heat and press of his body against hers, the smile that curved his lips when she responded and sought his tongue with her own.

As he deepened the kiss, his hands dropped hers

to hold her against him. One hand went to her nape, the other to the small of her back. Cassie's own hands clutched his shoulders, needing him to anchor her when it felt as if she might drift away with the tide, that she might dissolve into the kiss.

His body was hard and unyielding against her own softer curves. Cassie had never done anything so risky in years, and yet somehow his very solidity offered a sense of protection, of safety.

His mouth left hers and traced a path across her jaw, nibbling on her earlobe for a moment. His hot breath was raspy and seductive and sent a ribbon of desire straight to her groin to join the warmth that had been building there all evening.

Cassie arched her neck to give him access and his lips moved lower to trace her collarbone as the hand on her waist traveled higher, stroking over her ribs until he cupped the curve of her breast.

She knew where his mouth was headed, his lips were kissing along the path of the gold chain she always wore; the pendant that hung from it was resting between her breasts.

"Ronan." His name left her lips as a sigh when his thumb brushed over her nipple, already taut and straining for his touch against the lace of her bra.

The next moment, Cassie staggered slightly, unsure what had happened. She opened her eyes, blinking as she struggled to regain her equilibrium.

Ronan stood a couple of steps away, his hand running through his hair, staring out to the gently lapping ocean. He muttered swear words under his breath.

She felt drunk, drugged, as if the two beers she'd had with dinner had been laced with vodka shots. Her senses took too long to recover, but when they did, the awful embarrassment that flooded her made her wish she'd stayed dazed.

He shot her a glance. "Cassie, I…I'm sorry," he began, but then threw his hands up in the air and swore again. He turned away from her.

Cassie looked down at her disheveled dress. It was twisted around her waist and the neckline had been pulled askew. She straightened it with a shaking hand, tightening the belt and rearranging the collar. Her stomach leaped and dipped as her brain tried to catch up with what had just happened, worse than the turbulence from any flight.

She opened her mouth, but no words came out. What on earth could she say? Thank you for the most amazing kiss of my life? I'm sorry you hated it? Please don't take this as a reflection of my suitability as CEO of Country Style? Every inch of her skin flushed with the heat of humiliation.

Her hair was pulling uncomfortably. When he'd kissed her, his fingers had pushed through the knot of hair at her nape. The clip was now tangled and hurting. She reached behind her to pull it free, yanking the clip until it released, her hair tumbling down over her shoulders.

She was just shaking it out when Ronan turned back to her, his face full of remorse. But as he caught sight of her, he froze, whatever he'd been about to say dying on his lips. His look was hungry, raw and primal, so very different from the more calculated seduction his eyes had held before he'd kissed her. Cassie had a sudden feeling that she'd woken a sleeping tiger, and now she had no idea what to do to get him back in his cage.

"You tangled my hair," she said, her voice husky and defensive all at the same time.

He closed his eyes for a moment and swallowed hard. When he opened them again, she could see the restraint he forced upon himself.

A sudden thrill went through her at the realization, piercing the mortification that had been her initial response. She wasn't the only one who'd been affected by their kiss.

It was brazen, but Cassie couldn't help herself, and she let her eyes wander to Ronan's pants. The streetlight's yellow glow told her of his body's response to her. The very idea of it sent waves of anxiety and arousal through her.

Questions piled up inside her mind faster than she could process them. What would it be like to see him naked? To have his bare skin against her own? To have him touch her intimately, to have his weight on top of her, his body inside her?

"Cassie, sweetheart." His voice was a ragged plea. "You have to stop thinking whatever it is you're thinking, because otherwise I won't be held responsible for my actions." He sucked in a breath. "I'm trying so hard to do the right thing here."

Surely the right thing couldn't be denying this energy that thrummed between them. Even if it was the very last thing in the world she should be thinking about. He wasn't what she needed. She wanted safe, he offered reckless. She wanted stable and settled, he traveled the world for his work, no doubt had a girl in every port.

And yet.

They stood, staring at each other, for a moment that went forever.

Then the spell broke, a couple pushing a pram walked past, the sound of their voices and the baby's cooing babbles piercing the silence that had surrounded them. Cassie was suddenly aware of the rhythmic background noise of the waves, the call of a seagull, the fading sunset still a faint glow on the horizon. The smell of salt in the air and the hum of civilization, of people and buildings, just behind them.

Ronan took a step and, with a hand to the small of her back, steered them both toward their hotel. As soon as they were walking, his hand fell away.

The silence lasted all the way back to the hotel, all the way through the foyer, all the way into the lifts where Ronan pushed six for his floor and nine for hers. When the doors opened, he stepped out, but kept one foot inside to hold the doors for a moment.

"Cassie, I..." His eyes met hers for the first time and his words faded away. One hand raised and for a moment Cassie was sure he was going to reach out and stroke her hair.

She struggled hard to contain herself. Part of her wanted to throw herself at him, to beg him to take her to his room and make love to her all night—all her carefully laid out plans be damned. So what if Part Three happened before Part One was done? So what if he didn't match the description of the man she wanted? So what if he held her future with Country Style in his hands?

She couldn't help wondering what it would be like to let him know how devastatingly attractive she found him, how hard it was for her to resist him. But even if she somehow found the courage for that, she couldn't bear to take the risk that he might reject her. What if he kissed women like that all the time? Maybe it meant nothing to him.

Then somewhere inside, among all that anxiety and desire, a little voice reminded her more loudly that giving this man any more power over her was a really, *really* bad idea.

"Good night, Ronan," she said, proud that her voice was steady. She sounded professional, remote. As she should.

He took her cue. "Good night," he said, with a small nod of his head. He stepped fully out of the lift and the doors closed, taking him from her sight.

Cassie staggered back to lean against the lift wall and let out the breath she'd been holding. She felt like she'd run a marathon, her legs shook and her heart was pumping double time.

What on earth had she done? How stupid could one woman be?

Back in her room, Cassie paced the short length of carpet between the bedroom and the window, wondering what to do next. How could she have let what had just happened, happen? She needed advice. *She needed her head put back on straight.*

A quick glance at her watch told her it was almost nine, which made it almost midnight back in Melbourne. She should be tired after her early start. She should just go to bed.

Instead she picked up her mobile phone and dialed. The one person in her life she always turned to when she needed support. Graham.

He was awake, as she'd known he would be. The man slept barely five hours a night. It was the only way he managed to fit everything in.

"Cassie, my girl," he answered, no mention of the late hour of her call.

"Hi, Graham."

"Where are you?"

"Fremantle."

"Ah. How's the store there?"

"Looking great. They've done some fantastic stuff with their bedroom suite displays. I took some photos and I'll email them out to all the stores as idea starters."

"Good, good." He sounded a little distracted.

"They're having a few staffing issues," Cassie continued. "The new junior salesperson hasn't been very reliable and Brenda—she's the one who's been with them for years—isn't holding up well healthwise at the moment, so they keep getting caught short. I've suggested they put the junior on performance management and look at hiring a new senior to fill Brenda's shoes instead."

"You've got it all under control then," Graham said.

Cassie couldn't shake the feeling that he wasn't really listening.

"Look, Graham, I really called because I wanted to talk to you about the Conroy Corporation consultant—"

"Cassie, don't start this again," he interrupted, definitely listening now and annoyed. "I know you weren't thrilled about this right from the start, but I have my reasons."

"I know you do." Cassie fought to keep the whine out of her voice. Tiredness from the day was beginning to seep into her bones and she realized now that whatever she'd hoped to get from this conversation, it wasn't coming. Making the call had been a reflex, but it had been a bad idea. Graham wasn't going to call off Conroy Corporation because Cassie had almost let herself be seduced by their consultant and was now feeling confused about it all. And if she was looking for the sympathy, reassurance or fatherly concern that she occasionally sought from Graham, well, that wasn't coming, either. Because it wasn't as if she could tell him what had happened with Ronan down at the beach.

"Cassie, all I ask is that you cooperate with the Conroy consultant for now."

Cassie sucked in a breath and sternly told herself to put on her big-girl pants. She was feeling hurt and scared and she'd run to the next best thing she had to a daddy. Not really the behavior of a CEO.

"Of course, Graham. I'm working closely with him, giving him access to all the information he needs." And, seemingly, access to some stuff he *didn't* need, but she was trying her best not to think about that. Or about Ronan's expensive-smelling aftershave, or his soft lips or the slight bite of his stubble against her chin.

"Good. I know you'll do your best. I've got complete faith in you."

Cassie managed a smile. Praise from Graham always made her feel a little glowy. Perhaps because he didn't dole it out very often, or perhaps because he was the only family she had. But a little of the sharp edge wore off her anxiety. A very little.

"Thanks, Graham. I appreciate it. And will I see you at the Hawthorn store on Monday?" she asked. "For the opening?"

"Ah…" Graham hesitated. "Maybe. Probably. I'm not sure. I've got other meetings. Don't know if I'll make it. Have to see how I go."

"What's up?" Cassie asked, instantly concerned by the strange babbling. Graham Taylor was never uncertain about *anything*. Certainly not something as simple as whether or not he'd be attending a store opening.

"Nothing, nothing," Graham replied quickly. "Hopefully I'll see you there."

"Okay." Cassie shrugged. "I'll give you another progress call later in the week to let you know how we're going."

"Good stuff. Thank you, Cassie, my girl."

"Thanks, Graham, 'bye."

"Good night."

Cassie disconnected. She felt slightly calmer, but there was still a jittery, fluttery feeling under her skin. Ronan's touch, the heat of his body, the feel of his lips against hers—all the sensations were too easy to recall, sitting right at the edge of her memory. The very idea of what Graham might say if he knew what had just happened… It didn't bear thinking about.

She stripped off and took a cool shower, hoping it might pull the heat of the evening from her body. Unfortunately, Cassie had a bad feeling that cold water was no cure. The only cure for this kind of fever was a tall dark Irish-American called Ronan McGuire, and he wasn't available to her, not even on prescription.

CASSIE COULDN'T MANAGE to choke down the cold, soggy toast and lukewarm tea that the room-service breakfast presented her with. A knot of sick anxiety had wedged in her throat and wouldn't be dislodged. She was terrified of facing Ronan in the morning light, now that the previous evening's activities seemed so wanton and wrong.

She stared at herself in the mirror as she tied back her hair and tried to put on mascara. Her hand shook and a black smudge appeared under her lower eyelid, one to match the dark shadows her sleepless night had already put there.

She sighed in disgust.

"Get it together, Cassie," she told herself, giving a stern look to the mirror. She was getting good at lecturing herself. "Grow up. You've got another three days to get through. And Country Style means everything to you." As her life attested. "Get Part One of the Plan done before you think about what's next."

She was going to pretend nothing had happened. That was the decision she'd come to at some point around three or four this morning. If he mentioned it—which she hoped he wouldn't—she'd be casual and dismissive.

She stood straighter and peered at her reflection. She could do this.

"Oh, don't worry about it," she said to the mirror with a carefree wave of her hand. "It was nothing. Just a combination of beer and summer evening. Let's pretend it never happened."

Her eyes lit on the shaking mascara wand in her fingers and her shoulders slumped. She'd have to do something about that.

As it turned out, her rehearsal was for nothing—clearly Ronan had come to the same decision.

When she met him in the foyer he greeted her politely and coolly. He'd already snagged a cab, and he helped her lift her luggage into the boot. He was so professional, she half expected him to call her "ma'am" again.

On the plane, when they took off and Cassie's nerves threatened to take over, he didn't hold her hand again but he did make conversation that helped to distract her. It was all Country Style–related, but Cassie didn't mind. Besides, for the first time in her life, it honestly felt as if she had bigger problems than a possible plane crash. Funny how perspectives could change so quickly.

They were almost about to land in Sydney when Ronan snapped his laptop shut and pushed it under the seat in front. He sat still for a while, staring straight ahead, the only movement the tapping of his finger against the armrest.

His sudden stiffness pulled Cassie from the long-hand notes she'd been making about their upcoming store visits.

"What is it?" she asked, concerned. Her immediate thought was that he'd noticed something wrong with the plane. Just because she was hiding her fear better didn't mean it wasn't still there.

He turned his head and his eyes met hers, searching. "Cassie…last night…"

A clench of anxiety twisted Cassie's belly. The casual words she'd so carefully rehearsed in the mirror vanished into thin air.

"I owe you an apology." He sounded genuinely contrite, but his face was still professionally blank. "It was unprofessional of me and I hope it won't affect our working relationship. I'd…" His mask slipped as his forehead creased and his eyes became troubled. "I'd very much appreciate it if we could keep it between ourselves."

He was worried she was going to blab? As if she'd ever want anyone to know that she'd flung herself at the gorgeous Ronan, only to have him throw her advance back in her face. It wasn't quite the most humiliating experience of her life—that had been when she was seventeen and it was still etched in her memory in vivid, colorful detail—but it wasn't far off.

Her surprise at his request must have shown because his eyebrows knitted even further together.

"What?" he asked.

She tried hard to wipe her face of all expression. "Don't worry about it," she said. She tried that careless wave of her hand she'd practiced in front of the mirror, but she accidentally hit him on the arm and even the brief touch through the cotton of his shirt sent a surge of remembered longing through her that she tried hard to tamp down. "My lips are sealed."

It was the wrong thing to say. Ronan's eyes immediately went to her mouth, as if to check the veracity of her statement. His gaze was almost a caress, bringing back the memories of their kiss, of how soft and tender his lips had been against hers.

The plane bumped and dipped as it hit a pocket of turbulence and a strangled noise of fear left Cassie's throat before she could rein it in. The seat-belt sign dinged on.

She sat back in her seat, her eyes screwed shut. A now-familiar comforting warmth reached her as Ronan's fingers interlaced with her own. The feeling of his hand clasped around hers reminded her of their kiss, of how her body had responded to him, and that was as effective a distraction as any.

"Cassie, relax. We're just about to land. It's only a few bumps. Nothing to be scared of." His low, gentle voice continued in her ear, murmuring reassuring words while he held her hand just as tightly as she clasped his.

Cassie wasn't sure if she should be more scared of the plane crashing or of the man sitting next to her. But she didn't let go until they were safely on the ground.

CHAPTER SIX

ONCE THEY WERE OFF THE PLANE, Cassie fought the embarrassment of having held Ronan's hand so tightly her fingers still tingled. It seemed embarrassment had been her number one emotion ever since he had arrived.

For some reason, holding on to him calmed her, made the panic recede a little. It had been the same when they'd kissed and she'd almost lost herself—he'd been an anchor, keeping her grounded, keeping her safe, while she'd forgotten to be scared.

It was irrational to think that the man who could potentially undermine all her career hopes and dreams—who could ruin her Plan—was her safe port, her anchor, but then Cassie seemed to have been thinking quite a few irrational things since Ronan McGuire had turned up.

Ronan, for his part, was once again pretending nothing had happened. He was apparently good at that.

"Hang on a sec," she said as they passed a chocolate store in the airport on the way out to the taxi rank. She headed inside and found a large box of gourmet truffles.

Ronan gave her a questioning look.

"For Trent, the store manager at Moore Park. It's his

birthday today, and I wanted to take something he could share with the staff."

Ronan nodded and stood back to watch while the sales assistant wrapped Cassie's purchase in bright paper and a ribbon.

Cassie smiled as she thought about the visit ahead. She was looking forward to seeing Trent. They'd worked together when Cassie had first joined Country Style, and while Cassie's path had taken her into management, Trent had always loved the hands-on running of stores. He'd led some of Country Style's largest outlets, and had a reputation as a friendly if no-nonsense boss, a brilliant merchandiser, unrivaled salesperson— and for partying as hard as he worked. He and his partner, Matthew, had moved from Melbourne to Sydney a couple of years earlier so that Trent could take up the management role at the store. Cassie's limited social life had seriously felt their loss.

Outside, the temperature was cooler than it had been in Perth, but the humidity was higher. The long flight plus the time difference between the west and east coast meant it was already late afternoon—they'd only fit in the one store visit at Moore Park today. They had all of tomorrow to tour around the other Sydney stores, before they headed back to Melbourne the following day.

Ronan was silent in the taxi and that suited Cassie fine. It gave her time to pull herself together, to focus on the work ahead and remind herself of the points she needed to discuss with Trent.

The Country Style store was located inside a shopping center, a huge mall dedicated to home furnishings, decor and electronic goods. The store had an excellent position—one Cassie had personally negotiated with the center management—and as they walked toward it, Cassie couldn't help smiling. The window displays were perfect, showing off the latest range of dining suites. Trent must have taken personal inspiration for the display, because one setting was arranged as if it was about to host a birthday party—colorful streamers hung from a low chandelier, pretty glasses and crockery were set out as if waiting for champagne and birthday cake. A bright posy of flowers in the center of the table pulled it all together.

"Cassie!"

Cassie barely had time to wonder if Trent had some kind of watch out for her arrival before he enveloped her in a hug. She returned it as best she could with her handbag, the bag with the chocolates and her laptop all hanging from her hands and shoulders. Her wheeled case fell to the floor with a thump.

"Trent," she said. A lump rose in her throat, but she swallowed it away. What was with the emotion? Although the distance had meant they'd lost touch a little in recent years, Trent was one of her oldest friends. But she'd never felt like crying at a hug from him before. It must be stress, she told herself.

Trent put his hands to her shoulders and stepped back to look her up and down.

"Cassie, love, you look wrecked. Mel told me what's going on. Where's this wanker who's trying to prove you don't know what you're doing?"

"I guess that would be me," Ronan said, stepping out

from behind Cassie. She winced at Trent's impulsive words, but Ronan's face was impassive. "Ronan Mc-Guire." Ronan held out his hand.

Without missing a beat, Trent shook it and gave him an assessing look up and down. "Sorry about that," he said, without looking the least bit sorry at all. "It's just we're all pretty protective of our Cassie, here."

"I understand," Ronan said magnanimously.

Again, an irritating lump of emotion rose in Cassie's throat.

Trent gave her another quick squeeze before bending down to grab her abandoned case. "Come on, let's get your stuff out the back and then I'll take you around the store. We've done a few new things with the merchandising that I think you're going to like."

Cassie nodded, relieved to get things back on a business footing.

The next hour disappeared in an instant. Cassie had her usual chat with all the staff members, and Trent was keen to take her and Ronan around the whole store to view the new room-setting tableaus he'd created. He was showing off, being overly dramatic and excessively sycophantic toward Cassie, but she knew what he was trying to do. And she couldn't exactly pull him aside and tell him to cut it out while Ronan was standing by, watching.

For his part, Ronan continued to ask the reasonable, interested questions he'd asked the other store managers, and he didn't react to Trent's provocation at all.

When they arrived back at the counter area, the staff had already packed up the exterior displays and were about to lower the roller door to close the store for the night.

Cassie quickly grabbed the chocolates she'd purchased. "Happy birthday, Trent." She presented the gift to him in front of the team. "I thought I'd get something you might like to share."

Trent ripped off the wrapping paper. "Forget it!" he said, eyes twinkling with mischief. He held up the box and showed the expensive chocolate truffles to the gathered team. "You're not getting a single bite."

There was some good-natured complaining from the staff, mostly because they, like Cassie, knew that Trent was all bluster. Cassie was positive the chocolates would be opened the next morning for everyone to share.

"Right," Trent said, marshaling everyone together. "Drinks time it is. See you all at the pub. First round is on me."

Cassie frowned as the team began to scatter, picking up their belongings and heading for the door.

"Trent, I don't think—"

"You guys have to come, too, of course," Trent said, interrupting.

Cassie gave Ronan a look. Part of her wanted to join Trent for the celebration—she hadn't seen him in months and she knew it would be a fun evening. But she wasn't sure about the wisdom of taking Ronan to informal staff drinks—she couldn't control what the staff might say to him—or perhaps more important, what *Trent* might say to him. But she also couldn't see herself dumping Ronan alone at the hotel while she went out.

Ronan lifted his shoulders in a slight shrug. "It's okay with me."

"Of course it is," Trent announced, hustling them both toward the exit. "And even if it wasn't—" he linked his arm through Cassie's and shot a look over his shoulder at Ronan "—there's nothing you can do about it."

Cassie groaned. She wasn't sure if Ronan would overhear, but she leaned in and spoke under her breath to Trent. "You need to tone it down, Trent. Ronan's not that bad."

"Not that bad?" Trent didn't bother to lower his voice in reply. "My sweet, he's a wet dream on legs and that accent of his makes bits of me sit up and take notice, if you know what I mean. But no one messes with my Cassie."

Cassie sighed and looked over her shoulder. There was no way he hadn't heard that. Ronan quirked his eyebrow at her. Thankfully, an amused smile played at the corners of his mouth.

Good Lord. Cassie was going to have to keep Trent and Ronan apart all night, for her own sanity if nothing else.

Once they reached the bar they found the team had already snagged a large table with a padded bench surrounding two sides. She needn't have worried about Ronan talking with loose-lipped members of staff—none of the young crew around the table were remotely interested in speaking to him; they didn't even want to sit next to him.

Trent had clearly done some prep work to poison the well.

Cassie ended up sitting between Trent and Ronan at one end of the table, while the rest of the team huddled at the other. She wished she'd been sensible enough to refuse to come along in the first place. But they were here now and the best she could do was choke down a glass of the champagne Trent had ordered for her then make her excuses.

"So, Ronan, how's your visit to Oz been so far?" Trent asked, leaning over her.

Ronan smiled. "It's only been a couple of days, and most of those have been filled with work, but I love it. I'd like to come back and have a real vacation."

"Better than the old U.S. of A., would you say?"

"Well, I—"

Trent didn't let Ronan finish. "I mean, you guys know how to do a theme park, I'll say that. But the food's awful. When Matthew and I went to Florida, we couldn't find a decent pizza to save ourselves. Why do you think that is?"

Ronan smiled politely. Dangerously politely, Cassie thought. "I guess it depends on where—" he began, more patiently than Trent deserved.

Once again, Trent cut in over the top of Ronan's defense. "And the customer service! I'd heard that Americans were supposed to be so good at it, but we didn't see anything that was better than what we'd offer here.

Especially at Country Style. And you have to tip every-one just to get them to do their jobs."

Ronan sat stiffly, but didn't say anything, clearly aware that Trent wouldn't listen anyway. For his part, Trent seemed oblivious of the effect his careless in-sults were having, and he took a long sip of champagne before posing his next question.

"And what about Country Style? What are your thoughts so far?"

Just as Cassie had been about to interrupt, worried about just how much Trent could test Ronan's patience before Ronan decided he'd had enough, she stopped herself. Instead, she pricked up her ears to listen care-fully to Ronan's answer. It was a question she hadn't had the nerve to ask herself.

"Very impressive," he said smoothly, giving nothing away.

"That's Cassie's work, you know," Trent said. "Gra-ham's done bugger all in this business for the past five years. Every bit of growth and expansion is thanks to Cassie."

Cassie wasn't sure whether to blush or cringe. "Oh, Trent, it's not as simple as that. You know it's been a team effort and—"

"I have no doubts as to Cassie's skills and profes-sionalism," Ronan interrupted.

"But you must, or you wouldn't be here," Trent coun-tered.

"Trent, it's not Ronan's—" Cassie tried again.

"I have a job to do," Ronan responded. "Just as you do."

The two men were sitting forward, staring at each

other, a strange male dynamic pulsing between them. If Cassie hadn't known better, she'd have thought they were fighting over her. They were fighting for dominance, that much was sure. Two alpha males, circling each other, trying to work out who was pissing on the other's patch.

"Pretty crappy job, checking up on people, trying to find their weaknesses, undermining all the hard work they've done." Trent's voice raised in challenge.

"There's a little more to it than that." Ronan's voice, in contrast, dropped, becoming quieter and smoother. And far, far more threatening. That shuttered, cold look was back in his eyes.

There was no doubt in Cassie's mind as to who the winner would be in this battle.

"Well!" Cassie interrupted, raising her champagne glass. "This is a birthday celebration, so I think it's time to toast the birthday boy. Happy birthday, Trent!"

The staff picked up her cheers, and for a moment the testosterone levels around her lessened as the focus shifted and everyone raised their glasses. Even Ronan joined in, raising his untouched glass of champagne and smiling. Only Cassie would have noticed the way his smile didn't quite reach his eyes.

The last thing she needed was a fight between Trent and Ronan. What on earth would Graham think? It was imperative she keep things calm, just long enough so they could make their excuses and leave without seeming too insulting to Trent. He was her friend, after all, even if his behavior so far tonight had been less than exemplary. She knew it was well-intentioned, even if the execution was far from ideal.

She gave Trent a nudge with her shoulder. "How many birthdays have we celebrated together now, Trent? Ten?" she said, trying to keep the subject away from work.

Trent turned to Cassie and awarded her one of his winning smiles. "I think it might be eleven now, my sweet."

"Well, you're looking good for an old man," Cassie teased.

"I do my best, but it's hard to keep up with the young ones these days." Trent sighed dramatically and gestured to the other side of the table. The team had ordered another round of drinks, and two full glasses had appeared in front of Cassie and Trent; none for Ronan, whose first glass sat full and untouched on the table, anyway.

"You do okay," Cassie said reassuringly.

"I can't handle the clubs the way I used to. Matthew and I sit at home and if we watch a new-release DVD instead of whatever's on television we congratulate ourselves on having an exciting night." He gave a theatrical sigh.

Cassie gave the laugh he expected. "Well, eventually we all have to slow down. We're not the bright young things we used to be."

"Pah!" Trent waved his hand. "You, my sweet, will always be a bright young thing as far as I'm concerned." He smiled at her, and Cassie felt her cheeks heat with the unexpected compliment. "Ronan?" Trent leaned forward, and Cassie felt a moment of dread at what he might say. "Has Cassie here told you how she was my apprentice?"

Cassie's stomach did another of those turbulent swoops and she cursed herself. Trent knew a sizable chunk of her history, including parts she'd much rather Ronan not find out. Why hadn't she considered that before bringing up their past? Before agreeing to come to drinks?

She spoke hurriedly. "Oh, Trent, Ronan doesn't want to hear—"

"Apprentice?" Ronan interrupted. "Cassie worked for you?"

Trent nodded. Cassie could see he was about to launch into storytelling mode and her anxiety doubled. "Trent, please," she tried again. "There's no need—"

"Oh, darling girl, you're too modest for your own good," Trent admonished. He turned to Ronan to continue his story. "After Graham hired her, he assigned her to my store. Brought her around personally. A little waif of a thing she was! Just a scrap of a girl who needed a hug as much as she needed a good meal." Trent put an arm around Cassie's shoulders and gave her a squeeze.

Cassie winced. Experience told her there was very little she could do once Trent was on a roll. She gripped her half-empty champagne glass tightly, hoping he would remember what was at stake. "Trent," she said, trying to put heavy meaning into the single syllable. Trying to tell him to stop. "You don't need to go into *all* the details."

Trent gave her a pouty look. "Cassie doesn't want me to brag about her, but I'm gonna, my sweet, sorry." He switched back to Ronan who, Cassie noted, was sitting forward, paying careful attention. "There she was, and I thought, 'Oh, no, Graham's picked up a little charity case and he's landing me with her.' She was practically starved, and the first thing I did was buy her a sandwich and a coffee before we sat down to talk about her job."

That wasn't quite true. Graham had bought the coffee and sandwich that first day. Trent had bought her plenty of sandwiches since then, though, so Cassie wasn't going to quibble.

Ronan was frowning. "What do you mean, 'charity case'? Why was she hungry?"

Cassie tried to interrupt again, but neither man was paying her the least bit of attention.

"That brother of hers. Deserting her the way he did. Honestly, Cassie's far kinder to him than he deserves."

Cassie saved her breath trying to defend Pete. He'd spent two years of his life parenting a teenage girl, and he'd escaped as soon as he could. Who could blame him? He deserved a life. And she'd been okay. Eventually.

"Brother? The one in London?" Ronan asked.

Trent nodded. "After Cassie's parents died, Pete took care of her. But practically the day after she finished high school he ran off to London. Left her to fend for herself with two hundred dollars and the rent paid for a month. A month!" Trent repeated in outrage. "By the time she came to me, she was living in a shelter, down to her last five dollars. The girl was about to end up on the street." He shuddered. "And goodness knows what might have happened to her there."

"It wasn't like that," Cassie protested. But her voice held no conviction. Because that was pretty much exactly how it was. Except there had been no shelter—not by that time. By the time she'd run into Graham, she'd already been living in a squat for two weeks.

"It's just lucky she interviewed with Graham and he saw the potential in her—the potential for this future star of Country Style." Trent gave Cassie a pat on the head and she winced. "He gave her to me to train, and the rest is history!" he finished with a flourish. He raised his glass in the air and clinked it against Cassie's. "Just look at her now. You'd never know that she used to be a pitiful little orphan girl, saved from the jaws of drugs and prostitution by Country Style. I'm so proud of her." He beamed.

She gave him a feeble smile—he meant well, she knew that. Trent thought he'd just done her a favor. But her skin felt raw and exposed, as if she were naked while everyone else wore clothes.

She needed to get out of there.

Stumbling over her chair, she stood. "Happy birthday, Trent. Hope you have a great night. I need to—" she fumbled with her bags and case "—need to get to the hotel. Get stuck into my emails. The Hawthorn store opening on Monday still has a few details to iron out. And there's all the usual stuff. Also have to prepare for…tomorrow."

She was babbling and her hands were shaking.

Then, suddenly, her bags were smoothly lifted from

her, a firm, warm hand rested in the small of her back, steering her gently through the busy bar to the cooling evening outside. A cab magically materialized in front of her and before she knew it, she was sitting in the back and they were speeding toward their hotel.

He didn't say anything, but Ronan's warm, solid presence beside her was irrationally comforting, just like on the plane. He sat close to her, close enough to know that if she moved just a fraction to her left, she'd be able to lean her head on his shoulder. The idea was appealing, but she couldn't bring herself to show him how shaken she was. She wasn't quite sure why Trent's revelations had affected her so badly tonight. She'd put the skeletons of her past far back in her closet a long time ago.

It must be the stress. She couldn't afford for anything to disrupt her Plan—and everything was riding on Part One. Hearing her pathetic history rehashed, in front of the man who controlled *her* future, was unsettling because of what it could mean for the report. What if he decided that her past made her an undesirable leader?

Ronan got them checked in at the hotel, and Cassie stood back and let him, nibbling on her fingernails as she watched. She was trying hard to gather herself together, to pull her present-day, take-charge self back into place over the broken little girl that Trent's story had exposed. The little girl that always lingered just under the surface, no matter what Cassie did, no matter how much she achieved. No matter how hard she shoved those skeletons back.

"We have adjoining rooms," Ronan announced as he led the way to the lifts.

The doors opened at their floor and they stepped out. Ronan held one of the key cards out to her. Cassie grabbed it and they walked a short way down the corridor until a still-functioning part of her brain matched a door with the number on the cardboard folder that held her key. She fumbled, trying to slip the card through the reader, but her shaking fingers wouldn't cooperate and it fell to the floor.

Ronan swore under his breath, and in a blur of movement the card was picked up, her door was opened, and Cassie, her luggage and Ronan were in her room, the door banging shut behind them. It was a bad idea, Cassie knew, but she didn't feel strong enough to fight it.

He stood just a couple of steps from her, studying her. The emotion on his face was hard to interpret. Pity, frustration, anger. Anger with her or with himself?

"He was an idiot," Ronan said, tunneling his fingers through his hair. He shrugged off his suit jacket and lay it on the chair nearby.

He was angry with Trent? "He's my friend," Cassie said, feeling she had to put up some defense. She had too few friends not to value them, even when they unknowingly opened old wounds.

There was silence for a moment and Cassie watched from somewhere outside herself as Ronan waged an internal battle.

"Aw, crap," he muttered. One long stride and she was

in his arms, her cheek crushed to his chest, his arms tight around her. Cassie wrapped her arms around his waist and held on for dear life.

CHAPTER SEVEN

RONAN BURIED HIS FACE in Cassie's hair, pressing his lips to the crown of her head. The same two—seemingly opposite—feelings she seemed to evoke in him were once again at war. Desire. Protectiveness.

At least now the protectiveness he could explain. Ronan had always had a weakness for strays. His mother had despaired at the number of kittens and puppies and birds and, sometimes, other kids, he used to bring home.

Underneath that professional exterior that Cassie Hartman wore every day was a brokenhearted stray, a girl who'd been left to fend for herself far too soon. She wasn't weak, though. Ronan swallowed hard when he recognized the swell of pride in his chest at what she'd managed to do for herself. So many other people, faced with such circumstances, would have given up. Cassie had made herself into a success story.

It stirred something deep within him—especially when he thought of his own situation. He was a man of privilege, born into wealth, who, in comparison to Cassie, had had everything handed to him on a platter. Sure, he'd worked hard, and sure, his father hadn't given him any special advantage over anyone else in the firm, but he'd never had to struggle the way Cassie had. Not for anything as basic as food and shelter.

Could that be the root of his restlessness? Was it because he'd never really had to struggle to succeed that he felt as if he'd never accomplished anything in his life? Was that why he'd taken the risk with Sarah Forsythe? He realized, with sudden clarity, that he'd known the risks of sleeping with her. He'd known it could backfire, could jeopardize his career.

Had he done it just to push the envelope? To see how far he could go before his father cut him some slack? He put the thought away to examine later.

"It wasn't as bad as Trent made out," Cassie protested weakly, her voice muffled against his chest.

"No, I'm sure it was worse."

Ronan steered them to the bed—the only other place in the room to sit was a single desk chair. He leaned down and, scooping one arm under Cassie's knees, sat on the edge of the bed with her huddled in his lap. She didn't protest.

"Yeah," she breathed in answer.

Ronan stroked her back without speaking. Half of him wanted to know while the other half didn't.

"Graham was supposed to be my first trick," she said eventually.

Ronan blew out a breath. He didn't quite know why, but having heard Trent's version of Cassie's life story, he'd suspected something of the sort.

"He laughed at me when I tried to proposition him. Then he bought me lunch, and told me he'd give me a job. And if I wanted to live on the streets, that was fine, but wouldn't I like a career and a chance at a proper life?"

Cassie had filled out since those days, Ronan was sure; her lush curves were pressed against him right now as evidence. But he had no problems picturing a scared, skinny teenager, desperate to do what it took to survive.

"I met this girl at the shelter I went to when I couldn't pay the rent and the landlord evicted me. I didn't know what to do—I'd been trying to get jobs, but no one would hire me. She helped me. Let me stay with her at a squat she'd found when my time at the shelter was up. She…she told me what I had to do. It was the only way to get some money. She did it. She did it to pay for drugs. I just wanted the money for a place to stay. So I watched her, watched how she walked up to a man and what she said to him, then I stood on the corner and did what she'd done."

A shiver went through Cassie's body and Ronan held her tighter.

"I can't bear to imagine what my life might have been like if someone else had walked past at that point."

"It wasn't meant to be your fate," Ronan murmured.

"I owe everything—my life—to Graham. To Country Style."

He shook his head. "No. You owe him one lucky break. The rest you did yourself, with hard work and determination."

She was silent for a moment. Her body stiffened against his, as if she'd just realized where she was.

"I shouldn't be telling you this. I don't know why…"

She gave a short, bleak laugh and pushed against his chest, her head rising to meet his gaze. "I'm sorry. Seems like we've managed to have yet another night we have to pretend didn't happen."

She'd pulled herself together. She didn't look as frightened or vulnerable as she had before. But those feelings still lingered in her eyes, on the edges of that beautiful velvet-brown. And that combination of controlled and fragile, of certain and fearful, was potent.

Before Ronan could consider the wisdom of what he was doing, he'd lowered his mouth to hers, capturing it in a sweet kiss. Cassie's eyes went wide with surprise, but as he stroked her lips with his, the surprise faded and was replaced with desire, a hunger to match his own.

Her eyelids fluttered closed and she parted her lips, surprising him by taking charge of the kiss. Her tongue inexpertly surged to meet his own, her hand fisted in his shirt. A thrill shot through him and he responded in kind, turning the kiss blazing in an instant. Tongues, lips and teeth clashed as they tasted each other, fought to possess each other.

Ronan's hands went to her face, cupping her cheeks, tilting her head to suit his possession. They were both breathing raggedly, gasping for air before plunging back into hot, wet exploration.

His entire body strained to be closer to her. Her plump bottom on his lap was a tantalizing tease all in itself and, twisted as she was, her breasts brushed his torso in a way that wasn't nearly enough.

He dragged himself from her mouth, only so he

could press his lips to the sweet skin of her neck, trailing openmouthed kisses down that pale column until he met her fluttering pulse and flicked at it with his tongue.

His fingertips followed the line of her jaw and stroked the curve of her ear, before landing at the thick knot of hair at her nape. He lifted his head to peer at it, wondering if there was a pin or a clip he could undo, but the heavy curls covered whatever means she'd used to tie them back.

Ronan delivered a sucking kiss to her collarbone before muttering, "Let me see it." He tapped the knot of hair.

Cassie's hands moved without protest, tugging and pulling, and then it was loose. The sweet smell of patchouli filled his senses as she draped the beautiful, wavy curtain of hair over one shoulder.

Not touching it would be impossible. And Ronan also knew that as soon as he did, he'd be lost. He didn't care.

With a sudden move, he clasped Cassie around the waist and shifted on the bed, lying back on the pillows and pulling her over him. They were pressed belly to belly, and Cassie looked down at him, her face filled with questioning surprise. He didn't want to give her the chance to question, to think, to analyze—not yet. Not when he already knew the answers and didn't want to hear them.

Instead he threaded his fingers through that glorious brunette mane and brought her lips to his with a groan.

Cassie followed his direction willingly, opening

her mouth to him, stroking his tongue with her own. He tasted her thoroughly, exploring every sensitive little spot. His body craved more, reminding him that Cassie's pelvis was perfectly lined up with his own—just a few layers of clothing stood in the way.

Curiously, she hadn't moved against him, he didn't feel her body writhing to match her mouth's responsiveness.

He twisted, tumbling them both over, and Cassie now lay beneath him. Her legs parted under his weight and he settled in the cradle of her thighs. He gave an experimental thrust of his hips and Cassie's breath caught.

"Oh!" It was almost a cry of pain, but the way her eyes rolled back and her neck arched told him it was far more than that.

The invitation was impossible to resist, and Ronan lowered his mouth to the delicate skin under her ear.

Her fingers scrambled over his back as if she was unsure whether to pull him closer or push him away. Ronan kept up the pressure on her core, rocking against her, reveling in the way she tilted her hips to meet his, to magnify and concentrate the sensation.

It took only a moment to undo the buttons of her shirt and tug it out of those boring navy pants. The translucent pale blue lace of her bra was a pleasant surprise—he'd been expecting plain white cotton. That wouldn't have been a disappointment, but the lace revealed two strawberry-pink nipples straining for his touch.

His hand cupped one breast, pinching a nipple between thumb and forefinger, while his mouth dove to capture the other, nibbling wet little kisses through the lace before he sucked the peak into his mouth.

Cassie moaned and her back arched higher into him, her hips thrusting against his in ever-more-frantic moves. Ronan met her rhythm, letting her use him to seek the perfect position, the one that would give her the contact she needed. He felt it when she did, a shiver went through her body and her eyes flew open.

Ronan lifted his head from her breast and raised himself to kiss her lips again, making sure not to move his lower body as she pulsed against him. He pulled her bottom lip between his teeth, sucking it into his mouth before releasing it with a gentle pop.

Cassie's eyes went wide and her motions stilled. That fear, that panic, was back in her eyes.

"It's okay, sweetheart," he murmured, pressing a gentle kiss across her full mouth.

"Ronan, I—"

She broke off with a groan as Ronan jerked his hips against hers again. The zipper of his suit pants felt like it might become permanently etched into his skin, but he could sense the frantic edge of Cassie's desire. He'd let her have this, then they'd do it again, only slower and without clothes.

"Come for me," he whispered in her ear. "Take what you need and come."

Her eyes screwed shut and for a moment Ronan thought she might push him away, but then she moved against him again and her already ragged breathing became desperate gasps.

She bit her bottom lip with her front teeth, and the

action drew him back to her mouth. He flicked her lips with his tongue until she opened to him. Then he plunged inside, mimicking what his body wished it could do farther down.

He felt her climax building, her body tense, her fingers digging into his back, fingernails pinching him through his shirt. She wrenched her mouth from his with a gasp, then arched and froze, her face contorted in the bliss of her release. She cried out as spasms racked her body and Ronan caught her mouth again, swallowing her cries, still moving against her, drawing out her pleasure as long as he could.

The spasms turned to shudders and then her body relaxed, exhausted by her efforts. She lay beneath him, breathing heavily, her eyes still closed.

"So beautiful," Ronan murmured, peppering her face with gentle kisses. Her peak had increased his desire, and his restraint was costing him. His arms trembled as they supported his weight over her, and he ached for his own release with an intensity that bordered on pain.

He slipped an arm around her waist and fell to the side, bringing her with him so they lay facing each other.

It took a moment for Cassie to open her eyes. Her gaze was hazy and unfocused at first and Ronan smiled at her. "Was that good, sweetheart?" He stroked a lock of silky hair behind her ear.

A hundred emotions flickered through her eyes before one seemed to win out over the others. *Embarrassment*. Her already flushed face deepened to a rosy hue.

"Ronan, I don't...I've never...I didn't mean..."

"Shh." He kissed her to shut her up. Now wasn't the time. They'd already crossed the line. They could both worry about what that meant later.

But she didn't kiss him back.

He pulled away and frowned at her. "What's the matter?"

Embarrassment had given way to wide-eyed, unconcealed fear. She was scared? Of him?

"I suppose you need to..." She waved a hand toward his groin. "Unless you already have?"

He managed a chuckle. "I'm proud to say that I managed to hold on." He loosened the finger that he'd wrapped in her hair and traced it across her bare shoulder and over the curve of her breast, following the lacy edge of her bra. "Not that watching you didn't bring me very close to the edge." He lifted his head to press a kiss to her collarbone. She shivered and her skin prickled with goose bumps. "But I have a feeling that waiting for the real thing will be worth it," he whispered.

She stiffened and the fear in her eyes increased.

He searched her face. "What's the matter?" he asked again.

"Apart from the fact that we shouldn't be doing this in the first place?" Her voice trembled.

Ronan closed his eyes and blew out a breath. "Damn." He'd been so successful in pushing all that away—convincing himself she was conspiring with him in the deception. At her words, the little angel and devil on his shoulders reappeared. The angel pouted and frowned, arms crossed and foot tapping with displeasure. The devil tried to give him a high five.

He was losing it.

"Do you think you'll be quick?"

Her nervous question had him opening his eyes again immediately. Something wasn't right. "What?"

Cassie's hand went to the button of her pants and she fumbled to undo it with shaking fingers. She looked down. "If you'll be quick, then I guess it's okay."

His hand shot out and grabbed Cassie's wrist, stopping her from undressing. A cold shiver of dread trickled down his spine, extinguishing his desire. *Graham was supposed to be her first trick.* What else had Cassie been forced to do to survive on the streets?

"Don't you want…?" Cassie trailed off as she raised her head and her eyes met his.

"Cassie? What's going on?"

She swallowed hard. "Nothing."

"That's crap. I'm not making love to someone who wants it over and done with as fast as possible."

Tears welled in her eyes and Ronan cursed his harsh tone. He was just concerned. And frustrated.

"Is this something to do with your past?" he asked, his voice gentler this time. "Did someone hurt you?" The very idea of it sent ice water through his veins and made him clench his jaw. If he got his hands on them, he wouldn't be held responsible for his actions.

She shook her head. She looked down to where his hand still encircled her wrist. Ronan loosened his grip, realizing he was probably hurting her, and he stroked the soft skin of her inner arm with his thumb.

"Tell me." He didn't want to know, but he had to at the same time.

"I'm pathetic," she said, her voice breaking on an almost sob.

"You're not pathetic."

"I am. Some parts of my life are so good, so successful, but others… That's why I needed a plan."

"I don't know what you mean." Ronan frowned, genuinely confused. He had no idea where this was going.

"I'm not hesitating because something traumatic happened to me," she said in a rush, her eyes meeting his, wide with honesty, bright with tears. "I'm hesitating because I've never done this before and I don't know what to do."

A rush of relief washed over him, releasing the vise-like clasp that had gripped his chest. "You're a virgin?"

She nodded.

Ronan closed his eyes. Disbelief warred with relief. It could have been so much worse… If she'd been raped… He shuddered at the thought.

But a *virgin?*

This was already such a bad idea. He'd yet again let his dick rule his brain, and here he was, about to have sex with a client. Again. About to *deflower* a client. God only knew where that ranked on the ladder of sexual harassment. Take Sarah Forsythe's payout and add a couple of zeros, probably.

He rolled onto his back and groaned, scrubbing at his eyes with the heels of his hands.

Cassie, with her sweet mix of sophistication and naïveté, of control and vulnerability, got right under his defenses. Confused his radar and short-circuited his control.

How else had he ended up in bed with her? Bringing her to orgasm before fully intending to sate himself inside her?

The very last thing he'd expected from this trip was to hand his father even more ammunition about his unsuitability to lead Conroy Corporation one day. Hell, he'd be lucky if he got to keep a job in the mail room at this rate.

The bed moved and Ronan opened his eyes in time to see Cassie scramble away from him, hitching her disheveled shirt over her shoulders as she stood up and fastened the buttons hurriedly. She grabbed her hair with both hands, smoothing it away from her face.

"Cassie, wait."

She turned to him, but her eyes wouldn't meet his. They spent some time staring fearfully at the persistent bulge in his pants and then darted around the room, looking at anything but him.

She was breathing fast, but with nerves this time, not arousal. "Ronan, I'm sorry, I know it's not fair to leave you...*hanging* like this, after you gave me... But I just don't think I can..." She trailed off.

"I'm a big boy, Cassie. I can handle it." He propped himself up in the bed, leaning back against the headboard, arms folded across his chest. He had to face this, take the rap for his actions. He had to know what she intended to do. How fast would she report him to his father? "We need to talk."

Cassie grabbed her case and the other room's key, which Ronan had dumped on the counter near the TV.

"Let's not," she said. "It's something we never need talk about again." She was at the door before he knew it, her hand on the doorknob. "See you downstairs at eight-thirty in the morning for store visits." She didn't turn around as she spoke. "I'm sorry." The last two words were barely a whisper as she opened the door and disappeared into the corridor outside. The door shut with a bang behind her.

Ronan swore viciously and punched the bed with his fist.

What in hell had he done?

CHAPTER EIGHT

CASSIE WAS BOTH RELIEVED and unnerved that it took only a few steps before she could unlock the door to her room and close it behind her. She needed to escape fast, but the farther away she could get from Ronan, the safer she'd be. And next door wasn't nearly far enough.

She pushed her wheeled case inside before leaning against the wall. She didn't bother with turning on any lights. As she replayed what had just happened in her head, she sank down until she was on the floor, her head in her hands.

Oh, God.

Her breath was still coming in harsh pants and her heart hammered against her ribs.

What on earth had she been thinking?

The answer was clear: she hadn't.

It was way too soon to be moving to Part Three of her plan. And she couldn't have chosen a worse candidate to work with on it. The very man who threatened the achievement of Part One.

She drew in a shaky breath as she reminded herself of her carefully organized strategy. Thinking through her meticulous blueprint for the future helped to calm her down.

Part One was underway. She'd written the report for

Graham and he was considering it. Conroy Corporation had been brought in to ratify it.

Her stomach rolled.

No. Not going to think about Ronan or what just happened. Come on, Cassie, focus. Recap the Plan.

Part One was about building the foundation, creating a solid base from which everything else could grow. Securing her role, making sure it was as definitively locked-in as any job could be these days, was her first priority.

Part Two was the easy part—or so she hoped. An appointment with a stylist, a shopping trip with Mel and she'd not only *be* CEO, she'd look the part, too.

Part Three was to take steps to rid herself of the virginity that was beginning to feel like a burden. It wasn't that she was a prude. She wasn't uptight. It was just that since Graham gave her the luckiest break of her life, she'd focused on making sure she never ended up back on the streets. Making money, providing herself with a home, with security, had been more important than a sex life—more important than anything.

She shuddered as a slideshow of images from her life before she joined Country Style flickered through her mind. Cassie had managed to avoid a lot of things in those weeks she'd been homeless, living in shelters and the squat. Drugs, for one. Sex for another. But she'd seen plenty of both. And what she'd seen had repelled and disgusted her.

All too often, when she'd been in a clinch with one of the few guys who'd asked her out over the years, an image from her past would swim into her mind. And any interest she might have had in taking things to the next level would suddenly evaporate.

She'd never been so carried away she'd given up rational thought. Never lost herself in pleasure. Never felt so safe that she forgot to keep her guard up, that she let a man be so intimate with her body.

But then what had just happened with Ronan had no relation to those past fumblings, or to the mercenary, occasionally violent, couplings she'd witnessed all those years ago.

Cassie groaned and pressed her head back against the wall as she thought about what they'd done.

They hadn't even taken their clothes off. He'd been on top of her, but he'd handed over control. "Take what you need," he'd said in that low, sexy accent of his.

Is that why she'd been able to let go? Because she'd been in control just when she'd lost it completely? It had been the same when he'd kissed her. He'd been so gentle, so undemanding—at first, anyway—that Cassie hadn't felt threatened. She hadn't felt like she'd be losing part of herself by giving in to him.

A more important question: why was Ronan attracted to her? Did he try to sleep with every woman he spent more than a day with? The man could have any woman he wanted. Why her? His arousal had been real, Cassie was sure of that. Real and scarily...large.

She struggled to take in a deep breath and blew it out. Standing on trembling legs, she turned on the lights and went about getting herself organized. She put her case on the rack, pulled out her clothes for the next day and hung them in the wardrobe. She found her toiletries bag and headed for the bathroom.

Squeezing toothpaste onto her toothbrush, Cassie looked up and saw herself in the mirror. The toothbrush froze in midair.

In her haste, she'd buttoned her shirt incorrectly and it gaped wildly. Lucky the corridor had been deserted when she'd made the mad rush between rooms, or someone would have copped an unplanned eyeful. But it wasn't the disheveled shirt that made the breath stop in her lungs.

Her hair flowed loosely around her shoulders, the soft curls for once looking alluring and elegant instead of messy and out of control. Her cheeks were colored with a pink flush that extended down to her décolletage and her lips were swollen. Her eyes were bright. The red blush caused by a five o'clock shadow rubbing against the pale skin of her collarbone was beginning to show.

She looked like a siren. Sexy and mysterious. It was an image of herself she'd never seen before.

Ronan had done this to her.

Could there possibly be a crueler irony? The man who could destroy her was the only man she'd ever felt safe enough with, relaxed enough with to…to let herself go. He was going to do the sums and work out what value Cassie added to Country Style. And whether adding or subtracting her from the mix was the best for the future of the company.

When she'd first met him, she'd been grudgingly

impressed by his intelligence, by his business acumen and his insightful improvement suggestions. Oh, and if she was being honest she'd have to say that those good looks of his hadn't escaped her notice, either.

But now that they'd spent time together, she knew there was more to him than a whip-smart brain, well-cut suit and snazzy haircut.

She remembered his concern on the plane, how he'd held her hand and talked her through her fear. The way he'd taken over this evening when Trent had unwittingly exposed her past—he'd seen her hurt, taken her out of there and wrapped her in his arms to make her feel better.

He had that beautiful smile. A way of making people feel they were special. When he listened to her, it was as if there was no one more important.

With a heavy sigh, Cassie forced herself to continue her bedtime routine. She brushed her teeth, washed her face and snapped off the lights.

She slipped between the cold, stiff hotel-room sheets. She shivered—her skin was still oversensitive and the cotton was rough. How nice it would be to snuggle into a warm body.

Ronan's warm body. Skin against skin.

She wished she'd unbuttoned his shirt.

Did he sleep naked?

Cassie expected to have another sleepless night; her mind was in uproar. But as she settled into the pillows sleepiness overcame her. Another thing Ronan was good at, she thought as she yawned. Giving her a good night's sleep.

Sydney summer sunshine streamed through the curtains Cassie had forgotten to close the night before. She stretched and checked the clock; it was still early.

Memories of last night washed over her and left her confused, embarrassed and—disturbingly—aching for more. It could never happen, of course. The sooner she got that idea cemented into her head and traitorous body, the better.

Once she had showered and dressed, she headed to the dining room for breakfast—in all the excitement of last night, she hadn't put in a room-service order.

Her breath caught when she saw Ronan already sitting at a table. His hair was damp and he was reading a newspaper with frowning concentration.

His good looks struck her all over again. That effortless grace as he turned the page, the strong jaw, broad shoulders, piercing eyes. He was in dress pants and a white shirt—no tie. The dark hair revealed by the couple of undone buttons on his shirt made blood pulse hotly through Cassie's body, leaving her flushed and shaky. God, she wanted to see the man naked. Was that really so wrong?

"Table for one?" The waiter's voice interrupted Cassie's thoughts.

"Uh…" She paused. She *had* to sit with Ronan—claiming a separate table would be ridiculous. But she wasn't sure she was quite ready to face him—she hadn't counted on running into him until they met in the foyer for the day ahead—all businesslike and with boundaries clearly in place.

"No," she said finally. "My, uh, colleague is over there. I'll join him."

"As you wish."

Ronan's eyes met hers as she made her way across the dining room. He displayed no surprise at seeing her, but he didn't smile, either.

"Good morning," Cassie said, a little too brightly, pulling out the chair opposite and taking a seat.

He gave a short nod. "Morning." He folded the newspaper and laid it by the side of his plate.

The horrible mortification she'd felt last night, when he'd choked in disbelief over the word *virgin,* rushed through her again and her cheeks burned. This man was no doubt used to sleeping with models and starlets. Women with plenty of experience, who knew how to please him, and didn't ask him to get it over quickly or run away because they were scared of what was in his pants.

The waiter saved her from thinking of what to say next by appearing with silver pots in each hand. "Coffee or tea?" he asked.

"Tea."

He deftly poured tea into Cassie's cup and topped up Ronan's coffee after Ronan made a subtle gesture with his finger. Another example of his effortless ability to influence others. Cassie grabbed the white linen napkin and put it in her lap, as much to keep her hands busy as politeness.

"Help yourself at the buffet when you're ready." The waiter nodded and disappeared.

As soon as the waiter was out of earshot, Ronan

leaned forward, fixing Cassie with a steady gaze. His eyes were the blue of a stormy sea this morning, troubled and uneasy. "Cassie. About last night…"

CHAPTER NINE

RONAN SUCKED IN A BREATH. He could do this. "About last night. I wanted to say—"

"I'm sorry I ran out on you," Cassie blurted before he could continue. "I shouldn't have. I...I wanted to... make love with you." It had begun as a whisper and finished as little more than a breath. "I don't want to be a virgin anymore."

Ronan blinked slowly, positive he couldn't have heard her properly.

"Excuse me?" he said, for lack of any other words.

Of all the reactions he'd anticipated from Cassie, this wasn't one of them. It didn't even come close to the risk mitigation strategy he'd devised last night. Sleep, as usual since he'd arrived in Australia, had eluded him. Instead he'd been busy imagining every possible scenario that could happen as a result of the evening with Cassie, and how he'd manage it. Including how he'd submit his resignation to his father, imagining the disappointed but unsurprised look on Patrick Conroy's face. He'd written the letter in his head and been more than a little shocked at his own sense of loss and guilt at the idea that Conroy Corporation wouldn't be his.

Clearly he hadn't covered *every* possible scenario.

Cassie's eyes were firmly fixed on the napkin she

was twisting in her lap. "I think that's why I let it… But I know it was inappropriate and I never should have… I know you're probably used to more…" She broke off and swallowed hard. Ronan could see how much this conversation was costing her, but he was still too dumb-founded to find his feet.

"Anyway," she said in a rush, "I'm happy to forget it all happened if you are. No sense crying over spilt milk. It happened, we'll keep it between us and no one else ever needs to know. I'd really appreciate it if you could keep it confidential."

Finally she looked up and her eyes met his. The anxi-ety was still there, but a thread of determination had ap-peared. The determination that had got her from street kid to executive. Ronan was reminded of that strange pride and admiration he'd felt last night when she'd told him her life story.

She cleared her throat before continuing. "If you're okay with separating our…what we…*I did*…how I re-acted…from our work then we should be able to move forward without any issues."

He wanted to smile at her fumbling words, at her charming shyness as she described her responsiveness to his touch. It was so…*virginal*. But while his relief at her words was palpable, he couldn't explain the dis-appointment that shot through him at the same time. What, had he been expecting her to beg him to finish the job? Or was he such a masochist that he was disap-pointed she wasn't threatening him with a harassment suit?

Ronan let out a sigh and slumped back in his chair.

He looked over to the panoramic windows that graced one wall of the hotel restaurant. The view outside was of office buildings but a gap between two skyscrapers afforded a glimpse of sparkling blue water and part of the arch of the iconic Harbour Bridge. The sun was shining, the sky was cloudless—it would be another perfect summer day.

He turned back to Cassie. Her pleading eyes were his undoing. He remembered how she'd looked the night before, staring up at him, her breath catching in pleasure, her eyes bright and trusting, her hair spread over his pillow. Creamy breasts spilling from the blue lace of her bra. His body tightened in response.

It was a shock to realize he trusted her. He'd never trusted Sarah Forsythe, and look where that had got him. He knew now that he'd seen the edge of desperation in Sarah right from the start, he'd just chosen to ignore it—blithely assuming, as he had all his life, that everything would work out fine. It always had. Until recently—when everything he'd once been so sure of had suddenly begun to unravel.

Cassie had fallen silent, and Ronan was aware she was on tenterhooks waiting for his answer. It should be the other way around, he thought wryly. He was the one who'd been expecting to grovel for forgiveness, to plead for secrecy. He should be pleased she was taking this line. Not disappointed that he wouldn't get to see her naked.

"You want to forget about it all?" he asked, trying for a pragmatic tone.

She nodded, her bottom lip caught by her teeth in uncertainty. It made him want to kiss her.

He gave her a short nod. "Then that's what we'll do. We only have one more day in Sydney and then it's back to Melbourne tomorrow morning, right?"

"Yes."

"Then let's get through today and tomorrow and once we're back in Melbourne I'll only need to see you to ask questions to finalize my report. We won't need to meet face-to-face again until the store opening on Monday."

She swallowed again and nodded. "That sounds… fine." For a moment she seemed close to tears, but then she busied herself pouring milk into her cup of tea and managed to compose her face into a carefully neutral expression. Ronan did his best to copy her.

"It's going to be another beautiful day," she said, glancing out the window to the blue sky outside.

Ronan made a vague noise of agreement. The sunshine couldn't help the personal dark cloud that had suddenly settled over him. For reasons he couldn't explain, he wanted to go back to his room, slam the door and have a good sulk about the unfairness of life. Instead he took a bite of the breakfast that had been sitting untended in front of him.

"These eggs are awful," he said after one mouthful, tossing his fork on the plate with a clatter. "Where's the waiter? I want to complain."

THE STORE VISITS LINED UP for that day were perfunctory—on his side, anyway. Ronan had all the information he required, now he just needed time in front of his computer to write up his findings. There was no need to see more of Country Style's operations. But Cassie steamed through the schedule, bringing her particular brand of magic to each store they went to.

The staff greeted her eagerly. The managers always wanted a quiet word with her. Ronan guessed they were discreetly expressing their support for her—unlike Trent—away from the ears of the consultant. By the time they left each store, the staff were smiling, all the displays had been neatened and beautifully styled, and it seemed as if customers were flowing through the doors.

She was a retail Mary Poppins.

The only time the two of them were alone was during the cab rides between stores. And so far they'd each managed to keep busy while trapped in the car together. Cassie had made call after call regarding the new store opening, while Ronan had found checking emails on his PDA a handy avoidance tactic.

He pocketed his device, jumped out of the taxi and headed in to their last visit of the day.

This store was in an outer suburb—after this it was back to the hotel and their early morning flight to Melbourne the next day. Once back in Melbourne, he had five days before he returned to San Francisco. He had already submitted his interim findings, as per his father's joyless email; he'd be able to submit his final report within a day or two of arriving back in Melbourne. Now he needed to set up the meeting with Graham Taylor to present his recommendations. Taylor would be in town for the store opening, his father had told him, so likely it would be Monday or Tuesday.

So far, everything was as he expected. The deal Taylor had on the table was a good one. Country Style was a successful, medium-size, family-style business on the brink of something much bigger. The acquisition would open up the Australian market to the international buyer, and Country Style would slash its operating costs under the new management structure.

It was win-win. Taylor would walk away with a bucket load of money. The buyers would nab themselves a profitable business with excellent future growth potential. Ronan's report was pretty much open-and-shut.

Actually, it wasn't entirely win-win, Ronan amended internally. Some people would lose. Like Cassie Hartman. Like that flirty assistant of hers. Several of the store managers he'd met on this trip would likely also go. And those boutique suppliers Cassie had cultivated, like Brentons and their sick daughter, would lose their biggest customer as the conglomerate sought economies of scale from international providers.

Cassie hadn't once asked how Ronan's report was progressing. She hadn't even asked him for his thoughts on the final outcome—something most people didn't seem to be able to resist, in his experience. But she had to have an inkling of why he was there. Graham had said he'd kept the acquisition plans secret, but Cassie was smart—she knew the market, understood the current economic pressures, had written that damn report that had sparked the buyout idea in the first place—

she had to have heard a whisper of what Taylor had planned.

"Hey, Ryan, how are you?" Cassie shook hands with another staff member, a boy who looked barely old enough to be out of school and yet had a world-weary air about him. How did she remember all their names?

"Ryan, this is Ronan McGuire—he's traveling with me to get an insight into how we do things at Country Style."

"Nice to meet you," Ryan said, offering his hand. He seemed shy, but his eyes flashed with intelligence.

Ronan managed to pull himself out of his own head to greet the kid who held out a hand, seemingly growing more nervous with every second of Ronan's silence, matched only by Cassie's nervous body language.

"Nice to meet you, too, Ryan." He flashed his most disarming smile, not sure why Cassie was bothering to introduce him to such a junior member of staff.

Cassie gave the boy a reassuring smile. "Ryan, while I chat with the rest of the team, why don't you show Ronan around the store and tell him a little about your career at Country Style?"

"I'd be happy to," the kid replied in a stilted voice, but then shot Cassie a quick grin.

Ronan's antennae pricked up immediately—he was being set up. Something about their exchange seemed rehearsed. He gave Cassie a curious look—realizing as he did that they'd barely made eye contact all day— but she just gave him a blank smile that did nothing to hide the nerves she'd suddenly developed. Why was she nervous about *this* store visit when they'd seen so many already? Was there something wrong here?

"Mr. McGuire, I'll show you out the back first."

"Thanks, Ryan. I know you'll do a good job." Cassie's voice was low and warm, and the almost intimate smile she gave the kid made Ronan's hackles rise further. Not that he was jealous of a pimply teenager. It was just…unusual.

Ryan's acne-riddled face was already red, but he blushed a violent crimson as he turned and showed Ronan to the door that led out to the storeroom behind the shopfront.

"This is where we store our smaller stocked items," he said, spreading his arm wide to indicate the shelves and stacks of merchandise. It wasn't especially tidy, but there was clearly a system in place—it was the stockroom of a busy store with a high turnover.

"All the furniture is stored in a warehouse off-site," he continued. "Here we only keep some smaller pieces as well as soft furnishings and accessories like lamps and cushions and stuff like that."

"Right," Ronan said, nodding, though still puzzled. Why was he being given a personal tour by this kid?

"And this is the kitchen—we have our team meetings in here and it's, you know, a nice place to sit and have lunch. There's no coffee machine right now, but Cameron—that's our manager—said that if we meet next month's sales target he's gonna buy one of those cappuccino machines for us."

"That's…nice." The veneer of patience that Ronan had applied over his general irritability today was wearing extremely thin. What was the point of this tour? The store's purchase of a coffee machine for its staff was hardly important in the scheme of things.

Something about Ronan's expression must have communicated his bad mood, because Ryan's manner suddenly changed, and instead of being deferential, he looked bold. His eyes flashed with a defiance Ronan swore he recognized from Cassie. Were they related? Was that what this was about?

"Sit down."

Wait—the kid was ordering him around now?

"Please," Ryan added hastily. "Cassie wanted me to tell you about how I got to work at Country Style." He pulled out a chair at the battered table in the kitchenette and gestured for Ronan to sit.

Curiosity won out over annoyance, and Ronan sat.

"I've been working for Country Style for a year and a half. I was one of the first employees to join through Cassie's program and I help her run it now. Actually, I'm the Sydney coordinator," he said, and Ronan didn't miss the swell of pride in his voice.

"Sorry, I don't know what you mean. What program?"

"It's kind of like an apprenticeship Cassie set up for homeless and at-risk youth—you work in a store part-time and go to school to do a certificate in business management. Country Style pays for the course and, as long as you keep up a good attendance record and pass, you get a full-time job at a store when you're finished."

Ah, so that explained it. The young face with old

eyes. Ronan wasn't surprised, but he had to work to keep the smile off his face. It was just like Cassie—to find a way to help other young people who'd found themselves in the same situation she'd been in. And to give them the helping hand that Graham Taylor had—by mere chance—given her.

"So far we've had eight kids go through it and six have passed and ended up working in stores. There's two more currently studying—one in Melbourne and one in Sydney. They get a mentor to help them—I'm mentoring the Sydney kid." Again the pride in Ryan's voice was unmistakable. Not only had Country Style given him a job, they'd given him a purpose, a sense of self and a future.

Ronan made a mental note to ensure he mentioned this program in his report and recommended that it continued under the new ownership. It was a solid social-responsibility initiative and could be a valuable opportunity for publicity.

But it wasn't the idea of including it in his report that was causing a tightening of his chest.

"Sounds like you're a big help to Cassie," Ronan said, careful not to sound condescending.

Ryan shrugged modestly. "If I hadn't come to work at Country Style, I don't know where I'd be right now." A dark look crossed the boy's face. "Probably dead. Or in prison. Or just earning money however I could."

"And what's your role in the store?" Ronan asked, partly to distract himself from thinking about just what kind of things Ryan would have to have done to earn money on the streets. It was too close to Cassie's own near miss.

Ryan's face immediately brightened and he went on to describe his important role in managing stock and deliveries and making orders. "And just this week I've started out on the floor—Cameron's been training me in sales. I want to be a salesperson. I'm gonna do more selling this week, too. I'm gonna help us get that coffee machine."

A lump of emotion swelled in Ronan's throat at the gleam in Ryan's eyes as he dreamed of earning a coffee machine. Ronan could have bought the store a thousand coffee machines, but he recognized the pride and ambition that he could see so clearly painted on this young kid's face. He felt that way himself about his future at Conroy Corporation.

Except if that was the case, why had he almost thrown it all away with Sarah Forsythe? What was it that had made him push the relationship with his father almost to the breaking point? Why, when it came down to it, had his father been so instantly judgmental? Ronan hadn't even been given a chance to explain himself before he'd been packed off to Australia.

It made what had happened with Cassie last night even more indefensible. What on earth had he been thinking? Or was it like with Sarah—he hadn't been thinking at all? His experiences with Sarah and Cassie were worlds apart, both literally and figuratively. And yet at the same time, they showed that nothing had changed.

What did Cassie see in him?

Self-pity wasn't Ronan's thing, though, so he cleared his throat and stood up.

"I have no doubt you'll make a great salesperson," he said to Ryan, honestly.

"Thanks." Ryan cracked a smile that was much more suited to his young face than the haunted expression that told of a youth that had seen too much, too soon. "I hope you get to come back next month and I'll make you a cappuccino with our new machine," he said boldly.

Ronan couldn't help but smile back. "I have no doubt that you will."

CASSIE APPEARED SHORTLY after and they hurried through the remainder of the visit. Ronan found himself outside hailing a cab before he knew it.

"What's the rush?" he couldn't help asking. They had plenty of time—it was barely midafternoon.

"I asked Melanie to get me an earlier flight. I'm leaving for Melbourne in a couple of hours," Cassie said quickly.

Ronan looked across to her, but she was avoiding his gaze on the pretext of keeping an eye out for a cab.

"There are some issues with the Hawthorn opening that need my attention," she continued. "I figured you might like to have another night in Sydney—you could do some sightseeing—so I told Mel not to worry about changing your flight. You're still heading back to Melbourne tomorrow morning. That way tonight you can go down to the harbor and walk around, maybe have dinner at The Rocks." Cassie glanced at her watch.

"You've probably got time to find a harbor cruise if you wanted."

He couldn't blame her. He should be grateful that the only punishment for his behavior was to lose her company for a night. It could have been much worse. And yet he was perversely disappointed.

Discovering Cassie's innocence should have been a turnoff. But it wasn't. Instead, it had created a strange sense of possessiveness. The thought of another man with her left a bitter taste in his mouth. What if that other guy wasn't gentle with her? What if he wasn't skilled enough or patient enough to make sure she enjoyed it?

Why did Ronan think he had any right to even be *thinking* such things?

A thought struck him. "But what about the flight?" he asked.

"What about the flight?" Cassie frowned at him.

He remembered her pale face and stark terror when they'd experienced that turbulence on the way into Sydney. "Will you be okay by yourself? With the flying?"

She gave a short, dark laugh as a cab pulled up to the curb. "I always survive somehow."

CHAPTER TEN

THE AIRPORTS IN BOTH SYDNEY and Melbourne were chaotic, filled with Friday commuters desperate to get home for the weekend. It was almost enough to distract Cassie from the flight. Almost, but not quite. Especially when an approaching storm made the landing in Melbourne one of the bumpiest she'd ever experienced. Her hands still shook slightly from the adrenaline that had rushed through her.

She'd managed to distract herself by thinking about how Ronan had held her hand on their last flight—how he'd talked and joked with her to take her mind off what was happening. As much as she kept trying to put the gorgeous American out of her mind, he always seemed to find a way back in. Though, when thinking of him prevented her from having a panic attack during the landing, she'd indulged herself and let her fantasies run wild.

She sighed in relief as she closed her front door behind her and was surrounded by the familiar sights and smells of her home. Her little brick cottage in the broad, tree-lined street of Middle Park, a bay-side suburb south of the city, had been her haven for almost six years. Only this time the gentle colors and soft lines of her living room couldn't do more than dull the sharp edges of her agitation. Her home was her refuge. It had never before failed to slow down her breathing or lower her blood pressure. Perhaps she just needed to give it more time.

Cassie quickly unpacked her case and put her computer out on the dining-room table, ready to start work. But first she needed time out.

After changing into her favorite pair of worn jeans and a sloppy, pale pink T-shirt, she curled up in one of her oversize lounge chairs with a cup of tea. The blue-and-white-striped fabric of the chair was cool and soft against her hot skin, and the cream-colored shutters over the windows let in cracks of light while blocking much of the heat from the sun.

A basket of seashells she'd collected sat on the white-washed coffee table in front of her, next to a thick white candle that stood in a glass hurricane lantern waiting to be lit. On the walls, prints from her favorite painters and some elegant botanical drawings were framed in matching whitewashed and silver-gray timber.

Sitting on the mantelpiece, a photograph of Pete as a bucktoothed ten-year-old grinned at her. Next to that, her mum and dad smiled down at her serenely from a picture taken at the airfield just a few days before the plane crash.

"Argh!" Cassie made a stifled noise of frustration and buried her head in a cushion covered in colorful fabric from antique kimonos. After a moment she sat back and sighed heavily, her eyes wandering back to the photos above the fireplace.

It had been a few months since she'd heard from

Pete, but that wasn't unusual. When he'd first left her, he hadn't been in contact for six months. Then she'd received a letter and a check. By then she'd secured the job at Country Style and found a room to rent. It had taken her a year to convince him he didn't need to send money anymore.

Pete was only two and a half years older than her. When their parents died, he'd only just turned eighteen. He took on her legal guardianship even though he'd been about to go traveling. He got a job and supported them both when it turned out their parents' investments had taken a nosedive. There was very little money, but somehow Pete managed to keep a roof over their heads and food on the table. Cassie's feelings toward her brother were conflicted. He'd abandoned her when she needed him most and she'd been angry with him for a long time, but as she'd grown older she'd also come to understand the situation from his perspective. He'd been too young to be saddled with parenting a teenage girl. He'd had no time to process his own grief, and he'd been forced to sacrifice his own dreams while he supported her. Their contact these days was kept to Christmas and birthdays, polite, but Cassie sensed they both yearned for more. One day. Maybe that could be an addendum to her Plan—a Part Five—repairing the bond with her only remaining family.

Cassie looked around her comfortable, stylish living room. She'd paid off a good portion of her mortgage on the little Victorian cottage and made improvements to it that she knew had increased its value. She'd done everything she could to secure herself a home—to know that she'd never have to go without food or shelter again.

And for a while—until now—it had been enough.

Why did it suddenly feel empty?

It was warm inside, but Cassie grabbed a mohair blanket that had been artfully thrown over the ottoman beside her and cuddled up into it. She reached for her mobile phone, which was never far from her. She wasn't quite sure what it was that compelled her fingers, but she found herself finding Graham in her contacts list and pressing the button to make the call.

She was just checking in. That was all.

"Cassie, my girl."

Graham's familiar greeting was yelled over loud background noise that Cassie couldn't place.

"Graham? Can you hear me?"

"Hang on."

Cassie heard movement and then a closing door and the background noise receded.

"Where are you?" she asked.

"Out," Graham said curtly.

Okay, she could take a hint. "I was just calling to check in," she offered.

"Uh-huh."

Like the phone call in Perth, Cassie had the strangest feeling that Graham wasn't really paying attention. And, also like the phone call in Perth, Cassie realized that whatever she'd wanted from him, she wasn't going to get it. She and Graham had an unusual relationship, she knew that. It wasn't quite boss/employee, nor quite father/daughter. It was a mix of both. At work, they treated each other in a familial way. Outside of work, they treated each other in a businesslike way.

"Things went well in Sydney, I think," she said lamely. *Apart from the whole trying and failing to have sex with the consultant.* But she wasn't about to mention that. She went on to talk a little about the store visits and some of the information she'd picked up along the way.

She could practically hear Graham nodding. "Good. Good. Glad to hear it."

"And have you been able to free up your diary and come to the store opening on Monday?"

"Yes, yes, I'll be there. We'll have a chat when I'm there."

"Okay. That'd be good." Cassie swallowed hard. A chat? Just the ordinary, everyday kind of chat that she usually had with Graham? Or something else?

A wave of unnecessary guilt washed over her. There was no way he could know about what had happened in Sydney. As unsure as she was about a lot of things, she was certain that Ronan wouldn't have told anyone.

"Was there anything else, Cassie?"

"Not really." *I just wanted someone to make me feel better.*

"Okay. Have a good weekend."

Cassie was about to say goodbye and hang up when Graham spoke again.

"Cassie?"

"Yeah?"

"Is everything all right?"

Cassie sucked in a breath. "Yeah, I guess so."

"You sound upset."

"Do I?" And she'd thought she was good at hiding her feelings. "It's just been a stressful week. There's been a lot going on."

"I know. It's been tough on you."

Tears burned at the backs of her eyes at Graham's sympathy. She blinked hard to hold them in. "It's always good to learn," she said, conscious that now wasn't the time to admit that yes, it *had* been tough on her.

"You're a smart girl, Cassie, never doubt that. I knew as soon as I saw you that you could go far. And look at what you've achieved. I'm positive that you've barely scratched the surface of what you're capable of."

"Thanks, Graham." A tear slipped down her cheek, ignoring her attempts to restrain it.

"But, Cassie?"

"Yes?" A tendril of dread wound through her. *What?*

"If you have a fault, it's that you work too goddamn hard. Take a break. Go get a glass of wine and put your feet up. Consider that an order."

She managed a short laugh. "Okay. Wine. I can do that."

"Good. I'll see you on Monday. Take care, my girl."

"See you Monday."

They said goodbye and Cassie put down the phone with a heavy sigh. She felt a little better, but her house now felt emptier than it had before. She snuggled deeper into the blanket. There was an odd quiet in the air, an oppressive waiting. Even the birds were silent, perhaps hiding from the approaching storm.

She knew what her house was missing.

A man.

And not just any man.

Until she'd come up with her Plan, she'd thought all she needed was the security of her home and her job at Country Style. But then she'd spent New Year's Eve alone and the hollow celebration had clarified the missing element: a family and connections of her own. She'd not given a lot of thought as to who the man might be, other than someone gentle, sweet and stable.

But now?

Her traitorous brain supplied the images for her. Ronan emerging from the kitchen, laughing at something, carrying two cool drinks, the ice clinking. He'd put them down on the coffee table and Cassie would scold him for not using coasters on the expensive timber. He'd laugh at her but move the drinks because he understood how important it was to her. Then he'd flop down on the sofa, make a comment about the weather and prop his bare feet up on the arm.

What did his feet look like?

A pang of regret went through her, more powerful than the embarrassment she'd been feeling about the previous night. She wished she'd not been so nervous. How hard was it to undo a few buttons? Why hadn't she taken off his shirt? His pants?

Maybe, if she'd just explained things to him calmly and rationally, he'd have understood. Maybe he'd have taken care of her, made her first time something to remember fondly.

Maybe?

No, she was certain he would have.

He would be the perfect choice as a lover for any woman. For her.

Everything she'd seen of Ronan McGuire over the past few days told her that although he might seem to coast through life, flirting one moment, then coolly businesslike the next, the still waters of his blue eyes ran very deep indeed. He took his job seriously. He cared about people and what they thought of him.

His eyes that morning had been troubled—he'd been genuinely concerned about her response. Sweet, given that she was the one who really should be ashamed.

She felt an unexpected yearning, an emptiness in her stomach, as if she were hungry. But it wasn't food she needed.

She let out another long sigh as realization struck. It had only been four days—two nights—that she'd spent with Ronan, and yet she missed him. She missed his presence beside her.

And she knew, without doubt, that the small pang of regret she felt about not knowing what his feet looked like—not knowing what he looked like naked—was nothing compared to the regret she was going to feel when he left. When she let him go without ever having been brave enough to risk really being with him.

All her life she'd played it safe. She'd never left Country Style, even when she hadn't been particularly happy, scared of jumping from the frying pan into the fire. What if she wasn't successful in a new job? What if she couldn't pay the mortgage? It had taken a long time for her confidence to grow to the point that she stopped wondering whether she could succeed without Graham watching over her.

But now? Now she was fairly certain she could get another job that would pay enough to keep the roof over her head. She didn't want to—the thought of leaving Country Style still made butterflies mambo in her belly. But if the worst happened, she'd survive.

The few people who knew her life story—Graham, Trent, Mel—often called her courageous. They praised her bravery, her energy, the way she'd created a life for herself from nothing. If only they knew just what a coward she really was.

Cassie snuggled tighter into her chair cocoon. Perhaps some things were just not meant to be.

RONAN STOOD AT CASSIE's front door, cursing himself as a fool.

She'd run away from him as fast as she could, and here he was, chasing her. He'd just had to dig through a few documents to find her address. It was only so he could apologize properly—set the record straight—but still. This wasn't one of his proudest moments.

On the last-minute flight he'd managed to snare, he'd frowned as the plane hit some serious turbulence on the way into Melbourne. According to the pilot, the heatwave was about to break—a storm front was moving in and heavy rain predicted. The bumpy ride didn't bother him, but he hoped that Cassie's flight had been smoother—or that someone sitting next to her had helped keep her calm. Maybe held her hand for her, talked to her.

He pictured another traveler—some anonymous businessman—with his fingers entwined with Cassie's, stroking her wrist to soother her, just as he had. The air around him heated as if the sun had risen all over again. He muttered a curse under his breath, wrenched at his tie and pulled it free of his collar, stuffing it into a pocket.

He raised his fists to knock on the door, but hesitated for a moment. He was just going to clear the air—make sure things were understood between them—ensure there'd be no repercussions for Conroy Corporation as a result of his impetuous behavior.

And make sure she hadn't been too shaken by the flight.

His knock sounded incredibly loud in the quiet suburban street. Twilight had come early, thanks to the portentous clouds hanging low in the sky, bringing with them the smell of rain.

Cassie's face was the picture of surprise when she opened the door.

"But…I thought you were in Sydney?"

"Hello to you, too," Ronan couldn't help teasing.

She looked sleepy—he wondered if he'd woken her—and her already pink cheeks flushed darker at his quip.

"Hello, of course. Sorry, you just surprised me."

"I changed my flight." *Duh. You're a smart one, Conroy.*

"Clearly."

There was a moment of silence as they studied each other. Cassie wore soft jeans that hugged her every curve and an oversize pink T-shirt with a stretched-out neck that was slipping off, revealing the creamy skin of one shoulder and a coffee-colored bra strap. Her hair, pulled back as always, was messy, one long tendril hanging over her neck and curling down into her T-shirt…. No, probably not quite long enough to cover her whole breast. His fingers still itched to find out.

"I guess…you should come in," Cassie said eventually, stepping back.

Ronan wasn't sure how he felt about the hesitation in her voice. Disappointed? He *should* approve. No way should she be welcoming him into her home given the thoughts that were currently running rampant in his head.

"I won't be long," he promised, wondering at the same time if he was lying. "I just need a few minutes to talk to you."

Cassie nodded. She closed the door behind him as he maneuvered his case and laptop into the hallway and then stepped into her living room. A beautiful space that mirrored its owner. Cool and calm at first glance, then, if he looked closer, the splashes of passion became more obvious—a bright silk cushion, a lavish throw, the lush image of a spilling pomegranate framed in silver on the wall.

"Would you like a drink?" Cassie asked politely.

"Yes, please." Maybe he was dehydrated. Maybe that's why he wasn't thinking clearly. He hadn't needed to come in. He could have just said what he'd come to say on the doorstep and then left again. Hell, he could have done it over the phone. From Sydney.

"I'll be right back. Make yourself comfortable."

Ronan chose the light-colored sofa opposite the chair where Cassie had obviously been resting with a throw covering her. He imagined her curled up, her head resting on her arm, eyelashes fanned over her cheeks. If this was *their* home, he'd pick her up and carry her to bed; let her snuggle up to him all sweet and kittenlike. But once they got to bed, he'd rouse her from her sleepiness with a kiss and then—

"Here you go."

Cassie reappeared and handed him a glass of white wine, so chilled the outside of the glass had misted up. Ronan accepted it gratefully—he'd been expecting a glass of water. "Thanks." The dry wine slid down his throat far too easily.

Cassie settled in the chair opposite with her own glass.

"You have a lovely home," he said. His mother's conditioning in manners ran deep, but he meant it. He had a brief mental image of his own sterile, impersonal apartment and reminded himself of his determination to have it furnished. Something just like this would be perfect. He could see his father's approving expression already.

Cassie gave him a tight smile. "Thank you."

He couldn't blame her for her suspicion.

"Have you ever thought about a career in interior design? You've obviously got the touch."

Ronan didn't miss the play of emotions that crossed her face. Pleasure first, at his compliment. Then an angry fear.

"Why are you here, Ronan?" She was a stray cat spitting and hissing at an invader.

"I…" Why *was* he here, again?

She sat up straight in the chair and pinned him with a glare. "Because if you've come to tell me in your own obtuse way that I need to start looking for a new job, I appreciate the warning, but you can leave now."

"Oh." *Idiot.* "No, that's not what I meant at all." He couldn't possibly warn her. He'd already done enough to jeopardize this job. Revealing Graham Taylor's plans now would only count as another black mark. Besides, as talented and successful as Cassie was, she'd have no trouble getting another job. And if she worked well with the new owners during the takeover, they might even find a role for her within their organization. Ronan knew she'd be unhappy when the news came but, he rationalized, it might even be in her best interests to move on and gain experience outside Country Style.

Cassie relaxed slightly, but the wariness didn't leave her eyes. "Then what did you mean?"

"I was genuinely complimenting you. And I wanted to make sure you were okay. My flight was rough because of the storm, and I figured yours was, too." As if to underscore his words a low roll of thunder sounded outside.

"It wasn't the most pleasant experience of my life, but I survived."

Perversely, Ronan liked this prickly, no-nonsense version of Cassie. He'd seen glimpses of this side of her in the work environment, but never when it had been just the two of them together—then her nerves tended to get the upper hand. Being on her own home turf clearly made her more comfortable.

He stood and stretched, his muscles cramped from a day of cab rides and the plane flight. The restlessness that had been gnawing at him had seeped into his bones, making him feel caged, edgy. He took a couple of steps over to the fireplace. The grate was filled with a basket of fruit-shaped objects made of wicker. It should have looked silly, but somehow it worked—Cassie's magic touch again.

His eyes went to the mantelpiece and the row of framed photographs. "Is this your family?" he asked, picking up a portrait of a grinning boy.

"That's my brother, Pete."

"The one who lives in London?"

"Yes."

"And these are your parents?" He returned Pete's photo to the mantelpiece and peered closer at the photograph of two smiling adults standing in front of a tiny Cessna aircraft. For some reason he didn't pick up the frame; Cassie buzzed with a tension that told him not to.

"Yes. It was taken just before the accident."

"Accident?"

"My father was an amateur pilot. We all used to go flying. One weekend he took my mother up for a joy flight, and something went wrong with the engine. The investigators were never exactly sure what caused it."

Ronan froze for a moment as that information sunk in. "Your parents were killed in a plane crash?"

"When I was fifteen."

He shook his head. He'd been sympathetic about her fear of flying, but kind of amused by it, too. He had no idea what had caused it. "Cassie, I…" But there was nothing to say.

"My mum convinced Dad to have the picture taken—it was just the week before the accident. She said they didn't have any nice photos of them together. It was almost as if…" She trailed off.

"Almost as if she knew," Ronan finished softly.

"Yeah."

How could he express his sympathy without it seeming like pity? Sympathy, she'd accept; pity he knew she'd reject. "I'm so sorry for your loss. But, Cassie, you're an amazing woman. You've achieved so much in your life. I know they'd be very proud of you." He wasn't sure what made him say it, except once he had, he wondered if anyone else had ever told her that.

Cassie's eyes welled with tears and she quickly looked away from him. "Thanks," she said, her voice quiet. "I think my dad would be embarrassed about my fear of flying, but other than that I'd like to think they'd be pleased."

Ronan crossed to her chair and sat on the ottoman beside her. He put a hand to her cheek, forcing her eyes to meet his.

"Don't ever doubt that, Cassie. What you've done with your life, the career you've forged, how you've made yourself a home—" he gestured to the room around them "—it's definitely something to be proud of, no matter what happens with Country Style."

He knew he'd said the wrong thing as soon as the

words were out. Why did he have to keep bringing up work? Was it his own beaten-down logic trying to force him to remember why he'd come? He was supposed to apologize. Nothing more. Not get lost again in his admiration for what she'd achieved, or stare into those beautiful brown eyes and forget who he was. Or stroke the soft skin of her cheek because he simply couldn't help himself.

"You should have stayed in Sydney," Cassie blurted.

Ronan frowned. He hadn't expected to be greeted with kisses and streamers, but he'd never seen Cassie be rude before.

"I mean…" She sat back, away from his touch, and reached for her glass of wine. She took a sip and Ronan noticed that her hand was shaking. She lowered the glass to the table between them, sitting it on a square woven mat. "I mean," she began, her voice more controlled, "you missed the opportunity to take a look around, to play the tourist. I thought you'd appreciate a night to yourself to explore."

Ronan could see it for the ruse it was. She'd run from him, and he should have paid attention to that. He shouldn't have run after her like some adoring puppy or lovesick teenager.

Her eyes widened as she looked at him. While her words were pushing him away, her eyes were calling to him.

And just like that, all rational thought disappeared.

He dropped his voice. "There are other things I'd prefer to explore."

Cassie's eyes lit up. Fear and arousal warred inside

her, but this time, like in the hotel room the night before, Ronan could see that arousal was winning.

Her lips parted in a soft O.

"But, Cassie, are you sure? This has to be your choice." Was it some vestige of self-preservation or concern for Cassie that forced him to ask? He didn't want her to do something she didn't want to do. Her innocence meant she really didn't know what she was getting herself into. He needed to let her take the initiative.

The thought brought him up short. Had he actually learned something from his experience in New York?

Or maybe not, given the situation he was courting right now?

Cassie might be inexperienced, but he was experienced enough for the both of them. He should know better…but he wasn't going to think about that right now.

Her hungry look turned apprehensive. "What do you mean?"

"I mean the chemistry between us is dynamite, sweetheart. I know you don't have much to compare it to, but it could easily sweep both of us away."

She gave him a shy smile that told him she knew what he meant, gazing up through lowered lashes. Ronan barely stopped himself from leaping across the small space between them. He took a breath and let it out in a rush.

"I know it would be easier for you if I just seduced you and made the decision for you. Not that I'd do anything against your will," he added hurriedly. "I just want to be very clear that you know what we're doing here. I want you to understand the choice you're making."

"I…" Her throat worked as she swallowed. "I don't know if I can do that. If I think too much, if I let myself think about what it means…"

"Cassie, at breakfast this morning you told me you didn't want to be a virgin anymore. That's all this means. Nothing more."

She bit her bottom lip with her front teeth, clearly considering what he'd said. Ronan had almost talked himself out of whatever might happen next, but he felt he'd needed to put the truth out there. Now, if she accepted him but then regretted it, he could at least console himself with the knowledge that he'd tried to be a gentleman.

And perhaps he really was the immature idiot that his father thought.

"I… Ronan." She licked her lips nervously and the sight combined with his name in her breathy voice was enough to test any man's patience. "When do you go back to America?" she asked finally.

Ronan frowned. "Next week—Wednesday, I think. But, Cassie, you know this can't be more than—"

"I know," she said quickly. "And this is separate from work. We're keeping it separate, right?"

"Right. It's Friday night. The weekend. Work stops until Monday morning. Anything that happens between now and then is just about the two of us as people. Nothing to do with Country Style or restructures or acquisitions." Ronan cursed himself as his mouth ran away with him, but Cassie seemed too distracted to notice his slip.

"And you'll make it like before?" She studied him with wide eyes.

He grabbed her hand and stroked her wrist with his thumb. "I don't know what you mean, sweetheart."

"Like last night in the hotel. You made me…feel…"

He grinned. "Oh, I can do that again."

Cassie smiled back, tentatively, then bit her bottom lip again. "That's good, but that's not what I meant. I meant, you made me feel…safe."

"Safe?"

"Like I still had control."

Again, Ronan caught a glimpse of what Cassie's life must have been like. His chest tightened at the thought of what it must have taken to make this successful, proud woman so broken inside when it came to love.

Not love, he corrected himself. Lovemaking.

He met her eyes. "You have control, Cassie. Whatever we do, if it's not what you want, you say stop and we'll stop."

"But what if—"

"No what-ifs, Cassie." Anger at the men she'd known before rose inside him. "I don't know what kind of guys you've been around, but it's always possible to stop. Always. The goal is to feel so good you don't want to."

She smiled. "I don't think there's any danger of that not happening."

He managed a laugh. "I'm glad to hear it."

He stood and stretched, then headed back to the sofa. Cassie was already standing, a confused look on her face. "Don't you want to go to the bedroom?" she asked.

He fought not to let his amusement show as he kicked off his shoes, stretched out on the wide, comfy sofa and clasped his hands behind his head. "Not straightaway, sweetheart. I'm hungry. How about we get some takeout and watch a movie?"

"Oh."

Her barely concealed disappointment was so gorgeous he couldn't help but smile. "Don't worry, we'll get there. We've got the whole weekend in front of us. Right?"

"Okay." She sat back in her chair, feet tucked up underneath her, and began to reel off some of the takeout options in the neighborhood.

Ronan felt a welcome calm settle over him as he settled into the soft cushions. The first time he'd felt that way in…he couldn't remember how long. The little angel and devil on his shoulders tried to make an appearance but he brushed them away. So he was living down to his father's very worst expectations. So he was risking his career and reputation.

It would be worth it.

CHAPTER ELEVEN

BRUCE WILLIS'S KILL COUNT was mounting to the dozens. Cassie covered her eyes as yet another baddie bit the dust with a spray of fake blood. Violent films were not her thing, even ones as cartoon-silly as this one.

"You don't like the movie?" Ronan's sleepy voice asked. He was comfortably stretched out on her sofa as if he lived here, his eyes half-closed as he watched the screen. Cassie thought he looked exhausted and wanted to suggest he go to bed, but she knew he'd take that to mean something else. And because she kind of did mean something else, the butterflies started up their tango lessons in her belly all over again.

"It's okay," she said, wincing as another fight broke out. She knew it was staged, and yet that punch absolutely looked as if it had broken the other guy's nose. They were trying to blow up a plane or a building or something and Bruce was trying to stop them. She knew she was supposed to be barracking for Bruce, but she couldn't bring herself to care. She just wanted the hitting and shooting to stop.

"Are you scared?" he teased.

She rolled her eyes at him. "No, I am not scared. I just don't happen to like people killing each other all over the place."

"Aw. You're too soft. He's only killing the bad guys. They deserve it."

"I know." She sat back in her chair and folded her arms. She refused to admit that half the reason she wasn't enjoying the movie was that there was something she'd much rather be doing. Now that she'd made the decision to make love with Ronan and worry about regrets and consequences later, the anticipation was killing her.

She'd thought they'd go straight to bed. But no, first there was the copious order of Thai takeaway Ronan had asked for. It had taken ages to arrive and Ronan had eaten seconds of everything while Cassie could barely manage a few bites. Then he'd suggested they turn on the TV.

The movie had been going for almost two hours now.

The waiting was interminable.

Ronan yawned.

So did she. The stress of the week's travel had taken its toll and Cassie was exhausted. But she was too wound up to sleep.

She shifted in her chair, frustration mounting. He seemed so relaxed, so calm. She might think he wasn't so keen on her after all if it weren't for the fact that he was here, in her home. No, Ronan had been clear about what he wanted. Why wasn't he taking it now that it was available? Why wasn't he carrying her off to bed?

What, did he want her to *jump* him?

Cassie let out a breath as realization struck. That was it. He was waiting for her to make the first move.

GET 2 BOOKS

We'd like to send you two *Harlequin® Superromance®* novels absolutely free. Accepting them puts you under no obligation to purchase any more books.

FREE!

Return this card today to get
2 FREE BOOKS and 2 FREE GIFTS!

Harlequin
Super Romance

YES! Please send me 2 FREE *Harlequin® Superromance®*
novels, and 2 FREE mystery gifts as well. I understand
I am under no obligation to purchase anything, as
explained on the back of this insert.

❏ I prefer the regular-print edition
135/336 HDL FMG6

❏ I prefer the larger-print edition
139/339 HDL FMG6

Please Print

FIRST NAME	LAST NAME

ADDRESS

APT.#	CITY

STATE/PROV.	ZIP/POSTAL CODE

Visit us at:
www.ReaderService.com

▼ DETACH AND MAIL CARD TODAY! ▼

He'd said she had control. He said he wouldn't take her choice away.

He *was* waiting for her.

Great.

Butterflies turned into huge, stomping elephants.

Now that she had control, what exactly did she do with it? How did she approach him? Just crawl over and demand, "Take me, now!"

Debating with herself for a while, she cursed her lack of flirting experience. What could she do that was subtle but made her intentions obvious? Then she realized he'd just given her an idea.

On the TV, Bruce was sneaking up on some bad guys who didn't know he was behind them. It wasn't exactly terrifying, but suspenseful enough, she guessed.

Cassie grabbed a silk cushion and hugged it to her body, raising it to cover her eyes as the tension built.

"You *are* scared," Ronan crowed.

"Maybe a little," Cassie lied. *Well, not of the movie, anyway.* And then, before she could lose her nerve, she got up, circled the coffee table between them and lay down next to him on the sofa. The oversize furniture was still a tight fit for the two of them, but Ronan shifted across and before she knew it, Cassie was in his arms, her head tucked against his shoulder. His arm was around her and she rested her hand on his chest. His heart thudded rhythmically beneath her palm.

Suddenly Cassie could breathe again. When she was away from Ronan, her chest felt constricted, tight. In his arms, the world righted itself somehow.

A large, loud something exploded on the television, startling her.

Ronan chuckled. She felt his chest rumble with it, and his arm tightened around her.

"I thought that was just a ruse, but are you really scared?" he asked softly.

She couldn't see his face, but could just imagine the expression he wore. It didn't matter, but it prickled that he'd seen through her. "No, I'm not really scared," she admitted grumpily. "That noise just surprised me."

"Ah." He pressed a kiss to the top of her head. "Well, I'm glad you decided to pretend to be scared anyway."

Cassie flicked one of the throw pillows off the sofa with her foot. Slipping her knee between Ronan's, she no longer felt in danger of toppling off the couch at the next explosion.

Ronan sighed and made a muffled noise of contentment as Cassie snuggled closer. She couldn't help it. Just as she couldn't help her brain going off on a little fantasy. How lovely would this be when this was her life? When her grand plan was complete? She'd come home on Friday night after a busy, stressful week as CEO at Country Style, have a dinner of takeaway food and a cuddle on the couch with her man. Could life get much more perfect?

Of course, that man wouldn't be Ronan McGuire, but she'd think about that later.

Cassie closed her eyes, no longer interested in whether Bruce bested the baddies. Ronan's subtle cologne filled her senses. The solid muscle under her cheek should have been uncomfortable, but it was better than any pillow. The rise and fall of his chest, the thudding of his heartbeat, were wonderfully reassuring.

In the arms of the most dangerous man she'd ever met, Cassie had never felt so safe.

And just like that, she drifted off to sleep.

"CASSIE?"

Someone was stroking her cheek. It felt nice.

"Mmm?" Cassie mumbled, not willing to fully wake up. She was still tired and she was warm and comfy.

"Wake up, honey. We need to go to bed."

A sleepy awareness washed through her—nestled on the couch, warm and safe, she must have dozed. "Is the movie over?" she asked, still not entirely wakeful.

Ronan's chest moved in a breath of amusement. "Yeah. About four hours ago. We've both been asleep."

"Tired."

"Uh-huh."

Cassie let out a long breath and snuggled closer. She was more than happy to fall back to sleep. She'd been having a lovely dream. The store opening had been a phenomenal success and Graham had bought her a holiday to San Francisco as a thank-you present. Somehow, she was going to be able to get there without stepping on a plane.

"Cassie." Ronan's voice was more insistent now. "I'm sorry, sweetheart, but we have to move. I'm too hot surrounded by all these pillows and your lovely body, and I can't feel my arm." He gave her a gentle nudge.

"Oh. Right. Okay."

Opening one eye, Cassie came fully awake; remembered where she was and who she was with.

She sat up, suppressing a shiver as she left the warmth of Ronan's embrace. It wasn't cold in the room by any means, but the sudden change in temperature left her feeling bereft.

Ronan groaned as he stretched. He massaged his biceps with the fingers of his other hand, a grimace on his face.

"Sorry," Cassie said.

"Not your fault." He shrugged. "I guess we were both pretty dead on our feet."

Cassie moved to let him shift so they both sat on the sofa, facing her kitchen.

"Would you mind if I grabbed a quick shower?" Ronan asked. He picked at his shirt. "I'm feeling pretty ripe."

Cassie had just been sleeping next to his armpit and she hadn't noticed anything nasty, but she guessed it would be churlish to refuse. "Of course."

She busied herself finding a towel while Ronan rummaged through his bag and grabbed a few items.

"The bathroom's just here," Cassie said, showing him to the door between the house's two bedrooms. It had once been a tiny third bedroom, and she'd had it converted. The claw-foot bath with its gold-plated feet was probably her favorite thing in the house.

He shot her a quick smile as he grabbed the towel she offered and then disappeared into the bathroom.

"I'll only be a few minutes."

Still sleepy and overtired, Cassie's brain was running slow. It took a moment to process what was happening. Ronan. In her bathroom. About to shower.

He didn't close the door.

Cassie stood in the hallway as he began to undress. He had his back to her but she could tell he was undoing his shirt buttons. A moment later, the crumpled fabric dropped to the floor revealing a tanned, muscular back that narrowed to a waist that disappeared into his black pants. A clink told her his belt had been loosened, and then the unmistakable sound of a zipper…

The reality of the situation struck like thunder. Not only was she standing outside the bathroom like a voyeur, watching a man—her guest—undress, she was about to welcome him into her bed.

His trousers fell to the floor, the belt landing with a metallic thunk.

Cassie whirled around and marched herself into the lounge room, pressing the back of her hand to her heated cheeks. She busied herself with picking up their empty wineglasses and rinsing them in the kitchen.

What now?

Did she climb into bed and wait for him to join her there on the assumption that things would go as they'd discussed? Or had he changed his mind? He'd come here for sex and Cassie had forced him to have an uncomfortable conversation about it. And then, instead of seducing him the way he'd pretty much asked her to do, she'd fallen asleep on him.

She propped the clean glasses on the drainer to dry and stared out the window into the darkened backyard.

Maybe he was showering with the intention of getting dressed and going back to his hotel. Maybe she'd put one too many hurdles in his way.

Maybe she'd drooled in her sleep and turned him off.

She shouldn't be disappointed. She should be relieved that he'd decided to stop things now. At least Monday morning would be easier.

And then, in the reflection of the darkened window, she saw him approach. Naked except for black boxer-style underwear. Tanned skin and dark hair glinting with water. White teeth; he was smiling.

"You want a turn?" he asked, as he slipped one arm around her waist. He brushed away her ponytail to press his lips to her neck. "Although you smell pretty good to me," he murmured against her skin.

He stood closer, and as he kissed a line from her shoulder to her ear she could feel his arousal pressing against her.

A shiver rippled up her spine and she gripped the sink with suddenly trembling fingers.

"Yes, I think I will," she said, her voice sounding husky and sexy. She didn't even know she was capable of that kind of tone.

Ronan stepped back and then followed her as she headed for the bedroom. She grabbed her Chinese silk dressing gown and fled toward the bathroom. A backward glance told her that Ronan was emptying the pockets of his trousers, laying his belongings on one of the bedside tables. He'd chosen the right-hand side of the bed—not her side—and she couldn't help but smile at that, even as her stomach looped.

Setting the water to a tepid warmth, Cassie wished

she could wash her hair. It would be lovely to rinse out the lingering smell of airplanes, but the time involved in drying her mane was too much to bother with at— she checked the little carriage clock she kept on the bathroom shelf—two-thirty in the morning. Instead she tied it up into a knot on the top of her head.

She couldn't let herself think too much. The bottle of shower gel quivered in her hand and then, as she washed, rinsed, turned off the shower and dried herself, her whole body began to tremble. She shook her hair loose and ran shaking fingers through it in a futile attempt to bring some order to the riot of waves.

She hadn't felt this way since she and Pete had gone on a theme-park roller coaster on their last-ever family holiday. It had been one of those double-loop, big-dipper monstrosities and her parents had been cautious about allowing her to go on it—she'd only just met the height requirements. But she'd begged to be able to go with Pete—with his teenage-boy boasting, he'd said it was going to be the best thing ever. And he'd been right. It still ranked as one of the scariest, most thrilling experiences of her life.

And that was when it hit her. This wasn't just nerves. It was excitement. Anticipation. She wanted this. Yes, she was a little scared, but that didn't have to be bad. It was a different kind of fear compared to flying. To losing your family. To losing your home.

She was scared of feeling scared. She'd done a lot of work in her life in order to ensure she never felt fear again. Worked hard. Bought herself a house. Made a home. Kept her social life limited. Never allowed a man to get too close. The only thing she hadn't been able to avoid was flying.

And now this.

But she wasn't letting Ronan close. Not really. Physically, yes, but physically there was nothing to fear from him. There might be a little pain, but she doubted there'd be much anatomical evidence of her virginity left at this point in her life. And she knew he'd do his best to make it good for her.

Emotionally there was nothing to fear, either. They'd made it clear that this was a short-term deal. A weekend. A chance for her to once again experience the pleasure she'd felt in his arms the previous night.

That was something to be excited about. Not to fear.

"Are you okay?"

So much for not letting herself think too much.

She'd been standing in the bathroom staring at the wall having her little existential debate with herself for ages. He must be wondering what on earth she was doing.

"I'll be right there," she called back.

She wrapped the silk gown around her body, and the soft fabric on her skin made it hum with awareness. Her nipples hardened to visible peaks and the low-level thrumming that had been in her belly ever since she'd set eyes on Ronan McGuire stepped up a notch.

In the bedroom, Ronan had pulled the covers back on the bed and was lying on top, legs crossed at the ankles, hands clasped behind his head. His eyes darkened as she entered and he gave her a smile that was part reassurance, part predatory glare. Her stomach dipped.

Remember the roller coaster.

She smiled back.

He unclasped his hands and propped himself up on his elbows, studying her with a serious look. "Changed your mind?" he asked. "Because you can. If you want to."

The roller coaster left the station, and Cassie felt light and shaky and wonderful.

She stepped toward the bed and undid the tie of her robe.

"No, I haven't changed my mind. I want you."

CHAPTER TWELVE

RONAN HAD LEFT COHERENT thought behind long ago, but even if he hadn't, the sight of a freshly scrubbed Cassie, her hair tumbling around her shoulders and her nipples tight points under the silk of her robe, would have left his rational brain for dead.

She loosened the tie of her dressing gown, but didn't let it fall, climbing onto the bed next to him before her bare skin was revealed. His arms were around her instantly, pulling her into the tight embrace they'd shared on the sofa.

She was trembling all over.

It was enough to make him hesitate, to make him pause to see if this really was okay. But the look in her eyes told him everything he needed to know. She wanted this, in that determined way she had about everything. He almost laughed.

Instead, he lowered his mouth, and as their lips touched all the internal lecturing he'd given himself about taking this slow and perhaps even just giving Cassie another orgasm without going all the way evaporated into the warmth of the summer night.

He couldn't go another day without knowing the clasp of her body around his. Hell, he'd be lucky if he could go another five minutes.

He was overwhelmed by the trust she was placing in him. Not just with her body but with her self—the little girl who'd lost her family and her security far too soon. Part of him wondered if he deserved such trust, but another part didn't want to consider that too closely—he was determined not to fail her.

Her mouth opened to him and he deepened the kiss, finally sinking his fingers into the lush mane of hair that had been driving him crazy for days. It was just as thick and silky and soft as he'd expected and he groaned.

"What?" Cassie pulled back from his mouth and asked breathlessly.

"Your hair. It's gorgeous."

She smiled.

"Come here." Ronan rolled onto his back, bringing Cassie with him so she was splayed over his chest. He kissed her again as her hair fell around them like a curtain.

Cassie's robe gaped open and Ronan trailed a fingertip across her collarbone. In response, Cassie lifted her body, creating space between them, and his finger traced the valley between her breasts. She moaned in need against his mouth and he didn't hesitate to take the full weight of her breast in his palm, delighting in the pressure of her nipple against his skin.

"You're so beautiful," he said, pressing kisses over her neck as Cassie arched above him, pressing her breast more firmly to his grasp.

"You don't have to keep saying that." Her voice was barely a whisper.

Ronan wasn't paying close attention; his lips were about to meet that perky nipple that was just begging to be kissed. Then the meaning of her words sunk in.

His hand left her breast and cupped her cheek, pulling her gaze to his. "What? Why wouldn't I?"

"I know it's not true. But I don't mind," she added hurriedly.

"Why on earth would you think that? You're one of the most beautiful women I've ever known."

Her mouth parted as if to protest, but she seemed so genuinely confused she wasn't sure where to begin. "I've just…never… And Mel is so…"

Ronan frowned. *Mel?* Oh, that assistant of hers. How could she even begin to compare herself to Mel? The two women were like night and day. Ronan struggled to find the words.

"Mel is like a Japanese sports car," he said after a moment's thought. "Flashy, with curves in all the right places and easy to drive. Any driver can handle one of those. But you?" He pushed that mane of hair back over one creamy shoulder and surveyed all he could see, her body still half-hidden in silk. "You're a European convertible—classy, elegant, refined and a little wild where it counts. Those cars aren't meant for just anyone, but with the right driver they can wipe every other car off the road."

She considered him for a moment and one side of her mouth kicked up in amusement. "Did you just say I had a good motor?"

He chuckled. "More or less. Let's see if I can make you purr."

CASSIE HAD NO DOUBT that Ronan could do just that. He twisted under her and a moment later she was on her back staring up into those blue eyes. How could she ever have thought them cold? Looking down at her, they flared with passion, blue flames burning hotly. For her. She still couldn't quite believe it.

And then further thought was impossible as Ronan's lips closed around her breast and his hand stroked her belly, lower and lower, excruciatingly slowly. Cassie wanted to hurry him up, grab his hand and put it where she ached for his touch, but this torture was undeniably pleasurable, too, and she was torn between wanting it to stop and wanting it to go on forever.

Then his hand found its mark and Cassie jumped, unable to contain the shock of having someone else share that most intimate part of her. Ronan must have sensed her disquiet, because he murmured comforting nonsense words against her skin as he kissed his way back to her mouth, stealing her breath and erasing any trace of anxiety in the drowning pleasure of his touch.

Cassie arched as he stroked her center and her hands flew to his back, holding him tighter, pushing him away, clawing him, drinking in his very breath as he built her peak and sent her crashing over the edge.

She cried out into his mouth, her whole body taut against his, the world contracting to this room, this bed, this man, his fingers and what they did to her.

She was left panting. Ronan's hot mouth was on her ear and Cassie felt heat flush through her whole body. Should she be embarrassed about how quickly and how easily he could make her respond? She couldn't bring herself to care.

His hands roamed her body, learning her every curve, stroking the skin of her inner thighs, trailing light, almost ticklish touches over her stomach.

Her fingers still clasped his shoulders tightly, hanging on to him as if he were her anchor. Now that the storm had passed she delighted in the feel of him. Velvet-rich skin, a feathering of dark hair on his chest, the hard strength of muscle beneath.

"Cassie, I want you so much." His words were barely more than a breath in her ear. She could feel him through his boxers, hard and thick against her thigh, and she knew no more than a fleeting moment of anxiety. She hadn't lied. She wanted him. She wanted him with every fiber of her being. The ache between her legs had been briefly sated, but that respite seemed only to have stoked the fire of need even higher. Her longing to be filled, by him and only him, burned bright.

"I'm yours," she whispered back.

His eyes met hers and shone down at her—full of question, seeking reassurance. As an answer she slipped her hands down his back and into the waistband of his briefs, tugging as her fingers curved over the delicious swell of his buttocks. She leaned up, trying to push the fabric further, but it was caught on something.

He laughed when she frowned, and twisted onto his side.

Of course.

Cassie would have blushed again, but she didn't think it was possible for her skin to heat any more.

Ronan saved her embarrassment by quickly ridding himself of his underwear. Cassie used the opportunity to shrug out of the robe that was still tangled beneath her.

They were both naked.

And he took her breath away.

She didn't have much time to enjoy the view before he reached for the condom he'd left on the bedside table. After a few deft moves, he was ready.

Was she?

As if she'd done it a hundred times, Cassie's thighs widened to welcome him and her arms rose to wrap around his muscular back. It might all be new, but it felt *right,* as if she were a jigsaw puzzle and all her life she'd been missing this one essential piece.

But he didn't sink into her. Poised as he was, instead, his fingers were back, toying with her already aching core, his lips clasped around her nipple again.

Cassie groaned in pleasure and frustration, her fingernails biting into his skin. She understood what he was doing, but he was driving her mad.

"Are you okay?" The passion in his eyes was tempered for a moment with concern.

"Don't make me wait," she pleaded.

She could see the war in his eyes before they closed and he groaned. "Oh, Cassie," he muttered.

He moved, arranging their bodies, and Cassie tensed in anticipation. He murmured more of those comforting words, made silky by his accent, kissed her neck and ear, and then he was inside her, a gentle but inexorable thrust, pushing deep, connecting them in the most elemental of ways.

Cassie gasped. There was a moment of discomfort, but it wasn't really pain, more a slight stretching burn. She adjusted the angle of her hips and, as he slipped out and then back in, the pleasure turned her gasp into a moan of pleasure.

"Okay?" Ronan's tone was harsh; she could sense his restraint, could hear it in his voice, see it in his eyes, feel it in the trembling of his arms.

"Oh, Ronan," she said, because she didn't know what else to say. She lifted her ankles to link them behind his body, bringing him deeper into her, and he groaned in response. "Kiss me." She clasped his cheek with her hand, bringing his mouth to hers.

Their tongues met in a hot, wet kiss, mimicking the dance of their bodies, stoking the fires that burned inside them, spiraling their pleasure higher.

Ronan pulled away, breathing heavily, and Cassie shivered with the raw power of his body, the mastery he had over her, the effortless way he coaxed responses from her. His blue eyes bored into hers and Cassie had never felt more vulnerable or more protected. She'd given him everything, her life story, her insecurities, her body, and he'd taken it and cherished it.

She couldn't help her eyes drifting closed as the pleasure built low in her belly, a growing ache fueled by his body moving against her, within her, until she reached a peak more powerful than anything that had come before. She shattered, crying out, gripping Ronan's arms as she lost herself in blissful release.

She heard his own cry a moment later, felt the shudder of his body as he followed her over the edge, heard the rasp of his breath.

He collapsed on top of her and Cassie welcomed his weight; the press of him anchored her, restored her soul to her body.

As he fought to control his ragged breathing, he pressed a kiss to her neck, one hand reaching up to stroke the hair back from her face. "You okay?" he asked. Then he chuckled. "Apart from not being able to breathe?"

He rolled off her and turned away for a moment, taking care of the condom. And then he was back, his arms around her, settling her head against his shoulder.

Cassie twisted her legs around his and threw an arm across his chest, snuggling into his body, unconcerned by the warmth of the night and the throbbing heat of his skin. He smelled of soap and sweat and musk and Cassie thought she'd never get enough.

"Seriously," he started again, "are you okay?"

Cassie tried an experimental wiggle, noting a slight twinge between her legs, but nothing that dimmed the glow of pleasure that still sang from every nerve. "I'm perfect," she sighed.

He gave another of those low laughs and Cassie felt it vibrate in his chest. "Yes, you certainly are," he agreed.

His hand stroked the hair back from her face, arranging it carefully behind her shoulder.

"And I'm tired," she said, stifling a yawn. All she wanted to do was lie awake so she didn't miss a moment of this—of lying next to Ronan McGuire, of feeling her body hum with the afterglow of his glorious lovemaking. And yet sleep pulled at her, reminding her that it was the middle of the night, that she was in her own bed after an exhausting week of travel and upheaval, and that, for now, she was safe.

"Go to sleep, sweetheart," he urged, his hand still stroking her hair.

She arched her neck to meet his eyes. "We can do this again in the morning, right?"

His eyes twinkled his smile at her. "Yes, we can do this again in the morning, Cassie."

Reassured, Cassie curled up against his hot, hard body and thought she'd never felt more comfortable in her life.

CHAPTER THIRTEEN

WHEN CASSIE WOKE—LATE—on Saturday morning, she sucked in a deep breath and stretched. The air was thick with the musky scent of sex and Ronan's cologne, and the heat of the day had already begun to build.

But the rumpled sheets beside her were empty.

She felt a moment of panic before she heard off-key whistling coming from the direction of her kitchen.

She couldn't have handled it if Ronan had disappeared during the night—if, having made love to her, he'd got what he came for and left.

The storm front that had arrived the previous night had done nothing to break the heat; instead of raining it had lowered a curtain of oppressive humidity over the city. Even her silk robe seemed like too much clothing, so instead Cassie reached for a light blue cotton sarong she kept thrown over the chair in the corner and tied it under her arms.

"Good morning," she said quietly. A man in her kitchen wasn't new—she'd had guests before. But a man in his boxer shorts making her coffee after making love to her the night before? That was unheard of.

"Morning, sunshine," Ronan said cheerily, holding out one of her yellow-and-white-striped mugs. "Milk, no sugar, right?"

He was right, except at home she usually drank tea, not coffee. It didn't matter. He gave her a grin and a wink and then turned back to prepare his own drink.

Cassie stood rooted to the spot. That swoopy, tickly feeling in her belly was back, only she wasn't quite sure why. Perhaps it was just the reality of his sheer good looks and fantastic body standing right here, in her kitchen, that seemed so incongruous.

Forcing her feet to move, Cassie took a seat at the table near the window. She looked out into her backyard, a little overgrown from lack of attention. It was cloudy but bright, and the humidity left a shimmer of heat over the garden.

"Did you sleep well?" he asked, pulling out a chair next to hers and sitting down.

"Are you always this chirpy in the morning?" Cassie couldn't help asking, taking in his cheerful eyes and clear complexion.

He seemed to consider the question. "Not *every* morning." He grinned wickedly.

She rolled her eyes and took a sip of coffee, then stifled a yawn. She could sleep for days—the past week of travel, with the arrangements for the new store on top of that, had drained her to the point of exhaustion. Not to mention the emotional fatigue from sparring with the man opposite her now. And this was where that had got her. She couldn't bring herself to regret it. Not yet.

"Still tired?" Ronan asked.

"I slept like a log, but it's been a tiring week, and the weather doesn't help."

"No, the heat's tough," he agreed. "But I heard that it's supposed to change today."

"Good."

He studied her for a while and Cassie began to feel self-conscious. She patted her hair. "What? Do I have bed head? I can't control it—it has a mind of its own."

He took her hand in his, drawing it away from her hair. "You look beautiful. Sexy and gorgeous." He pressed a kiss to her palm before setting her hand down on the table.

Cassie knew it wasn't true, but she wasn't anywhere close to getting sick of hearing him say it.

She took a moment to do some admiring of her own. She hadn't had much of a chance to look at or touch him—too wrapped up in her own anxiety. And he'd been so generous, making it all about her, not asking anything from her in return. But oh, how she wanted to touch. She wanted to lay him down and explore every inch of his skin, to squeeze those arms and feel that hard muscle beneath, to follow that trail of hair down his belly that right now disappeared behind the table in front of her.

His gentle laugh brought her back to earth. "Honey, sometimes you get this look in your eyes and I wonder if you're going to devour me whole."

Cassie's cheeks burned. She stared at the table, concentrating hard on her coffee.

His finger reached out to tilt her head up until she met his gaze again.

"I like it."

She had no idea what to say to that, so she smiled

instead, convinced she seemed goofy and awkward. Nothing like the women he usually dated, she was sure. Still, maybe that wasn't a bad thing.

"What would you like to do today?" she asked, changing the subject.

He shrugged. "As long as I spend it with you, I don't care."

Oh, those smooth lines of his. She'd recognized him as a player from the very start, when he'd walked up to her outside the warehouse and introduced himself—to Melanie. But now there was a sincerity there that she'd not noticed before. He genuinely seemed to want to be with her. Or was she kidding herself? Ronan had promised her a weekend—nothing more. She'd do well to remember that.

"We could walk to the beach and then down to St. Kilda," Cassie suggested. "There's lots of nice places there to eat and things to look at."

"Sounds good."

A HALF HOUR LATER, RONAN was walking along the beach hand in hand with Cassie. He was thankful he'd used the time at Sydney airport waiting for his flight to do some shopping—the cargo shorts and T-shirt he'd purchased were far more suited to this activity than the business shirts and trousers he'd brought from home. As far as footwear went, though, he only had his sneakers or work shoes. So sneakers it was. But Cassie had shaken off her sandals as soon as they'd reached the sand so he'd joined her in going barefoot, and they were now hooked over his fingers.

The water was cool but not cold as shallow waves washed over their feet. It was overcast and the wind was picking up, but the air was still heavy enough to keep a sheen of perspiration across his skin.

"That's St. Kilda Pier," Cassie said, pointing out into the water to a long wooden pier with an ornate-roofed building at the end. "It burned down a few years ago, but they rebuilt it."

She was taking her role as tour guide seriously and had told him all about her neighborhood and some of the landmarks they'd walked past. She seemed so comfortable and at-home, Ronan was happy to let her talk.

"What's that?" he asked, pointing to a tall white timber structure in the distance.

"Luna Park," she said with a smile. "It's an old theme park with rides and a fun fair. We can walk around there."

"Sounds like fun."

"But breakfast first?"

Ronan's stomach rumbled in agreement. "Definitely breakfast first."

Cassie took him to a restaurant with a view of a fast-food outlet across the road. Ronan queried her choice with a raised eyebrow.

"Not the most beautiful view, but the food's good, I promise," she said.

They each ate huge breakfasts of eggs, bacon, mushrooms, spinach and toast, sitting at an outdoor table next to the sidewalk. The wind changed direction as they were eating, bringing a cool breeze in from across the water. The relief was so palpable Ronan could almost feel the city let out a sigh.

"Let's take a walk up Acland Street to help the food go down," Cassie suggested once they'd finished eating, "and then we'll stop in at Luna Park on our way home."

Ronan was happy to be led around. Contented and relaxed, he was aware they were feelings that had been foreign to him for a long time. The quirky stores and even quirkier locals they saw as they walked along the street were fun. He could easily see himself living in this city with its brown river, gray bay and changeable weather.

"Do you mind if we look in here for a moment?" Cassie had paused in front of a bookstore.

"Not at all."

They spent a long time wandering through the shelves, each pointing out their own favorite reads before drifting into their own areas of special interest. Cassie was drawn to the design section, of course; Ronan could have guessed that. He'd picked up a new leadership and management tome, but wasn't really paying attention to it. Instead his attention was constantly drawn to Cassie as she buried her nose in thick books filled with architectural photos and drawings.

Giving in to the inevitable, he shelved his book and walked over to her. "Do you want to buy it?" he whispered in her ear.

Cassie started at his voice, so absorbed in her reading she hadn't heard his approach. She smiled and closed the heavy volume she'd been studying. "No. It's really expensive."

"I'll get it for you."

She shook her head. "Thanks, I do appreciate the offer, but I also don't want to have to carry it home." She lifted it up and let it fall on the counter with a thud in demonstration of its weight.

"Fair enough."

"Shall we keep walking?"

Ronan nodded and took her hand as they emerged back into the sunshine and clamor of the busy street.

They walked past other shops and about a dozen bakeries with windows filled with all kinds of delicious-looking pastries. It was lucky he was stuffed from breakfast, or the temptation could have been too strong. Besides, X-rated thoughts involving Cassie and cream-filled pastries were enough to distract him from the idea of actually eating one himself.

Having done a loop and doubled back, they reached the beach end of the street again and the theme park stood in front of them.

"Luna Park was built in the 1920s, I think," Cassie said as they walked toward the park entrance. The entrance archway was constructed to look like a giant laughing face, and they passed through the mouth, below a row of even white teeth.

It was busy—Ronan guessed everyone was taking advantage of their summer weekend—though it was no Disneyland. Everything was worn and a little shabby, but it had a certain old-fashioned charm. The white timbers he'd seen from the distance supported a roller coaster that groaned and creaked as the car went past. He cringed just listening to it.

"Let's go on it," Cassie suggested, pointing to the car as it swooped down a dip. Her eyes sparkled at him. She'd tied her hair back into a ponytail this morning and wore no makeup. She looked young and pretty and fresh and Ronan hoped just a little of that might wear off on him. Lately he'd been feeling so old and tired.

"Okay, let's do it." He grabbed her hand and half walked, half ran over to the ticket office, Cassie giggling beside him. Ronan felt his heart growing lighter with each step.

The rickety roller coaster actually appeared much safer once he was on it—he could see the modern additions that enhanced protection for its passengers. Cassie laced her fingers through his as the car slowly—creakily—left the dock.

He turned to smile at her and squeezed her hand.

She looked halfway between terrified and thrilled, which he guessed was appropriate for a roller coaster, only they hadn't even started yet. And this wasn't exactly a triple-twister corkscrew on top of a fifty-story building à la Las Vegas. It was called the *Scenic Railway,* and really it offered a view of the beach with a few little hills and dips, as far as he could see.

They rounded the corner, passing the minaret-style top of the entrance gates, and Ronan looked out over the bay. The car approached the first dip and Cassie's grip on his hand tightened. It reminded him of her reaction on the plane and he looked over to make sure she was okay. A smile was plastered on her face, almost as broad as the one they'd walked through as they'd entered. It made Ronan's stomach flip in a way that had nothing to do with the ride.

The car reached the peak and Cassie gasped as it began to free-fall. It only lasted a second or two and then the old thing was groaning its way up the next incline.

"How you doing?" he asked, shouting over the noise of the roller coaster and the wind that whipped around them.

"I'm great!" Cassie's eyes were wide, although Ronan didn't entirely understand why she was so excited.

Later, as they made their way back to Cassie's house, he asked her about it. "Is that the first time you've been on a roller coaster?"

"My second time," she replied. She skipped a step to catch up with him and took his hand in hers. "The first time was years ago, with my brother."

"At Luna Park?" He'd never been one for public displays of affection, but holding hands with Cassie and walking along the sand was so comfortable he barely gave it a second thought.

"No, at a theme park in Queensland. It was a proper one, with safety bars and twists and loops. It was terrifying."

"But you seemed to really enjoy this one."

"I did."

The wind had picked up to an unpleasant strength, whipping sand around their legs. They had kept their shoes on for the return journey, walking along the firm wet sand, giving the lapping waves a wide berth. The bay had turned a churning brownish color and the cloud cover had deepened, adding a distinct chill to the air.

"You know, apparently there used to be a ghost at Luna Park," Cassie said after they'd walked in companionable silence for a while.

"Really?"

"In the early nineteen hundreds, or so I've heard. It was on the roller coaster—it would pop up in front of the cars just as they were about to go down the big dip and scare everyone."

Ronan chuckled. "Sounds like a ghost with a sense of humor."

"I know. It could have hung out in the ghost train, but no, it went for the roller coaster."

"What happened? Is it still there?"

Cassie shook her head. "No, I don't think so. It hasn't been seen for decades. I think it's gone now. It must have got sick of scaring people." A mysterious smile played around her lips. "Or maybe people just got sick of being scared," she added in a small voice that he almost didn't hear.

There was more to her comment, he knew, but a couple of fat raindrops hit his face and distracted him. "What's going on with this weather?" he asked instead.

"Welcome to Melbourne," Cassie said with a laugh. "If you don't like the weather, just wait a minute. We're the city that has four seasons in one day."

"So we've had summer, what's this?"

"Winter!" Cassie shrieked as cold rain suddenly pelted down from the sky.

CHAPTER FOURTEEN

THEY BROKE INTO A RUN, the corner of Cassie's street just up ahead. It was less than five minutes before they were standing on her porch as she searched for her key, but both of them were soaked and shivering.

"This is ridiculous." Ronan shook the water out of his hair and then bent down to take off his saturated shoes.

"I know." Cassie flicked her sandals off and squeezed her ponytail, sending a trail of water onto the decking. "I'm soaked."

"Me, too." His brand-new T-shirt and shorts were drenched, his skin was beginning to prickle with the cold, and a trickle of icy water ran from his hair down his back.

Cassie smiled at him and he'd never felt better.

"Come on." Cassie opened the door and headed straight for the bathroom. Ronan followed, his wet socks squelching along the floorboards. Leaning over, she turned on the taps in the deep tub and sent him a grin that shot heat straight to his groin.

Straightening and turning to face him, her hands went to the hem of the light cotton dress she was wearing, now plastered to her skin, revealing puckered nipples and the outline of her underwear. With one motion she stripped the dress over her head and dropped it with a wet slap on the floor, leaving her standing there in matching pink bra and panties.

Ronan's chill was instantly forgotten. In fact he absently wondered if there might be steam rising from his skin—he'd never met a woman who inspired such an instant and extreme reaction inside him. In a few seconds flat he ached to have her.

"I thought we could have a bath to warm up," Cassie said shyly, her quiet voice a contrast to her boldly almost-naked body. "And maybe we can have some hot chocolate afterward."

"Sounds great." His voice felt as strangled as his gut. Why wasn't this desire for her fading? He'd thought part of his near obsession with Cassie, the impulse that had compelled him to track her down at her house, was the perverse need to have something he shouldn't. Over and over this past week he'd told himself she was off-limits, and in doing so, he'd amplified his craving for her.

But, to put it crudely, he'd had her now.

Taken her body, taken her virginity, made her scream and arch with pleasure more than once.

It should have been enough. It wasn't. Not nearly.

"My bubble bath is rose scented, sorry," Cassie chatted as she attended to their bath. "I hope you don't mind smelling like flowers. But I thought it would be nice to have some bubbles."

If it meant getting naked with her again, Ronan would happily have smelled of cow dung. He wrestled his wet T-shirt over his head and stripped off his shorts and underwear.

He loved that she blushed so easily. As soon as he was naked, her eyes darted around the room, landing everywhere but on him, and he couldn't help smiling.

"It's okay, Cassie." He took a few steps closer to her. "You can look."

She let out a nervous laugh. "Sorry. It's just, I…" Clearly flustered, she flapped one hand in the air in place of her missing words.

He stepped closer still, close enough to lean over and press a kiss to the tip of her nose. "You can look while I take care of this." Reaching around her back, he felt for the catch of her bra. He deftly unhooked it and trailed his hands over her shoulders and down her arms, taking the straps with him.

Her breath caught as he lifted the garment away and dropped it on the floor beside them.

He'd felt her eyes on him and now tentative fingers reached for his chest and stroked a line from shoulder to belly, following her gaze. He wanted to lift her onto the bathroom counter and take her right now, but forced himself to wait. His hands tightened into fists by his sides as her touch moved lower, becoming firmer as her confidence grew.

His eyelids fluttered closed as she grasped him, her fingers still cool from the rain. He leaned his head back and groaned as she began to move; her sweet mouth lowered to his chest and pressed kisses across his skin, her tongue darting out to flick against one of his nipples before her lips claimed it.

"Cassie." He wasn't sure if it was warning or encouragement. A longing to touch her filled his every pore, but he knew as soon as he did, he'd be hoisting her against him and thrusting inside her, and he wanted to give her this, a chance to explore a man in a way she'd never done before.

"Your body's so hard," she murmured against his skin. "Everywhere."

Her fingers moved over his length in agonizing pleasure while her other hand ran down his back and skimmed over his buttocks, tracing their curves. A shiver went through him, testament to his restraint, every muscle taut to the point of pain.

Abruptly she released him. "You're cold."

He sucked in a breath and opened his eyes, meeting her concerned gaze. "No, baby, I'm very, very hot."

She laughed, almost a giggle, and her eyes dipped away. "Let's have a bath anyway." She shuddered. "I *am* cold."

It took more self-control than Ronan knew he possessed to step into the bath, watch as Cassie stripped off her panties and then have her climb in, resting back against his chest, her soft bottom pressed in tormenting intimacy against him. He drew in a ragged breath and congratulated himself on his self-discipline. He really should get a medal for this.

The bath oil had made the water slippery and bubbles floated across the surface. Ronan grabbed handfuls of suds and brought them closer. "Look, you've got a bubble bikini."

She laughed but it turned into a groan as his hands

met her skin, splashing warm water over her chilled shoulders before cupping both breasts.

Her neck arched as she laid her head on his shoulder. "It feels so good when you touch me," she whispered.

"It feels so good to touch you," he replied, twisting to press his lips against the pulse point in her neck. She sighed and a wet hand rose out of the water to clasp his head to her.

As delectable as her full breasts were to touch, Ronan couldn't help continuing his exploration, one hand moving lower in the water, toying with the curls at the juncture of her thighs.

Her legs parted and Ronan could just make out the sound of his name on her lips. But as his fingers delved deeper, her body stiffened.

"No, wait."

Cassie plucked his hands away from her and laced her fingers with his.

She twisted around to meet his eyes. "I want to do this when I can see you and touch you, too."

"Cassie, I don't mind—"

"I know. But let's just get warm here and then we'll go back to bed, okay?"

He studied the determined look on her face. This woman of his was stubborn, no mistaking that. Stubborn and willful. It was what had made her a survivor, and his chest filled again with that bizarre pride at what she'd achieved.

He chuckled and gave her a little dip of his head. "Yes, ma'am, whatever you say."

"Good." Cassie turned and rested back against him,

wrapping his arms around her. She played with one of his hands, absently following the veins that traced his skin. "Ronan?"

"Hmm?"

"Can you lift your feet out of the water for a minute?"

"Why?"

"Because I want to look at them."

"What?"

"You said I could look." Her tone bristled with defensiveness.

"At my feet?"

Her shoulders shrugged against him.

Puzzled, Ronan complied, lifting his legs so his feet stuck up on the edge of the bath, dripping water onto the floor on either side. "My feet, ma'am, for your viewing pleasure."

A soft laugh rippled through her. "Thank you."

He flexed his ankles and wiggled his toes, showing off, having no idea why she might be so fascinated. As feet went they were pretty ordinary, he figured.

"They're very nice feet," Cassie said quietly after a moment. "Now you should put them back in the water so they don't get cold."

"Okay."

A companionable silence fell, broken only by the occasional splash of water as one of them moved position, and the continuous drumming of rain on the roof.

"So what's the story with the roller coaster?" Ronan asked after a while. He wondered if she'd tell him.

She hesitated before answering. "What do you mean?"

"I mean, I get that you enjoyed it, but it seemed like there was something else going on."

No answer.

"Did you see the ghost?" he added as a joke.

"I saw lots of ghosts." She let out a long sigh.

"I don't understand." He gave her a gentle nudge as if he could physically make her talk.

"I…don't know how to explain it." Her fingers had gone still against his hands.

"Try."

Another sigh and then, haltingly, she began to speak. "Last…last night, before we…" She waved a hand, sprinkling water over them.

"Made love," Ronan supplied.

"Yes, that. I was…scared. But I realized that fear and excitement can feel the same sometimes. Like a roller coaster. And when I was on the roller coaster today, I realized that I've missed out on things in my life because I didn't know that. Lots of things that might have been exciting, I stayed away from because I was scared."

Ronan didn't know what to say so he just squeezed her tighter, encouraging her to continue.

"I made this plan. I knew my life wasn't working, and I had to do something about it, so I created a plan that was all about staying safe. I wrote that proposal for Graham because I need my work at Country Style to be my foundation—that was the first step. I knew I couldn't move forward if that wasn't secure."

The breath froze in Ronan's lungs as she spoke. But she seemed to have forgotten the reason he was there in the first place, and she continued without pause.

"Then I was going to get Mel to give me a makeover. I know I could do more with my fashion sense and my hair and makeup and all that."

Ronan wanted to reassure her that she was beautiful just as she was, but he was still reeling from the kick-in-the-guts reminder of what he was here to do. In a few days' time, he'd be responsible for Cassie losing her job—the very foundation she was trying to secure. Hell, Graham might even ask him to fire her personally—it had happened before.

"And then I was going to try to meet a man and have a family," Cassie continued. "They were steps three and four. I had it all worked out and none of the steps could happen out of order, because that would have been too risky."

She twisted in the bath, turning to face him. Her velvet-brown eyes were both serious and joyful, brimming with possibility.

"But look at what I've done—just in the past twenty-four hours. I've been on a roller coaster again. I've been with you. And I've been safe both times. Even though I was scared, it turned out okay. I didn't lose anything."

Or anyone, Ronan wanted to add. Because he knew that was the real key to her fear. She hadn't lost anyone—yet. But she would soon. Ronan would do what he'd been hired to do and she'd lose the only family she had left—her Country Style colleagues. And then he'd fly back to San Francisco, to his sterile apartment, and take up his hard-fought-for partnership. The thought left him feeling empty.

"Oh, sweetheart," he said, clasping her head and pulling it to his chest. He pressed a kiss to her crown and stroked her back. "What a big day you've had."

It would be crueler than he could imagine to tell her now that soon her plans would all come crashing down. He swallowed down the bitter taste of his betrayal.

What he could give her was this weekend—a weekend to learn how beautiful she was and just how much a man could desire her. Telling her what the future held would only cause her anxiety and grief. But he promised himself that first thing Monday morning he'd come clean—tell her exactly what Graham was planning, give her time to steel herself for the blow. What it would mean for Conroy Corp, he didn't know. He'd deal with that—and his father—later.

He pushed Cassie's shoulders, turning her away from him. "Let me wash your hair for you." It gave him more time to neutralize his expression.

Slowly Ronan wet Cassie's hair, lathered shampoo into it, rinsed it and followed her instructions to apply some kind of conditioner that didn't need to be washed out. By the time he'd finished he'd managed to push Country Style to the back of his mind and reconciled himself to his decision.

In the bedroom, Cassie looked up at him with her trusting brown eyes, and he blinked. Coward that he was, he couldn't bring himself to tell the truth. Selfish as he was, he couldn't bear to tear himself away from her. Instead, he kissed a path down her body, used his mouth to bring her to her peak, and then lost himself inside her until all that remained was the sight, sound, taste and touch of Cassie Hartman.

CHAPTER FIFTEEN

CASSIE HAD NEVER KNOWN weekends like this existed.

She'd done no work, except field a couple of calls about last-minute issues with the store opening on Monday. The rest she'd let go through to voice mail. Compared to a usual weekend—when Country Style stores around the country were filled with customers and a hundred and one queries seemed to need her personal attention—that was nothing.

And the world hadn't ended. Stores were still open. Customers were still buying furniture in droves.

After their bath, she and Ronan had spent the rest of Saturday in bed, listening to the rain, eating whatever she could rummage from the freezer, sharing a bottle of wine, making love again, falling asleep in each other's arms.

This morning they'd woken and Cassie had decided that since Ronan hadn't taken the opportunity to do any sightseeing in Sydney, she'd better give him at least a taste of what Australia looked like outside of furniture stores and hotel rooms.

"We really didn't need to hire this car," Cassie said as Ronan sped along the highway toward home from the Yarra Valley, the picturesque wine region just outside Melbourne where they'd spent the day.

"*You* didn't need to hire it. I *did*."

He looked so pleased with himself, sitting behind the wheel of the ridiculously expensive European convertible, Cassie didn't bother pursuing her protest. She smiled and shook her head, watching the scenery whip past. Ronan was a confident driver, sure and decisive. It reminded Cassie of when he'd compared her to this kind of car. He was a master at bringing out the best in both of them, it seemed.

After the storm the day before, Mother Nature had managed to provide them with a perfect summer day. Warm, but not too hot, with a gentle breeze and blue sky that rivaled Ronan's eyes.

"Do you want to stop for one more wine tasting before we leave the valley?" she asked.

He shrugged. "I don't mind. We can stop if you want."

Cassie thought about it. The sun was beginning to lower in the sky now and she felt sleepy and comfortable. She stretched languidly. "I don't think I can be bothered." She stifled a yawn.

Ronan shot her a quick look. "That's what drinking in the middle of the day will do to you."

"I know, I know." Cassie had enjoyed a full glass of champagne at their last stop instead of the minimal tasting that Ronan had done. The alcohol wasn't entirely responsible for her tiredness—she hadn't had much sleep the night before—but it was contributing to her lethargy. She yawned, not bothering to stifle it this time.

"Don't go to sleep on me," Ronan warned with an

indulgent smile. "I don't know the way back to your place."

"You could just follow the signs back to the city and wake me when we get there," she suggested.

"Assuming I remember to drive on the left-hand side of the road."

"Oh, yeah." Cassie sat up straighter. Perhaps she should stay awake. Just in case. Ronan must be tired, too. A car accident would not be a pleasant way to end this weekend.

Cassie's stomach clenched. She didn't want to think about the weekend ending. She wanted it to go on forever, to live in this fantasy where Ronan was hers and the rest of the world didn't matter.

"What was your favorite animal?" she asked, as much to make conversation as to distract herself.

"At the sanctuary?"

"Yes." Along with the wineries, Cassie had taken Ronan to an animal sanctuary—where he'd been thrilled to meet real, live kangaroos, koalas and a grumpy-looking goanna. They'd laughed at a kookaburra to try to encourage it to laugh back, but he'd remained annoyingly silent.

"I liked the koala, of course. But I think my favorite was that little rabbit-looking thing."

"The bilby? Really?" Cassie was surprised.

"Yeah. It was cute, but also looked like it was sad, like it needed a home."

Not something Cassie would have expected the high-flying business consultant to say. "Do you have any pets back in San Francisco?"

"Nope. I'm not there enough to take care of one. Otherwise I probably would. There's a stray cat in the neighborhood that I feed occasionally, but I don't think that counts."

"What sort of pet would you have?"

"A dog. And a cat. Two dogs and a cat if I could manage it."

"You like animals."

"Yeah, you?"

"Yes, but—same as you—I'm not home enough to take care of one. I'd love to have a dog. I'm jealous when I watch the people walking theirs along the beach."

"Maybe you can—" He cut himself off.

"What?" Cassie prompted.

He shook his head. "Nothing."

"Did you have pets as a child?"

His mouth curved in a smile that gave Cassie her answer.

"Yes. Lots. A menagerie. My mother complained the whole time, but she secretly loved them, too. All kinds of animals—especially ones that were hurt or injured. I'd find them and bring them home, and Siobhan would pretend they were patients and patch them up, and somehow we'd never get around to setting them free again."

"Sounds messy." *And wonderful.* "What about when you get your partnership? Will that mean you'll travel less and would have time for a dog?"

His mouth compressed into a thin line. "Maybe," he said sharply.

So did that mean he'd ever be traveling in Australia again? Or once he was back in San Francisco, was that it? Cassie bit her lip to stop herself from saying anything more. They'd been very clear. This weekend was all they had, and on Monday morning it would be as if it had never existed.

She wondered if Ronan's thoughts were taking a similar path, because his hand reached out and rested on her leg, giving her thigh a squeeze. Her body responded to his touch, just as it always did, but there was something about the moment that was too colored with sadness for Cassie to enjoy it properly.

She wished she could throw a rope around the sun and stop it from sinking any further. If only there was a way to keep this day from ending.

Shifting in her seat, she gave herself a scolding for her childish thoughts. The only way to get through this was to make the most of every second while it lasted. Soak it in enough so that the memories would sustain her.

No, not just sustain her—strengthen her.

This weekend had shown Cassie that she was capable of attracting a man, of flirting with him, touching him, caressing him, making love to him. She loved hearing Ronan's noises of pleasure and knowing she was the cause.

That had to count for something, right? That had to mean that when the right man crossed her path, she'd be ready, prepared to grab him with both hands and hold on. Didn't it? Because surely if she felt this way with

Ronan, it meant she could feel this way with someone else?

Cassie didn't want to think too hard about the answer.

She covered Ronan's hand with her own, tracing his knuckles and threading her fingers between his.

"You know what?" she said.

"What?" he asked, the ghost of a smile on his lips, as if he knew what she was going to say.

"You know what I want to do when we get home?"

"What?"

Cassie leaned over and whispered some of her naughtiest ideas into his ear. When she leaned back in her seat, she was pleased to see the flush on his cheeks.

Ronan groaned. "Sweetheart, did you really have to tell me that when we're on a freeway and there's nowhere to pull over?"

Cassie gave a laugh. Sexy and a little devious. She was proud of herself.

Ronan shifted in his seat. "How long until we get home?"

RONAN HAD KISSED HER as they'd parked the car in front of her house and Cassie wondered if she'd be receiving any reprimands from her neighbors as they'd realized their little display really, *really* needed to move inside. They hadn't even made it to the bedroom— Cassie knew she'd never look at the coat pegs that she'd clung to on the wall just inside the front door in quite the same way ever again.

But as the sun slowly faded on Sunday evening and they relaxed in her lounge room, having demolished another order of Thai food, anxiety began to creep back in. It was a remembered sensation from childhood, the realization that fun time was almost over and it was back to school tomorrow.

And it wasn't just her. She could practically feel the tension beginning to vibrate from the other side of the room. The television was on, but Cassie was sure neither of them was paying attention. Ronan was lying on the sofa, his bare feet propped up on the arm, just as she'd once pictured. His hands were tucked behind his head and he looked for all the world as if he were simply relaxing after a lovely weekend. But although she'd only known him a week, Cassie knew better. There was a stiffness in his jaw, a set to his shoulders that clearly showed this was a man who was not at ease.

He took in a deep breath and Cassie braced herself, although against what, she wasn't entirely sure.

"I should probably go back to my hotel," he announced, fanning that tiny spark of anxiety into flames that lit through her body. "No doubt you have an early start tomorrow."

She forced herself to sound carefree. "Yes, I want to be at the store around six. There'll be the last-minute tweaks to make—there always are. But the staff seem on the ball and when I called on Friday everything sounded as if it was under control. There's a chance Graham might visit this week—he often comes to new-store openings. Seems to be the only thing that still interests him about Country Style. I'll have to be on my toes." She was babbling and forced herself to shut up.

He turned his head away from the television and his

eyes locked with hers. There was a long pause before he spoke again. "Cassie? I need to talk to you," he began.

Something in his eyes troubled her and she would have given anything for him to stop speaking.

"Cassie. I…" His throat bobbed as he swallowed. "Cassie, I lied about my name." He winced, as if he'd been expecting different words to come out of his mouth.

Cassie was confused for a moment. She'd thought they were about to have "the talk"—the one about how their weekend agreement was about to come to an end, how tomorrow they'd have to go back to their established roles, how he'd never kiss her again. The idea started an ache in her stomach, the ache of a sensation she knew only too well: grief.

But *he'd lied about his name?* It was the last thing she expected.

She shook her head. "I don't understand."

"I know. I'm not sure I do, either," he added in a low voice.

Ronan twisted his body until he sat upright, elbows on his knees, looking at her. An ad on the TV screamed about the world that would open up if only you used a particular deodorant. He searched out the remote control and turned off the background noise with a flick. "I only did it when I came to Australia. I just…I had something to prove when I came here. That I could succeed on my own."

"But I'm sure you're very successful." At least this puzzlement was a distraction from the gnawing ache in her belly.

"I am, but…" He stood up and paced, tunneling his fingers through his hair. The calm, controlled Ronan McGuire—or whatever his name was—was no longer so calm and controlled.

"What is it? You are Ronan, aren't you?"

He drew in a deep breath and let it out in a sigh. "Yes, I'm Ronan—Ronan Conroy. My father is Patrick Conroy, the head of Conroy Corporation. McGuire is my grandmother's maiden name." His blue eyes burned intensely. "It wasn't anything to do with you. I made the decision to do it before I'd even met you."

"Okay." Cassie felt a little hurt that he'd lied to her, but she couldn't really see why it was such a big deal.

"I decided to take a different name while I was here because I'm sick of the baggage and expectations that come with being Patrick Conroy's son. I just wanted to prove myself on my own."

"I guess I can understand that."

"But it was a mistake. It doesn't mean anything. I was being egotistical and unrealistic, thinking my name would make a difference to who I was, to how I behaved."

Cassie didn't want to talk about work. Not now. She wanted it to wait for Monday morning, as they'd agreed. But the strain she could read on Ronan's face was real and she wanted to take him in her arms and smooth it away. "Ronan, you're very good at what you do. Insightful, articulate, intelligent. I'm sure you've done an excellent job with your analysis of Country Style. You don't have anything to prove. I've seen your work, and I know you're incredibly talented. I know what you do for Graham and for Country Style will be brilliant, as well."

Instead of soothing him, her words seemed only to increase his burden. He closed his eyes for a moment and shook his head. "Oh, Cassie. Don't say that."

"But aren't you about to become partner? Surely that's recognition of your achievements."

"Yes, my partnership," he echoed bitterly. "Do a good job here and I get rewarded with what should have been mine in the first place. A partnership leading to vice president, and then, when my father retires, taking over the company from him. Except I know now that I was never really sure I wanted it. My father saw that more clearly than I did."

"You don't want to be partner?"

"I don't know." His voice betrayed his turmoil. "I thought I did. But maybe I didn't. I did everything I could to jeopardize it, to push my father's patience to the limit. Maybe I was unconsciously trying to sabotage myself." He sighed again. "Maybe I still am."

Cassie knew what he was talking about. Being with her. He'd told her more than once that they couldn't risk getting involved. He'd tried to push her away as firmly as she'd tried to push him away. They'd both failed.

"Ronan, I know we shouldn't have…" Words deserted her. How could she describe what had happened between them this weekend? It was more than just making love. She'd fallen for him, she knew it now—had probably known it from the very moment he turned up on her doorstep, if not from the moment he'd appeared outside the warehouse. There was no way she could let him know she'd broken the terms of their agreement by falling in love.

She gulped as the knowledge sunk in.

Love.

She'd gone and fallen in love with Ronan, regardless of his last name.

"I know we shouldn't have had this weekend together," she began again. "But I promise you that it won't affect our working relationship. Tomorrow morning, when we're back at Country Style, it will all go back to normal. I know what we agreed and I'll stick to it. I'll behave as if this never happened, I promise."

Cassie wondered if she should cross her fingers behind her back. Could she keep that promise? *She had to.* Country Style could not be put at risk by her inability to keep away from a gorgeous man. By her inability to stop herself from falling in love with him. "You'll go back to evaluating my performance and I'll go back to trying to prove to you that I'm the best person to lead Country Style. Just like old times." She finished with a little laugh that sounded weird and strangled. She would simply have to pick up the pieces later.

Ronan shook his head. "Oh, Cassie." He raked his hands over his face, scrubbing at his unshaven jaw.

His anxiety ate away at her. She hated seeing him like this, torn, uncertain. It was so different from his usual brash confidence. More than anything, more than her own sadness and loss, she wanted him to feel better. If that didn't tell her she loved him, nothing did. "If you really don't want to go back to Conroy Corporation, why don't you get a new job? Start up a company of your own? I'm sure you'd be very successful."

Cassie felt uncertain about her advice and was sure it showed. What did she know about advising someone on their career? A girl who'd spent her entire working life with one company? For the first time, Cassie wondered if she *had* limited herself by staying with Country Style. What possibilities were out there that she'd never let herself consider? She'd never wanted to be vulnerable enough to make love with someone, and now that it had happened she couldn't believe she'd denied herself the pleasure for all these years. What if the same principle applied to her work? What if fear of leaving Country Style had trapped her just as much as it had protected her?

Ronan shook his head. "I can't. I don't want to follow someone else's plans for my life, but I can't leave Conroy Corporation. I never knew what I wanted before, but now I realize I've been taking things for granted. It wasn't exactly a sense of entitlement, but I…" He broke off and spun away from her, pacing back and forth as if he could no longer contain his energy within.

Cassie shelved her self-reflection for another time. "Ronan, if this is what you really want, your father will understand. He's your father. He loves you. He'll want what's best for you."

He shot her a bitter smile over his shoulder. "You don't know Patrick Conroy."

"No, but I know he should be grateful to have a son like you."

"And I should be grateful to have a father, right, Cassie?" he spat, spinning to face her. "That's what you mean, isn't it? Suck it up, because it could be worse—he could have died in a plane crash."

She shrank back from his anger, so unexpected and unexplained.

"Oh, God." He swore under his breath. He took a step toward her, then hesitated. "I'm so sorry, Cassie." His voice dripped with regret, his low tone shamed and guilty. "This isn't about you. I just can't stand…" His fists tightened by his sides as their eyes met.

They looked at each other for a long moment. There was too much going on in his eyes, Cassie couldn't read his expression. Pain, regret and yet, through all that, desire. He still wanted her, and Cassie wanted him with a hunger that was sharp enough to devour. Could they have just one last moment? One last time together before he had to go?

Cassie stood up and took a step toward him, her hand reaching out uncertainly.

His eyes darkened, desire beginning to edge out the rest. But then the shutters came down. "I have to go," he suddenly announced, turning away from her. "This isn't fair," he muttered.

"What isn't fair?" Cassie stood helpless, watching as he gathered his belongings from the bedroom and shoved everything into his overnight case. Her hands hung by her sides, paralyzed by confusion.

He strode over to her and clasped her cheeks with his hands. He pressed a hard kiss to her mouth, forceful, as if he was trying to leave his imprint on her somehow. He drew back and stared at her.

"Cassie, whatever happens, I want you to know that it wasn't about you. You're beautiful, incredibly sexy. You're an amazing woman, and you're fantastic at your job—one of the best I've ever seen. If the world was different—if I was different..." He drew in a breath. "But it's not and I'm not." The back of a finger stroked her cheek. "Take care, Cassie. You're so strong. Stronger than you think."

Cassie blinked and then he was gone. He whirled away from her, grabbed his case, and then the front door closed with a thud behind him.

Her knees weakened and she sank back into the chair behind her.

What had just happened?

He couldn't be gone. Not like that.

No, this wasn't how she'd expected this part of the weekend to work out at all. She'd imagined kissing him on the doorstep, sadly waving goodbye as he loaded his case into a taxi outside and then disappeared. Perhaps she'd shed a few tears once she was back inside on her own. It would be sad, she knew that. But then she'd be able to wrap herself up in the memories of the weekend they'd shared. That would be enough to see her through.

But this sour note, his anger and confusion... That wasn't how it was supposed to go. Now she felt not only bereft, but bewildered and hurt.

Why had he lied about his name? She still didn't understand. It didn't make any difference, though.

Her time with Ronan McGuire—Ronan *Conroy*—was over. She needed to remember that they'd only ever had the weekend. However it had ended, it had ended.

CHAPTER SIXTEEN

THE DOORS OF THE HAWTHORN store had been open for four hours. So far most things had gone according to plan. Cassie's eye for detail picked out that the car-park signage still wasn't quite right, but most people wouldn't notice. A couple of staff members were spending more time chatting than working, and Cassie knew she'd be having words with them before the end of the day. One of the lighting features in the dining room display area wasn't working, but an electrician was on the way to check it out.

Other than that, things were good. Apart from the blisters. Cassie winced and cursed herself for not sticking to her usual uniform. The impulse that had possessed her that morning and compelled her to whisk her hair into a complicated French roll and pull out a skirt and three-inch pumps instead of her normal trousers and court shoes now seemed like the worst kind of self-indulgent foolishness. Although she'd pretty much given up on her four-stage plan—her weekend with Ronan had made it redundant—today had been the wrong day to choose to work on Part Two's self-makeover section.

"Cassie! There's something wrong in the tearoom!"

Cassie sighed as she finished rearranging a bedding

display that had just been upturned by an enthusiastic customer who had wanted to look at the timber bed "without all the frills in the way." And who had then walked out without buying anything.

Tweaking the last pillow until it sat on just the right angle, she turned and made her way quickly to the sales desk and through the door behind that led to the back of the store and the staff tearoom.

A hassled-looking Mel met her there. "I think we need to call a plumber," Mel said, throwing her hands up. "There's a problem with the tap."

"How can there be a problem with the tap? It's brand-new," Cassie huffed.

"I tried to turn it off, but it just wouldn't turn," a wet-looking junior sales assistant said, gesturing to the small stainless-steel sink in the kitchenette. "And then I tried to take it apart to get to the washer, but I just got sprayed."

Cassie looked the girl up and down. "Sharon, isn't it?"

Sharon nodded miserably.

"Don't worry about the tap," Cassie ordered crisply. "Go get yourself dried off—use the hand dryers in the staff bathroom. And perhaps iron your shirt again to get the water out of it. We'll take care of this—we need you out on the floor."

"Okay." The bedraggled girl disappeared.

"Right." Cassie turned to face the tap that was spewing water into the sink, splashing everything in the vicinity. She swallowed hard around a lump in her throat, cursing herself as she did. This was *not* worth crying over! A stupid broken tap! Everything else was going so well—a problem with the plumbing was nothing in the scheme of things. What was wrong with her? She usually took things like this in her stride.

"Do we know how to turn the water off?" she asked Mel, forcing her voice to stay steady.

Mel shook her head. "I can go out back to look."

Cassie nodded as she studied the tap. If she just… "Okay. Let me see if there is anything I can—*crap!*" Cassie's attempt ended with the same result as Sharon's had—Cassie was sprayed with water from head to waist.

"Oh, Cassie." Mel looked horrified, but then began to giggle.

Cassie looked down at her chambray shirt, one side of it saturated and clinging to her skin. She could feel her for-once carefully arranged hair hanging lankly against one cheek. It reminded her of getting caught in the rain with Ronan and the lump in her throat rose again. But she looked at Mel's smiling face and what bubbled out of her was laughter, not tears. It was slightly hysterical, but at least it was better than crying.

"Excuse us, ladies."

It was Graham who spoke, but when Cassie looked over to the three men who'd just appeared, Ronan was the one who drew her gaze immediately. He was immaculate, in the same gray suit and red tie he'd worn the first day she'd met him. But in contrast to that first impression of cool confidence, today he practically vibrated with tension and he didn't meet her eyes. Graham Taylor stood to his right, a disapproving frown across his face. The man who stood on his left Cassie had never seen before, but the set of his shoulders, the shape of his face and the blue of his eyes told her instantly that this was Patrick Conroy, Ronan's father. Had Ronan known he was coming?

Mel recovered first. "We've got a little plumbing problem, Graham."

"Then I suggest you turn off the mains and call a plumber," he said drily.

"I'll go do that now." Mel disappeared quickly toward the back of the building.

Graham's frown softened to an indulgent smile as he looked Cassie up and down. "Cassie, my girl, I know you like to think you can take care of everything, but some things really do require an expert."

Cassie bristled at his words, even though she knew he meant no harm.

"I'll call a plumber," she said, trying to keep her tone even. Being caught by her boss in the middle of a crisis, even something as simple and clearly not her fault as a broken tap, wasn't how she would have liked things to go. Especially not when the consultant responsible for evaluating her performance was standing right beside him. A sick sense of foreboding settled in her stomach.

Graham held up a hand as Cassie headed out to find a telephone. "Before you go, Cassie, I know you've met Ronan Conroy, but I wanted to introduce you to Patrick Conroy, president of the Conroy Corporation and my old friend. We met when I worked in the U.S. many years ago."

"*Many* years ago," Patrick Conroy echoed with emphasis. "It's a pleasure to meet you, Ms. Hartman." He took a step forward and offered his hand.

Cassie wiped her wet hand and then shook his, momentarily dumbstruck. Patrick Conroy's grasp was firm and his eyes sparkled with amusement. She could see that this was not a man to cross, a man with determined and definitive opinions. But she sensed a kindness and warmth in his manner. He wasn't laughing *at* her, but with her. There was also no mistaking that Conroy charisma—was that genetic? It was a view into the future, because this was surely how Ronan would look in thirty years. Still earth-shatteringly handsome.

"It's, uh, a pleasure to meet you, too, Mr. Conroy," Cassie managed to stutter.

"Perhaps we'll leave you to sort this out and come back later," Graham suggested. "Patrick and Ronan and I are going to have lunch and then we'll come back and see how things are going." His look turned suddenly serious. "Then we'll have a talk about…the future."

Cassie clasped her hands together to hide the tremor she couldn't control. "Certainly. I'll have this fixed up before you return." She forced a smile.

The three men began to leave. Ronan gave her a quick glance, meeting her eyes for the first time since he'd appeared. His look was shuttered and distant, and then, with a short nod, he was gone.

Cassie sank into a chair as soon as they disappeared from sight, her knees weak. The pressure of the store opening, the wariness she felt with Graham now watching her every move, and the idea of an upcoming "talk" about the future was enough to sap her last speck of energy. And that was without facing Ronan again after their weekend. Without remembering his face as he smiled, as he slept, as he lost himself in pleasure. Cassie felt drained to the point of nervous exhaustion.

Faintly she registered that the constant gush of the tap slowed and then stopped. A few moments later Mel reappeared. She reached for a tea towel and wiped her dirty hands and then sat down opposite Cassie.

"Finally found the tap," she said. "Are they gone?"

Cassie nodded.

"Geez, I'd forgotten how gorgeous that Ronan was. Phew!" Mel fanned herself dramatically. "I don't know how you managed to spend the week with him without spontaneously combusting. I'd have jumped him for sure."

Cassie gave a rueful snort. Because what could she say?

"I know, I know. You don't do that sort of thing. You're way more professional than me. But the man is *so* hot. I wonder if he has a girlfriend."

Cassie realized she'd never thought to ask. *Did* he have a girlfriend? They hadn't discussed his romantic past—only hers. The extent of her vulnerability hit her—he knew so much about her. Her family, her past, her insecurities, her inexperience—he knew it all. What did she know about him, really? Until last night, she hadn't even known his real name.

She couldn't keep thinking about it or she'd go mad. Abruptly she stood. "I'd better go clean up." Without waiting to see Mel's expression she dashed for the bathroom.

Her shirt took only a few minutes to dry under the hand dryer in the bathroom. Her hair was another matter. The machine fluffed it up into a messy cloud. Because of her decision to pin it up that morning she now had only bobby pins to secure it with, but the wild locks were beyond her abilities to tame without a cupboard full of product. All she could do was pat it down as best she could and leave it loose.

The noise when she stepped back out into the store was enough to startle her. In contrast to the relatively quiet morning, it seemed as though every person in Melbourne had decided to visit the brand-new Country Style outlet at the same time.

"Where do you want me?" Cassie asked Steve, the store manager, as he bustled past.

"Um…" He looked around. "Actually, could you do a lunch run? I can't let people take breaks when the store's like this, so they'll have to wait till later. Some drinks and sandwiches out in the tearoom would be good so the team can grab something on the run."

"No problem." Cassie had no issues with being the errand girl. In times like this, it was all hands on deck and rank meant nothing.

"Oh, and make sure to get a few bottles of water, too," Steve added with a grin. "Seeing as we don't have any coming out of the tap."

"Good thinking." Cassie winced. She should have thought of that.

Scooping up her purse, she headed for the café a few doors down, glad to have a purpose, glad to have something to distract her.

THERE WERE DAYS FROM HELL and then there were days from a very special region of the ninth circle of hell, Ronan thought as he sat at the white-linen-covered table between his father and Graham Taylor and picked at the stupidly expensive lunch in front of him.

Patrick Conroy's surprise visit wasn't exactly welcome. Ronan could only thank whatever lucky stars he had that he'd actually been in his hotel room when the receptionist called the night before to announce his father's arrival. It could have been much worse. He could have still been at Cassie's. He could have been *caught*.

His father's insistence that he'd come to visit his old friend Graham had rung entirely false. Ronan knew Patrick Conroy was really in Australia to check up on his son's performance. It would only have stung more if he'd actually been innocent.

And that, Ronan thought, was the *real* problem here.

The two older men talked away, reminiscing about old times and catching up on recent achievements. Their shared history and unsubtle one-upmanship left Ronan out of the conversation and sunk in his own thoughts.

Would he admit to his father what had happened between him and Cassie? There was no need to. She'd given her word she wouldn't say anything and he trusted her.

So what now? He'd give his due-diligence report and walk away. Country Style would be sold. Graham Taylor would make a bundle. Conroy Corporation would invoice a substantial fee for Ronan's work. Cassie would lose her job.

It wasn't his problem.

But then why did he feel so terrible?

His only comfort was that at least this was all coming to an end. Within a day or two he'd be on a plane and all of this would be half a world away.

"Ronan?" His father's tone told him he'd missed something.

"Yes, sir?"

"I said, have you sent a final copy of the report to Graham yet?"

"I haven't seen it," Graham added with a frown.

Ronan shook his head. "No, not yet. You'll most likely have it tomorrow—certainly before I leave for San Francisco. I was going to complete it this morning, but your arrival upset my schedule," he said, looking pointedly at his father.

Patrick Conroy gave a small laugh. "Aren't you glad to see your dear old dad?" he joked.

Ronan smiled because he knew it was expected and that Graham was watching. "Of course. I just hadn't planned for it, that's all."

"So can you give me an overview? What did you discover?" Graham leaned forward, his elbows on the table, keen to hear every word.

Ronan forced himself to focus. Business. He pushed aside a mental image of Cassie, instead picturing the words of his report on his laptop screen.

"Cassie Hartman's competitor analysis was accurate," he began. "Her suggestion that Country Style has to dramatically expand in order to maintain its position in the market is correct, or it faces losing out to its larger competitors—and new international players."

Graham nodded. "I knew she'd called that right."

"Cassie proposed Country Style expand through opening a large number of new stores in untested markets. That's certainly one option, although it does carry a significant element of risk. What Cassie didn't look at in her report, which you picked up on, Graham, is that instead of expanding under its own brand, Country Style can merge with a competitor and increase its reach with the power and resources of global buying and advertising supporting it."

Patrick Conroy made a "hurry up" gesture with his hand. "Those are the two options. We knew that. What's the recommendation?"

Cut to the chase. Typical of his father.

Ronan's stomach clenched. He was about to deliver the death blow to Cassie's career with Country Style. He studied the two older men who were staring at him with such expectant looks on their faces.

"Strategically it makes more sense to merge. The international consortium you've been dealing with, Graham, are the perfect partners in terms of market sector and product positioning. My report should be sufficient in terms of due diligence for them." He sucked in a breath before pronouncing the final verdict, feeling like an executioner about to swing the ax. "You should sell Country Style."

The grin on Graham Taylor's face was obscene. Ronan could almost see the dollar signs in his eyes.

His father rapped the table with his knuckles. "Good work."

Ronan supposed he should be pleased by the praise.

"Right, right, right," Graham muttered almost to himself. Then, looking between Ronan and Patrick, he began tapping his fingers against his jaw. "The buyers want to move fast. They're keen to get in while this new flagship store is in its infancy. If we get on top of things quickly, they could rebrand it and make it their first Australian outlet."

"Makes sense," Ronan said. Because from a business perspective, it did.

"And what about the structure once the deal goes through?" Graham asked him.

"Their recommendations in terms of management, organization line management and support services are sound."

Graham glanced at Ronan and then studied his hands, taking great interest in picking at a fingernail.

Patrick Conroy cleared his throat after a long pause. "I assume they're going to consolidate the Australian head-office staff with their own management. Is that a problem, Graham?"

"No, no, it's not a problem." Graham sounded uncertain.

"Why the hesitation?" Patrick Conroy pushed.

"It's...my operations manager, Cassie," Graham began hesitantly.

Ronan sat up straighter in his chair. "What about her?"

Graham gave him a searching look. "How would you describe her skills, her competency?"

Ronan had a bad feeling about where this was going, but he had no choice but to answer. "She's a very talented manager. Her history with the company gives her an unrivaled knowledge of its workings. She has a flair for picking trends in interior design and ordering accordingly. And she has built a very engaged and loyal workforce."

"But?" Graham pressed and Ronan wondered what in his words or tone of voice had given away that there was a *but*.

"But…she has limited experience," Ronan admitted reluctantly. "None outside of Country Style. She's managed it excellently up to its current stage of growth and I have no doubt she'd continue to manage it well into the future. However, if the company is to grow internationally under the new management, it needs someone with broader experience and global expertise."

It was the truth, but that didn't stop his betrayal of Cassie from curdling his stomach. The food he'd just eaten turned into a solid lump.

Graham rubbed a hand over his face. "So you don't think the new buyers will offer her a management role?"

"I seriously doubt it. And even if they did, it wouldn't be on par with the CEO role she was pitching for."

Graham took another bite of his lunch and seemed to chew over his thoughts as well as his food. He put his cutlery down and leaned forward, as if about to reveal a confidence.

"I have a little problem there."

"How can we help?" Ronan's father asked. Always the consultant.

"Cassie…well," Graham began hesitantly, "Cassie is kind of like a daughter to me. She had a tough upbringing, fell on hard times and I just happened to…meet her at the right moment."

Ronan was grateful that Graham respected Cassie's privacy. He knew she'd be horrified if Graham had told business colleagues about exactly how they'd met.

"You gave her a job?" Patrick asked.

"Yes, yes. I got her back on her feet, helped her to find her way and supported her while she got herself sorted out."

"How decent of you."

His father's obsequious tone made Ronan want to gag. He wanted to jump into the conversation, yell at them to take care of Cassie, but he couldn't. What would he say, anyway? *Graham, don't sell the business because I don't want Cassie to lose her safety net at Country Style?* They'd laugh. And then ask why. Admitting he'd slept with Cassie wasn't the worst part of it. The worst part would be admitting that he'd already done enough to shake her carefully constructed foundations, and he wondered if she could take any more. His strong, willful, beautifully fragile Cassie.

"She's worked hard, make no mistake," Graham said, "and she's certainly added value to Country Style. But she really should have moved on long ago. She needs to spread her wings, to grow. I've tried to push her a couple of times, but she's never taken the bait. I know she could be incredibly successful, but she's too scared to leave the safety of the job she knows."

"This decision will be hard for her, then," Patrick summarized.

"Yes. Very. In the long run, I think it will be for the best, but she won't take it well."

"Conroy Corporation has a great deal of experience in situations like this," Patrick jumped in before Ronan could speak. The older man leaned back in his chair, nodding with what Ronan knew was a practiced expression of concern. "We have vast resources in the U.S. to assist individuals impacted by organizational change to shift their perspective and embrace uncertainty and realize possibility. I'm sure Ronan can find similar support services in Australia and make them available to all your staff who'll be outplaced in the merger."

It was the usual consultant lingo to cover the fact they were talking about people, their lives and families, their emotions.

Graham looked at Ronan. "I assume you had no problems working with Cassie over the past week? Even though she wasn't aware of the true purpose of your investigation?"

"There weren't any issues from a work perspective," Ronan answered carefully. From the corner of his eye he saw the flash in his father's eyes as he picked up on the unsubtle caveat in his words, but Ronan kept his gaze trained on Graham Taylor.

"So are you able to stay and assist with the transition?" Graham asked.

"What kind of assistance do you need?" Ronan asked warily. He felt his only comfort—that he would be leaving soon—beginning to slip through his fingers.

"I think it's clear," Patrick interrupted. "Graham needs your help to make the announcement. You can arrange the support services, facilitate the initial conversations with the new buyers and then we can step out of the process and let them take over once the paperwork is done."

It was all very standard. A very normal, ordinary engagement for Conroy Corporation.

Ronan felt the bile rise in his throat. "You want *me* to fire Cassie?"

CHAPTER SEVENTEEN

"YOU CAN GIVE HER THE NEWS initially," Graham said. "It'll go down better coming from a third party rather than from me. And then I'll talk to her once she's had a chance to think about it."

Ronan took a long drink from the water glass in front of him. It was the perfect opportunity to come clean. To declare that he had a conflict of interest. He couldn't fire a woman he'd had a sexual relationship with. Apart from anything else, if Cassie decided to sue for wrongful dismissal and disclosed the details of their liaison, it would create a shit storm that would have employment-rights lawyers rubbing their hands in glee.

A lawsuit for Conroy Corporation because Ronan hadn't been able to keep his pants zipped? It was some wicked déjà vu.

They'd been here before and his father had had to buy a way out of it. It wasn't going to happen again. Better to be honest now and deal with the consequences than to have it explode like a land mine later. Not to mention that he still had no idea how he could bring himself to face Cassie and give her the news that would destroy her.

Ronan waited to see what would come out of his mouth. Nothing did.

"I know it sounds like I'm getting soft in my old age." Graham gave Patrick a manly slap on the arm as if to prove to his friend that he was still young and fit. "But this girl really is like a daughter to me. I just can't bring myself to give her the bad news."

"I understand," Patrick said smoothly.

Suddenly, unexpectedly, Ronan found himself leaping in with his true thoughts. "I think that if you want to protect your relationship with Cassie, Graham, if you really feel this way about her, you should respect her enough to give her the news yourself," Ronan said. It wasn't just because he was too cowardly to do it—he genuinely thought Graham Taylor should man up and give Cassie the respect she deserved.

"What?" his father asked sharply.

Graham gave him a considered look. "Hmm. Maybe you're right."

Ronan ignored his father's angry expression. He shouldn't be contradicting the client, he knew that already, but this was too important to let go. "I'm happy to be there with you when you do it." No, he wasn't, but he'd do it because it was what a Conroy Corporation consultant—partner—should do. "But I think in the end, she'll be grateful to you for having the courage to face her directly and give her the news yourself."

Graham nodded his head slowly. "Yes, okay. I think you're right."

Ronan was pleased to see the scowl slip from his father's face. *As long as the client was happy...*

"You've obviously got to know Cassie pretty well this past week," Graham said. It wasn't a question.

"Enough to know she'd appreciate hearing this kind of news from you."

"I suppose it will be best for her in the long run," Graham repeated, and Ronan wondered who he was trying to convince.

"I'm sure, I'm sure," Patrick soothed. Then he changed the subject. "Do you remember that damn-fool marathon we tried to do back in seventy-eight? Nearly killed us, but neither of us were willing to admit it!"

Both older men laughed and the topic of conversation moved away from business for a while as they continued to reminisce.

After a few minutes, Graham looked at his watch. "I have to get back to the store—a few things to take care of before we, well, before we do the deed. Why don't you take some time, have a father-son catch up and I'll see you back there in a while?" He stood.

Ronan's father nodded. "Great idea. See you soon."

Ronan frowned. Since when had his father been interested in father-son catch-ups?

Once Graham Taylor had disappeared out the restaurant's front door, Patrick leaned forward and studied Ronan closely. "It's good to see you, son."

"Uh-huh." Ronan's every nerve was on alert. Something was definitely up.

"Have you enjoyed visiting Australia? What do you think of Melbourne?"

"It's a nice city," Ronan replied carefully.

"And did you miss San Francisco much?"

"Not much to miss. Mom and Siobhan, of course, but otherwise…" He left that thought hanging.

His father didn't even blink. "And what about the work? That all went smoothly, right? Graham seems quite pleased with the job you've done. I'm glad to see that you're capable of seeing a job through to the end."

Ronan's patience was stretched to the limit. "I've always been capable of that, Dad. You've just never seemed to notice before."

His father leaned back, a surprised look on his face. "What do you mean?"

"Forget it." Ronan threw his napkin on the table and gestured to the waiter for the check. He wasn't about to sit there and whine and complain in a way that would only reinforce his father's already low opinion of him.

Patrick sat forward suddenly, hands clasped, a frown creating deep creases between his eyebrows. "No, son, I want to hear what you have to say."

Ronan felt as if a desk had suddenly sprung up between them.

"Why now? Why after all these years would you suddenly want to listen to me?"

His frown deepened. "I've always listened to you."

"And heard only what you wanted to hear."

"Ronan, I—"

Ronan blew out a breath and stood up suddenly, interrupting whatever platitudes his father was about to utter. He'd heard them before.

"Do I qualify for my partnership now?" he asked.

"I wanted to talk to you about that. I've got a proposal for you to consider."

"Great," Ronan muttered. He grabbed his wallet from his back pocket and headed to the front desk of the restaurant. He couldn't wait any longer for the waiter to bring the bill. Not if it meant listening to his father come up with yet another hurdle he had to overcome, yet another test of his skill and dedication before he'd be considered a suitable candidate to head Conroy Corporation.

"Ronan?" his father called out, following on his heels.

"I've got to get back to Country Style," Ronan said. Go back and face the most unpleasant experience of his life to date. If that wasn't cast-iron proof of his dedication to the firm, he didn't know what was. Pity his father would never realize the magnitude of Ronan's commitment.

He was about to go watch Graham Taylor fire Cassie. Take the one thing that Cassie held precious and crush it in front of her. Ronan knew how Cassie felt about Country Style. Hearing this news was going to be nothing less than a full-body blow.

And as soon as she heard she'd know... She'd know that he'd been lying to her, that he'd looked her in the eye and lied.

And suddenly nothing about his life had any kind of glow about it.

"Let's talk again tonight, at the hotel," his father said, as the waiter sorted out the payment for their meal, oblivious to Ronan's torment. "After you've sorted things out with Graham and this Cassie."

"Fine," Ronan said numbly, not entirely sure what he was agreeing to.

"You've got some work to do this afternoon." Ronan braced himself as his father gave him an affectionate slap on the shoulder. "Job's not finished yet."

Ronan let his father lead the way out of the restaurant. He wished more than anything that this was over. That he could fast-forward time and get out of here. Get home to his creaky sofa and smelly stray cat and pretend this had never happened. He had the horrible feeling that no matter how hard he tried, this task would be beyond him.

CASSIE HAD BEEN RUNNING ragged ever since she'd got back from the café with sandwiches and water. She'd even been serving, finding herself a little rusty on some of the pricing details, but strangely enjoying being back on the floor.

"Cassie, are you free now?"

She didn't miss the edge of irritation in Graham's voice. He'd been repeatedly asking her to meet with him since he had returned from lunch—and that had been almost an hour ago. Cassie had been exceptionally diligent at finding reasons she couldn't talk just then. Mostly because standing right behind Graham's shoulder each time he asked was Ronan, looking stony-faced and blank.

Even as she'd made her excuses and flittered around the store she'd been conscious of his presence, watching him from the corner of her eye as he sat and talked quietly with Graham, the two of them waiting for her.

The idea of meeting with him, trying to keep her expression composed and businesslike, was just too overwhelming. Flashbacks from their weekend taunted her: his smile, his touch, the way his long eyelashes rested on his cheeks when he slept.

She figured she just needed a little more time to work up the courage, but as the day wore on and her nerves didn't disappear, she began to realize she needed to get it over and done with. Whatever the outcome, surely it would be better to know than to live with the anxiety that was twisting her belly and making the blood pound in her head.

Although she wasn't ready *just yet.*

"One more moment, Graham," she said, her courage failing her. Again. She pushed an annoying strand of hair back from her face. This was why she wore it tied back. "I just have to shift this lamp over to—"

"Cassie, now." Ronan's low command brooked no protest.

Cassie put the lamp back down and wiped her hands of imaginary dust.

This was it.

The moment that would define her future. Part One of her tattered plan was about to come to fruition.

Or not.

"We'll use Steve's office," Graham said, gesturing to the door in the far corner.

"Okay." Cassie managed a short nod and led the way as both men stepped back to let her in front of them. It gave Cassie a moment to try to school her face into a mask of polite curiosity. Surely that was an appropriate expression for a future CEO? As she reached the door and walked through it, her stomach swooped.

Fear.

Excitement.

She remembered the ride on the roller coaster at Luna Park. She remembered walking into her bedroom to find Ronan lying on her bed.

Fear and excitement.

They battled for supremacy inside her.

If things went well, this could be the most exciting moment of her life. Well, one of them, anyway.

She had to remember that.

Steve's office held a desk and a small round table. The table had three chairs around it, as if someone had prepared it for this meeting. Someone probably had.

Cassie took a seat, clasping her hands in her lap to hide her nerves, hoping that her face was still schooled into her practiced mask of calm anticipation.

Graham took a chair as Ronan closed the door behind them and then he finally sat, too. The table was small and with their chairs pulled in, Cassie could feel the heat of Ronan's knees just beside her. He seemed tired, dark smudges under his eyes betraying the lack of sleep he'd had over the weekend. Cassie wanted to reach over and stroke his face, to pull his head into her lap and hold him until he drifted off to sleep.

A ridiculous compulsion given the circumstances.

Ronan met her eyes and held them for a charged moment before he looked away, adjusting one of his cuff links unnecessarily. She remembered the moment in the meeting room back at the warehouse when he'd taken off his jacket and rolled up his sleeves. Now she knew what he looked like naked. How the sinews and muscles of his arms entwined all the way up to his broad, round shoulders. She knew the noises he made when…

What was wrong with her?

She forced herself to focus. This was the most important meeting she'd ever attended. There was no room for fantasies or regrets. They'd had their weekend. That was that.

The table was clear of paper, Cassie noted as she turned her attention to the business at hand. No copies of Ronan's report, or her own, ready to be discussed. Did that mean anything?

"Cassie, my girl…" Graham began. Then he paused for a while, picking at one of his fingernails before he looked up. "You've done such a good job of the store here, Cassie," he said.

"Thank you, Graham." Cassie smiled, pleased, as always, with Graham's praise.

"You've done a great job for Country Style and I know the company wouldn't be the success it is today without your hard work and dedication."

So far so good. Cassie allowed herself a glimmer of hope.

"As you know, the market is getting more and more competitive. We not only have to compete with the local guys, but there are international players who want a slice of the action. And then there's the internet—and no one really knows what's going to happen there."

Cassie nodded. "Absolutely. As I mentioned in my

report, one of our options is to set up our own online store, and differentiate ourselves from others by providing interior design advice, not just products." She made an effort to sit straighter. Even though Graham was saying good things, she still had a feeling she wasn't over the line yet.

"Yes, you did. That was a good suggestion."

So far Ronan had stayed silent, but there was a pained expression on his face and he moved restlessly in his chair. Was he simply having as much difficulty separating their weekend from business as she was? If she'd known how hard it was going to be... Nope. She would have done it anyway.

"And as I'm sure Ronan's report revealed," she said, giving him a quick smile that he didn't return, "there are plenty of opportunities for us to grow our market share in the areas where we already have a presence."

"I agree," Graham said. "And I'd like to talk more to you about that. When you said that Patricia in North Sydney was successful with that direct-mail campaign, I think that's the kind of thing we should look into further."

"Absolutely," Cassie said, warming to her topic. "She had an excellent response rate and I think it's something that would work very well in lots of our other stores. Probably ones that have a similar demographic, like—"

Ronan cleared his throat, interrupting. "I think we're getting off track," he said.

Cassie gave a rueful smile. It didn't take much to have her launch into a conversation about her favorite topic. And when it was Graham on the other side of the table—there was always so much to talk about.

"Sorry," she apologized. "I get carried away." She decided to go all in. "I just love this business, as you know. There's so much for us to achieve, and I can't wait to be part of it."

Graham blew out a heavy breath and slumped back in his chair. Suddenly Cassie's fear won out over her excitement. He didn't look like a man who was about to make her dreams come true.

Graham sent Ronan a strange, pleading look.

Cassie looked from Graham to Ronan and back again, unnerved by the silent exchange between them, suddenly sure it didn't mean anything good for her. She rested her eyes on Ronan, begging for the truth. She needed to know. Now.

Ronan closed his eyes for a moment, and when he met her gaze his expression was more closed off than she'd ever seen it.

"Cassie," he began. He leaned forward and folded his hands on the table in front of him. "There's been an offer made for Country Style. A generous offer that would see Country Style's stores rebranded and become part of an international chain. Graham has decided to sell." His voice was dulled, missing any kind of light and shade.

Cassie tried to listen as he explained some of the details of the deal. Rebranding. Shared services operations for administration. Merged management. The white noise in her ears made it difficult to concentrate. Country Style—gone? And then her second thought…

"What does all this mean for me?" she blurted.

"Cassie, I'm afraid there would be no need for duplicate local management," Ronan said in that same blank, robotic tone. "Once the deal goes through, there will no longer be a position for you."

No longer be a position...?

"You mean you're firing me?" She searched Ronan's face, looking for the man she'd trusted so much she'd bared herself, body and soul, to him. He wasn't there. That was almost as soul-destroying as the news itself.

"I don't have a job with Country Style anymore? Is that what you're saying?" she asked again, her voice slightly shrill with disbelief.

The silence was all the confirmation she needed. Her gaze flicked from Ronan to Graham and back again. Graham's sheepish expression and Ronan's impassive stare that didn't quite meet her eyes were just as damning as their sudden speechlessness.

The quiet in the room stretched on into infinity as Cassie struggled to understand what had just happened. That the blow had come from *Ronan* of all people...

Everything around her became hyperreal—the soft give of the chair that supported her, the faint buzz from the fluorescent light above. The smell in the room—a lingering scent of fresh paint, the plasticky smell of new laminate furniture, Ronan's aftershave. Through the thin rectangular window in the door, Cassie could see customers testing out a sofa as if nothing had changed.

Nothing *had* changed, except for her, she realized. Her world had just been upended. It was as if gravity had suddenly been switched off. Everything that had held her feet on the ground, everything that had given her solidity and security had just been ripped away.

And she was left feeling…numb. Numb and paralyzed by the shock.

"Cassie." Graham broke the silence and practically leaped across the table. He grabbed her hands out from her lap and held them in both of his. "I want you to know that this is nothing to do with you. I'll give you the best reference anyone has ever seen. Or, if you want, you're welcome to take another look at joining my luggage business. I know you said it didn't interest you, but I'm sure I could find something for you there."

She shook her head, not necessarily a denial, but she couldn't even begin to think about another job right now.

"Okay," Graham said hurriedly. "But I'm sure we can work something out and of course there will be a generous severance package that will give you plenty of time to find your next role. I could even ask Ronan to write you a reference. Since he got here and started work on the report for the buyers, he's been telling me that he was very impressed with your abilities." Graham waved a hand at Ronan. "Ronan, tell her about all those service thingies that Conroy Corporation has to help people find new jobs."

Cassie's eyes cut to Ronan's and she swore she saw a streak of pain cross them.

Finally the truth sunk in. He'd lied to her. He'd been lying all along.

The purpose of his visit had always been to ratify Graham's plan to sell Country Style, not her plan to lead it. She waited for the spike of betrayal to stab through her, but her numbness was all-encompassing. It left no room for anything else. She was staring at Ronan, she knew it, and probably her every thought was written on her face for him to read, but he was busily studying the wall behind her, sitting stiffly in his chair, his expression closed.

Before Ronan could begin his doubtlessly well-rehearsed spiel about Conroy Corporation's outplacement services, Cassie turned back to Graham. "What about the others. Mel...?"

Graham looked sheepish. "We won't know until the deal goes through," he mumbled.

"When..." Cassie couldn't manage to finish the question. She looked to Ronan for the answer, unable to stomach the apologetic look on Graham's face, asking for forgiveness she was nowhere near ready to grant.

"Quite soon," Ronan said. "We need you to keep this confidential for the next day or so while we work out the final details and sign the contracts. Then we'll need to come up with a strategy for informing the staff. The new owners want to take over this store within the month."

A month. So fast.

Cassie extracted her hands from Graham's grasp. He seemed upset by her obvious distress, but Cassie couldn't bring herself to find words to reassure him. She knew she should say, "Don't worry, Graham, I'll be fine," or something like that, but it would be a lie.

She got to her feet, prompting both men to stand, too. "I'm going to..." *What?* What was she going to do? Without finishing her sentence, she headed for the door and walked out into the store.

Behind her she heard Graham say, "We should go after her."

Ronan's voice was low and cold. "No. Just give her some time. I'll check on her in a few minutes."

CASSIE WALKED THROUGH the store to the back, somehow finding herself in the tearoom. The world seemed insubstantial around her, as if it would all come crashing down just as easily as her grand plan had done.

One of the junior staff members rushed in and grabbed a bottle of water, muttering rushed thanks before disappearing again. Cassie felt as if everyone was on fast-forward while she was stuck in slow motion.

"Cassie? Oh, there you are. I managed to find a plumber, but he can't get here for…" Mel broke off and stood directly in front of her. "What's wrong?"

Where to start? Her lover's betrayal? No, that part of it hadn't even begun to sink in. What about the fact that Mel herself would most likely lose her job soon? She had a right to know. She had a right to the warning that Cassie herself hadn't received.

But she couldn't do it.

"I have a headache," Cassie muttered, unable to meet Mel's eyes. God, the guilt was overwhelming.

Ronan had looked her in the eye.

Ronan had kissed her, seduced her, made love to her, and all the while this knowledge was in his head.

She could barely comprehend the magnitude of his deceit.

Mel clucked and fussed. "It's no wonder—all the stress you've been under. The store opening, Graham's investigation, dealing with that consultant. Here, sit down."

Cassie sat because she didn't know what else to do. She wanted to go home and curl up under a blanket and pretend the world didn't exist, but that wasn't an option. Even though she'd been fired, she still had a job to do.

Mel opened a bottle of cola and pushed it into Cassie's hands. "Drink this. Apparently caffeine is good for headaches."

Cassie took a few sips, finding it hard to swallow. Her throat was thick with…*what?* Tears? Rage?

Her limbs felt heavy, her brain fogged.

"I think I need some fresh air," she mumbled.

"Are you nauseous?" Mel's concern faded for a moment as she grinned. "You're not pregnant, are you?"

Cassie knew Mel was asking as a joke—her friend knew the sorry state of Cassie's nonexistent love life. But the question made her stomach swoop dangerously. She wasn't pregnant—Ronan had taken precautions. But Mel didn't know what had happened over the weekend, that Cassie had finally let someone through the castle walls she'd built around herself, that all her defenses had been breached.

And he'd ended up being a Trojan horse. She'd let him in, only to have him destroy her from the inside.

Cassie got to her feet blindly, still clutching the

bottle of cola. "Mel, I'm just going to sit out the back for a while. Come find me if you need me."

Mel frowned again and reached over to grab her hand. "Cassie, are you sure? You really look terrible. Do you want me to take you home?"

"I'll be fine." Cassie shook off Mel's sympathy; she didn't deserve it. When Mel learned the real reason behind the "headache," she'd feel as betrayed as Cassie did now.

"Okay," Mel agreed, sounding uncertain. "Well, take care. Take your mobile with you and text me if you need anything. And, Cassie?"

Cassie paused as she headed out of the tearoom.

"You look really pretty with your hair out like that. You should do it more often."

Cassie managed what she hoped was a smile and muttered a thank-you. She walked out to the car park behind the store, not seeing the world around her. Everything still felt unreal.

She found her car and sat in the driver's seat with the door open. Melbourne had turned on one of its perfect summer days, and the sun shone brightly while a cool breeze rustled through the shrubs and trees in the car park's freshly dug garden bed. There were bushfires burning somewhere that lent a haze to the sky.

What would she do now?

Everything she'd worked for was about to be wiped out. No more job at Country Style. *No more Country Style.* The only home she'd known, the only family she had. Even when she'd come up with her Plan, shoring up her role with Country Style had been her first priority.

She'd survive.

She'd survived before and she'd do it again.

But right now, she wasn't sure if she wanted to.

The back door of Country Style opened with a bang, bouncing off the concrete wall beside it. A shadow emerged, stepping out into the car park, shielding his eyes from the sunlight.

Cassie didn't need to see his face to know it was Ronan. Even shadowed in the doorway she'd recognized him instantly.

She saw the moment that he spotted her, his long legs striding over, purposeful and swift. Cassie wanted to run away, but she couldn't find the energy to close the car door, let alone start the engine and drive off. She stared at the steering wheel in front of her.

"Cassie?" he called out from a few steps away. His tone had an urgency that matched his strides.

She didn't look up.

"Cassie? Are you okay?" He reached the car door and opened it wider, resting his hand on the car roof to lean down and peer in at her. "Mel said you were sick."

His words didn't penetrate the fog Cassie found herself trapped inside, but his scent did. That musky male fragrance and expensive cologne reached out and surrounded her, reminding her of the touch of his skin against hers, of how it felt to be caught up in his arms.

Safe.

She'd thought she was *safe*.

How wrong could she have been?

"Cassie, sweetheart, I know you've had a shock, but you're scaring me. Are you okay? Say something." He crouched down beside her.

Oh, now she was *sweetheart?* Numbness swiftly became anger, a white-hot rage that scared her in its intensity.

"Cassie, please." He reached inside the car to take her hand.

Cassie snatched it away. "Don't touch me!"

She'd never known she could growl like that.

He jerked back in surprise. "Cassie?"

Cassie managed to turn her face in his direction. She wasn't sure she could look him in the eye, but when she did, all she saw was anxiety and pain. Giving her the worst news of her life had been painful for *him?* Ha!

"I'll save you the trouble of hiring an outplacement service for me, Mr. Conroy," she spat. "How about I resign? Would that make things easier for you?"

He swore under his breath and stood in a sudden rush, raking one hand through his hair. He was silent for a moment, just the sound of his breathing and the crunch of gravel under his feet as he took a few paces back and forth. Then he swore again, more viciously this time.

"Cassie, I know what you're thinking. But you have to believe I didn't plan this."

"Because I should start believing you now?"

"*Damn.* Cassie, I didn't—"

"You lied to me, Ronan." Cassie's voice broke as the anger inside her softened and began to turn into a feeling that was far more dangerous to her self-control:

sorrow. "I thought you were here to confirm that I could head up Country Style. You let me think that. Instead you were here to sell it out from under me. Did you know all along that I'd lose my job?" She wasn't sure why she needed to know, but she did.

He closed his eyes for a moment and Cassie knew what he was going to say before he opened his mouth. "Yes, I knew it was a likely outcome."

"And after everything I told you, everything we shared, you never thought to tell me."

His hands tightened into fists by his sides. "Cassie, you don't understand. It's my job, it's work. The partnership. I couldn't say anything."

"But you could still sleep with me."

He spun on his heel, muttering under his breath. He took a few paces away then turned and came back. "I know we shouldn't have been...*close*...like that. We should never have... You know I didn't want to..."

Cassie gasped as if he'd slapped her.

Ronan thumped his fist on the roof of her car. The vibration rattled through Cassie's whole body.

"Damn it, Cassie, you know the connection we had! You know what it meant to both of us, even though we only had a weekend. We said that the weekend had nothing to do with work. That we'd put everything aside and then things would go back to the way they were on Monday. Well, it's Monday, Cassie, and this is reality. As much as it sucks for both of us, this is it."

"It sucks for both of us?" Cassie held on to her anger. The heat of it was keeping her from freezing over inside. She raised her voice, embracing the mindlessness of rage as it stopped her from thinking about everything crumbling around her. "I lose my job and you go home to your partnership? Doesn't sound like life sucks for you right now."

Ronan made a frustrated growling noise in the back of his throat. "I'm not saying the right things here."

"It's okay, Ronan, I'm getting the picture quite clearly anyway." Cassie would like to have been standing, to yell at him face-to-face, but she was grateful for the car seat because she wasn't sure her shaking legs would hold her up. "You were more concerned about your work than me from day one. Even after the hotel room in Sydney, the first thing you wanted to be sure of was that I wasn't going to turn you in for unprofessional conduct. What, do you make a habit of sleeping with clients?"

It was an off-the-cuff insult, but Ronan's wince told her she'd hit a nerve.

"Oh, my God, it's true, isn't it?" Cassie breathed. "I'm not the first." This was too much. Too much to process on top of everything else. Anger. Rage. *Hang on to them,* she reminded herself. They would see her through this. She wouldn't crumple in front of him. "So what would happen if I told Daddy what went on this weekend? How likely would Patrick Conroy be to make you a partner knowing that your main goal for Conroy Corporation is to turn it into your own personal bordello?"

At least he had the sense to look contrite, ashamed. "Cassie, it wasn't like that. You know it wasn't," he insisted. "I might have done the wrong thing in the past, but…" He broke off. "What happened between us was different. You know it was special."

Cassie gave a short, bleak laugh. "Yeah, you had to work to get me into bed. Probably the first time you've ever had to do that. That's all that made it 'special' to you." She reached across him for the door handle. She couldn't bear this for a moment longer.

"No, Cassie, wait." Ronan grabbed the door to stop her from closing it.

"Let go, Ronan."

"Not until we work this out."

"What's to work out?" She couldn't risk looking at him. "Go inside and tell Graham that you made sure I was okay and that I've gone home to consider the news. I'll talk to him tomorrow. You've done your job."

"And what about…" He swallowed. "What about us?"

"There never was an 'us,' was there?" She blinked to force back the tears. She couldn't drive if she was crying. "The weekend never happened. I won't tell anyone about it if you don't. Does that put your mind at ease?"

He looked shocked, shocked enough for her to have time to pull the door shut and start the engine.

The Country Style car-park sign flickered past as she drove out to the street. Even amidst her turmoil, a flash of guilt at leaving the store went through her. Disappearing in the middle of the first day of a new store opening? It felt wrong. But old habits die hard, she figured. Besides, what was the worst that could happen? It wasn't as if Graham could fire her twice.

She snorted a tragic laugh at her own black humor and drove out onto the street, refusing to look in the mirror to see Ronan one last time.

CHAPTER EIGHTEEN

RONAN RAN THROUGH EVERY swear word he knew and then invented a few more for good measure. How could he have screwed that up so monumentally? He prided himself on being able to control himself even in the most difficult conversations—he'd managed multimillion-dollar merger negotiations, fired unethical CEOs, advised politicians on make-or-break speeches. And he'd never been provoked to shouting or reduced to begging.

What on earth was wrong with him?

The sun beat down on the asphalt around him, heating the air. His nostrils filled with dust and car exhaust and the vague scent of smoke, appropriate for the ruin that he'd just made of things.

He'd tell his father to shove the partnership up his ass. If Patrick Conroy wanted to put him through more tests like this one, Ronan didn't want any part of it.

This was too hard. Too much.

He'd resign from Conroy Corporation and find a new job—go to Europe maybe, find something in London. Make a fresh start. See if he could put all this behind him.

The idea left him feeling worse—if that was possible—than he already did.

Graham Taylor stood in the door that lead out from the store and called out.

Ronan straightened his shoulders and strode over. He would be cool and professional even if it killed him.

"Where's Cassie?" Graham asked.

"She decided to go home," Ronan said, schooling his voice into something that sounded close to normal. "She wanted time to think." It was almost the truth.

"Was she okay?"

"About what you'd expect."

"Hmm." Graham's grunt told Ronan that he'd anticipated Cassie's meltdown.

"She'll be fine. She's strong," he said, wondering who he was trying to convince. Whoever it was, he doubted they'd be swayed by his uncertain tone.

Graham stepped back to let Ronan inside and closed the door behind them. He gave Ronan a rueful smile. "I suppose it's for the best. Like a Band-Aid—rip it off quickly."

Ronan made a noise that he hoped sounded like agreement.

His father appeared then, emerging from the shadows of a stack of furniture. It made Ronan instantly wary—the man had a way of fading into the background when it was convenient. Had he witnessed any of the conversation out in the parking lot? But when Ronan studied his face, nothing seemed out of the ordinary.

It was time to get out of here. "Graham, did you need me for anything else today?" Ronan asked. "If not, I'll go back to the hotel and get that report finished for you."

"Yes, yes, good idea," Graham said. "I'll hang around here seeing as Cassie's gone. Not that I can do anything to help, mind you!" he added with a wry chuckle. "That girl knows everything about this place and I don't know a thing."

Idiot. Imbecile. Fool.

The words echoed in Ronan's head as they stayed unspoken. He wasn't sure if they were meant for Graham or himself.

Lost in his own thoughts, Ronan was barely aware of catching a cab with his father back to their hotel and stepping into the elevator. It was only when he reached out to press the button for his floor that his father stopped him with a hand on his wrist.

"No. Come to my room. I want to talk to you."

His tone told Ronan there was no point protesting.

He didn't have the energy for an argument anyway. Maybe it was finally time to say all the things that needed to be said. Maybe it was time for Ronan to say that he was no longer willing to play his father's games and that he was no longer willing to fight a losing battle for leadership of Conroy Corporation.

It wasn't just this afternoon—telling people they no longer had a job was part of life as a consultant, and he knew that. But having to do it to Cassie—if only he'd been able to talk to his father, explain…but no. And now Patrick Conroy would tell him what his next task was going to be—a new maze for Ronan to solve on the twisted and seemingly never-ending path to the top of Conroy Corporation.

They rode up to the top floor in silence, and stayed silent even after his father opened the door to the lush suite. Ronan went immediately to the windows; the view out to the bay was breathtaking. Kitesurfers dotted the sparkling blue water with bright primary colors, while a busy tree-lined road carried a stream of traffic south. The rest of the world continued as normal, while Ronan felt as if his entire life had just taken an unexpected turn.

"Here."

Ronan accepted the glass of Scotch his father offered, without drinking.

"To a successful job." Patrick held up the glass for a clink that didn't come.

Silence.

"Ronan? What's going on? I thought you'd be happy."

Ronan took in a breath and let it out in a rush. He didn't have any other option. "I'm resigning."

He'd expected at least a bit of astonishment, but his father's expression stayed neutral. He was using his poker face, honed in playing against opponents in hundreds of negotiations over his thirty years in the business.

Then suddenly, he reached for a chair and sat down. "I wondered when this day would come." The mask fell away. He looked old, Ronan thought, old and tired. Like a man nearing sixty who still worked a sixty-hour week *should* look.

"Are you okay?" Ronan asked, possessed by concern that overrode his surprise at his father's unexpected comment. He wasn't ready for his father to be old, to die. He didn't want to lose his family the way Cassie had lost hers—he loved them too much.

The idea stopped him short.

"I'm fine, I'm fine." Patrick Conroy waved off his concern, the Scotch sloshing in the glass before he took another sip.

"You're not surprised by my resignation?" Ronan took a sip of his own Scotch, welcoming the familiar burn. Who knew, if he drank enough of it, it might just take the sharp edges off the world.

Patrick shook his head. "No. I knew this was coming. I've done everything I can to stop it, delay it, but I could see it." He gave Ronan a reluctant half smile. "You're too much like me. Want to go out and conquer the world for yourself. Following in my footsteps, leading the empire I built—I've always worried that it wouldn't be enough for you."

Ronan reached for a chair himself, shock making him clumsy. He'd never heard his father talk like this. He sank into the chair, draining his glass and setting it down on the table beside him.

"Sending you here was a last-ditch attempt…" Patrick shook his head and gave Ronan a sad smile.

"Attempt? At what?"

Patrick swirled the amber liquid in his glass for a few moments before answering. "I've decided to open an Asia Pacific regional office," he said. "We need to take advantage of the emerging markets in Asia and we can't do that effectively from the U.S. We need staff in the region, familiar with the local culture and business issues. Headquarters will be in Melbourne." He stopped for a dramatic pause before continuing. "I thought *you* might like to lead it."

"What?" Ronan took a moment to process what his father was saying.

"Of course, your mother is furious with me for suggesting you move to the other side of the world, but I think it would be just the ticket for you." He grinned. "Partner, *and president,* Asia Pacific Operations. How does that sound?"

"So, let me get this straight," Ronan said slowly. "You send me over here to do a covert investigation that's going to result in Country Style being sold out from underneath all the people who've worked hard to make it successful. With that part done, you're now going to make me do your old friend's dirty work and fire Cassie Hartman and most of her staff. And as a reward I get to run a new regional division of Conroy Corp?"

Patrick Conroy gave him a wide smile. "That's about the size of it."

Ronan paused for a moment. This wasn't his father's usual challenge. For once, he was actually giving Ronan a reward, a carrot instead of the stick. "Me?" was all he could say.

"You've earned it. I think you're the best man for the job."

"But you've never…"

"Never what?"

Suddenly Ronan couldn't hold it in any longer. All the disappointments and hurt of never measuring up, of his work never being quite enough no matter how much he tried, began tumbling out. "For my whole career you've made me work harder, longer hours, given me more difficult assignments. I've had to fight for every raise, for every promotion. No one else in Conroy Corporation has worked as diligently as I have—and I've watched them pass me by as they climbed the ladder and I stayed still."

His father seemed confused by his outburst. "But that was all necessary."

"Necessary?" His fists clenched in anger. "I should have been made partner *before* I went to New York. But you always have *just one more thing* I have to do before I'm good enough to deserve it. I'm never good enough for you." Ronan forced his mouth closed. He'd never spoken this way to his father—never expressed these thoughts aloud before.

Patrick Conroy sighed heavily. "Oh, my boy. I think perhaps we should have had this conversation some time ago."

"Would it have made any difference?"

"Well, I thought you understood…but clearly I was wrong."

"Understood what?"

His father leaned forward and gave him the penetrating look that had seen him rise to the top of his profession and stay there for the past thirty years. "You *needed* to work harder than everyone else. You had to work harder and longer than everyone else, just to have a level playing field."

Now it was Ronan's turn to be confused. And, much as he didn't want to admit it, hurt. "You think I'm that bad at consulting?"

His father rolled his eyes. "I think you're that *good.* You're smart, son, smarter than me even. If you'd progressed according to merit, you'd have already shown me the door." He gave a small chuckle. "But the board would never have taken you seriously—you'd never have won their confidence."

"I don't—"

"I've been preparing you. Making sure that when your time came, when it was time for you to step up to lead Conroy Corporation, there wasn't a chance in hell that you wouldn't be the best candidate, blood or no blood. With what you've done, what you've achieved, there's no way the board could turn you away. There's literally no one else in the company with your kind of record."

Ronan slumped back in his chair. "You could have told me," he said, shaking his head. All that anger, all that hurt—instead of thwarting him, his father had been looking out for him. Albeit, in his own slightly twisted way. Ronan wondered whether it would have made a difference if he had known about his father's plans.

He might have thought twice before sleeping with Sarah Forsythe. But Cassie... He really didn't know how he could have changed what had happened with Cassie. His future with Conroy Corporation hazed into insubstantial mist whenever he was close to her, whenever he had the chance to get closer to her.

"I really thought you might go for starting up a new division," Patrick said, his tone rueful, "that way you'd have the opportunity to build something of your own."

Ronan's mind was still on Sarah and Cassie. "But why would you do that after everything? After...what happened in New York?" Ronan hesitated to bring it up. His father bailing him out; his own poor judgment. Sarah Forsythe had been a mistake, Ronan could see that now. He'd been riding high on the success of the job, sure that this time his father *couldn't* argue his promotion.

But then, a little voice had whispered to him, he was going to be head of Conroy Corporation one day, so what did it really matter?

Had he run that risk deliberately? Pushed the boundaries just to see what he could get away with? Just to test whether his father really did see him as a son and not just a willful employee?

Yes, he had to admit, he probably had.

He wanted to slap himself for his own arrogance and stupidity.

"You were sending me a message in your own way," Patrick said. "I knew then we'd reached a tipping point. Mind you, I don't condone what you did with that woman," he added with a paternal frown.

Sending a message? Had he been that obvious? Sabotaging himself—making himself so undesirable as an heir that his father would have to take action to prove Ronan was special? So he knew his father really wanted him to head Conroy Corporation—that he wasn't just one of a hundred possible candidates?

Ronan found it hard to believe—his father knew him better than he knew himself. A grudging respect for the old man's wisdom and experience renewed itself in Ronan. He only wished his father would respect him in return—and there was no way that would happen when Ronan told him this next part.

"Dad, there's something else you need to know."

His father nodded, taking another sip of Scotch. Good, Ronan thought. *You'll need all the fortification you can get for this.*

"I don't deserve to head Conroy Corporation— whether the Asia Pacific division or the company as a whole."

Yes, he could admit now, he'd known that having any kind of intimacy with Sarah Forsythe was a risk. He'd known it with Cassie, too. And yet he couldn't— *wouldn't*—put the two women in the same category. What he'd shared with Cassie was nothing like what had happened with Sarah. He'd tried everything to resist the pull Cassie had over him. He was a compass and she was his north—it would have been against his very nature to not be with her.

"Go on," Patrick said.

"I…Cassie Hartman." Ronan dipped his head, but whether it was in shame or just to hide his emotions from his father, he wasn't sure. "Cassie and I…"

"You were involved with her?"

He ignored his father's sharply indrawn breath and tried to ignore the feelings stirred up at the word *were*—at thinking about his time with Cassie in the past tense.

"Yes. And I've hurt her badly." His teeth clenched as he remembered the shattered expression on her face as she sat in the car and listened to him stammer his excuses. He left the chair and paced, unable to contain himself.

"Country Style means everything to her—losing her job is going to tear her apart. She can do anything—I know she's talented enough and determined enough to make it—but she doesn't have anyone to help, to fall back on. She's all alone."

He pictured Cassie sitting in her living room as she probably was right now, curled up in a ball on that over-size chair, bereft and broken.

And it was his fault.

He stared out at the view before him, blinking hard. "I lied to her and I don't think she'll ever forgive me."

Ronan hadn't realized his father was standing behind him until he felt the heavy weight of a hand on his shoulder. "So what are you doing here?" his father asked.

It took a moment for the meaning of his words to sink in. "Huh?"

"Why aren't you with her, making your apologies? Trying to win her forgiveness?"

Ronan spun around to face his dad. "What? Where's the lecture? Where's the call to the lawyers?"

"Son." Patrick shook his head. "When you had that problem in New York, you never talked like this. Frankly, it was your attitude toward the poor woman that made me so angry. You didn't care what happened to her. You didn't express the least bit of sympathy that she'd been caught up in your little self-destruction plot." His father's lips compressed into a thin line of disappointment. "Your mother and I raised you better than that."

Ronan considered his father's words and knew they were true. That only made his actions more despicable, not less.

And to have done it again with Cassie? She was so innocent—or she had been, until he'd come along. "Cassie deserves better than me," he muttered, tunneling his fingers through his hair.

"Do you love her?" Patrick asked.

Ronan had never had this kind of conversation with his father. He wasn't sure if he'd describe their relationship as close, but they had a strong bond that came through business and talking about Conroy Corporation and, occasionally, their mutual love of sport. It was his mother who had handled all the teen angst and broken hearts of his life. So the question sounded wrong coming from his father's lips, and yet…the answer suddenly seemed so obvious.

"Yeah. Yes. I love her." The knowledge clicked into place, setting part of him at peace. He loved Cassie Hartman with every cell of his body. If he couldn't get her to forgive him, if he couldn't win her back…

"Then go and get her," Patrick said, giving Ronan a gentle push. "Everything else we can work out later. Business stuff can wait."

"But…" Ronan hesitated. Was there any point?

Would Cassie listen to him? Would she even let him in the door? And then there was Country Style, the report, the sale negotiation, the informing of staff—he still had a lot of work to do. And some of that work involved Cassie. It was an absolute, stinking mess. He'd lied to her from the start—how could she possibly let that go?

"Go. You think something like this happens every day?" Patrick stood with his hands on his hips, a determined look on his face. "I've loved your mother for almost thirty-five years. I'd give up everything for her without a second's hesitation. She's the reason I get out of bed in the morning. Everything else is gravy."

Ronan stared at his father a moment longer, not quite sure what to do with this version of Patrick Conroy. He'd chosen to see his father as an impediment, a roadblock to his own future. But he could see more clearly now. What his father really wanted was for him to be happy—even if he hadn't always gone about it the right way.

"Thanks, Dad." Ronan gave his father a quick, fierce hug, unable to remember if they'd ever done that.

"You're welcome. Now go get her and bring her back here. I want to get to know this little gal everyone's told me about. She sounds like a dynamo."

CASSIE'S HOUSE WAS GOING TO be so clean she'd be able to eat off every surface. She'd started by pulling out the handful of antique teacups and saucers she had on display on the mantelpiece in the dining room and carefully washing them in hot soapy water. But her hands were shaking too much and she worried about breaking them.

So instead she put on rubber gloves, grabbed the bleach and headed for the bathroom. She'd just started in on the tiles when she banged her head against the side of the tub with a loud clunk. Blinking back tears that stung her eyes and pressing a hand to her forehead, she was swamped by memories of the last bath she'd taken and suddenly couldn't stand to be there a moment longer.

Next she dragged out the vacuum cleaner and sucked up the sandy footprints in the hall, doing her best to ignore another set of memories. She focused on the carpet, on the mindless rhythm of the vacuum, back and forth, back and forth. It was almost enough to empty her mind.

She made her way to the spare bedroom at the back of the house, covering every inch of the carpet there even though the room was rarely used.

Then the vacuum died.

"I did knock."

Cassie let out a little squeak of fright and turned to see Ronan standing in the bedroom doorway, his foot still balanced on the vacuum's off switch.

He was the last person she'd expected to see. Her traitorous body responded just as it always did—her heart raced, her stomach swooped and every nerve tingled with the urge to walk over and press herself against him.

How good it would feel to be wrapped in those arms, to lean against that strong body. To be comforted by him after her whole world had been shaken. To feel safe again.

Pity it could never happen.

"Go away, Ronan," she said, proud that her voice stayed reasonably steady. "We've said everything that needs saying."

"You might have, but I haven't even gotten started."

"What, want to iron out more details about my severance package? Need to talk about my superannuation entitlements?" The bitter comments were out before she could hold them back. She wished she could be flippant, carefree, but he'd know it was an act anyway. Being forced to leave Country Style was nothing less than devastating and he knew it.

"I want to talk about us. You and me."

Cassie yanked on the vacuum, pulling it away from him. "I don't. 'Bye." She pressed the switch and began to furiously work at the carpet under an antique dresser, her back to him.

The vacuum died again.

"Come on, Cassie. I know I don't deserve it, but please just hear me out."

What was there to say?

His hands clamped around her upper arms and tried to force her to turn around to face him. She resisted even as his touch warmed her skin.

"Cassie, please."

He pulled on her more forcefully until she staggered. She twisted and stepped forward out of his grasp, spinning around to look at him. "You really want to do that? Add a physical harassment charge to the rest?"

He flinched as if she'd slapped him and dropped his hands to his sides.

It was a bluff, of course. She'd never be able to use what had happened between them for a lawsuit. Their time together had been too special—for her, anyway.

"Please. Just let me talk. Ten minutes, that's all I ask. Then you can kick me out and never speak to me again. I promise."

If nothing else, Cassie needed to get him out of this room. It was too small and Ronan was too large, and the neatly made-up spare bed loomed large in the corner of her eye. How easy it would be to sink down onto it and beg him to make love to her just one more time.

Perhaps she was truly a masochist at heart. It was the only explanation for her warped impulse to let him hurt her again.

"Go into the lounge room," she said, her eyes fixed somewhere over his shoulder.

"Will you come with me?"

"In a moment."

He hesitated but then seemed to figure out that was the best he was going to get, so he turned and she heard his footsteps on the wooden floorboards, muffled as he reached the thick rug in the living room.

Cassie let out a shaky breath. She could do this. Listen to his stumbling excuses, let him tell her—yet again—that they'd only promised each other a weekend. She'd known the deal going in. She just hadn't known the cost.

Her heart.

She loved Ronan Conroy—she couldn't deny it. She

knew the way his eyebrow would quirk up just on one side when he was amused or interested. She knew the changing colors of his eyes reflected the sky. She knew he was a proud man, a man with exemplary manners, a man who'd rather die than show weakness to an opponent. She knew he had a mole shaped like Tasmania on his left hip and that he was ticklish behind his knees. Cassie could hardly believe she'd known him less than a week.

She knew she loved a man who couldn't love her back. A man who was leaving for San Francisco in a day or two.

He wasn't a man who left things unfinished. He was here because he wanted to reassure himself there'd be no consequences for him as a result of their affair. He wanted to say goodbye.

She could manage that. Couldn't she?

Straightening her spine, Cassie headed out into the living room, blinking a little at the brightness after the dim bedroom.

Ronan was sitting on her sofa, the place he'd effectively staked as his own during their weekend, his head in his hands. He looked up as soon as she stepped closer.

"Cassie, I…" he began before breaking off and jumping to his feet, eyes wide. "What have you done?"

His warm fingers were pressing gently on her forehead and Cassie winced as he reached her hairline.

"Sit down," he ordered before disappearing into the kitchen.

Cassie sat in the spot he'd just vacated, gingerly exploring her own head. She found a lump the size of a golf ball.

That explained the headache.

"Here." Ronan reappeared holding a dish towel filled with ice cubes. "Put this on it."

"Thanks," Cassie mumbled as her cheeks heated. This wasn't how she'd imagined the conversation. "I bumped it when I was cleaning the bathroom."

Ronan shook his head. He looked as if he were about to scold her, but instead he simply sighed and sat beside her on the sofa. Careful to maintain the distance between them, Cassie noted.

Best to get this over with.

"Ronan, you don't have to worry about anything. I'm not going to tell anyone about what happened between us. And I won't tell anyone about what's happening to Country Style, either—not until we've been able to draw up a proper communication plan to make the official announcement." *Oh, God.* Tears threatened every time she thought about it. She blinked them back—she was not going to lose it now. "You don't have to worry. I won't do anything that would risk your partnership. We agreed not to see each other personally after the weekend and I'm okay with that."

She risked a glance at him. He was staring out toward the kitchen, a faraway look in his eyes and she wondered if he'd heard her.

"Cassie," he said, his voice quiet. The sound of her name on his lips always sent a thrill through her. This time it was bittersweet, knowing it might be the last.

"I've been so unhappy with my life. Back in San

Francisco, I felt trapped. Everything was laid out in front of me. Work my way up through Conroy Corporation until my father retired and I took over. Marry the daughter of one of my mother's friends and produce grandchildren. Settle down in a pastel-colored Victorian somewhere near my parents. A vacation home in Napa or maybe down the coast. There was no excitement, no risk, nothing that I'd really be able to claim as my own."

Huh? Cassie wondered if the bump on her head had affected her more than she'd thought.

"I'm grateful to have my family, believe me, I am." He glanced at her and she saw the sincerity in his eyes. "But I've been doing everything I can to rebel against that path. I don't even have a proper home—not like this." He waved a hand around to indicate the room they sat in. "I travel all the time so I can avoid the endless blind dates my mother sets up. I've even tried to sabotage my career at Conroy Corporation—that way I could continue to blame my father for my failures, instead of realizing that it was all about me."

He ran his fingers through his hair before twisting on the sofa to face her.

"It's time to stop all that, Cassie. I've never felt as much at home as I have here. I like this city and its stupid weather." He gave her one of those endearing lopsided smiles. "My father has offered me the chance to head up a new Asia Pacific division of Conroy Corporation. It's going to be based here in Melbourne. There'll probably be some travel involved, but there's so much opportunity to make a difference in this part of the world. And… It gives me… I have a chance to build something of my own, with choices that I've made. It's what I want—what I need."

Nausea rose in her throat. Ronan was staying in Melbourne. Cassie wondered where the office would be, where he'd decide to live. Which areas of the city would suddenly become off-limits to her? At least if he'd been going back to San Francisco she wouldn't have to worry about accidentally running into him and breaking her heart all over again.

But she couldn't deny him this. He was a caged tiger returning to the wild—to the freedom that he'd always needed. Loving him meant letting him go.

She nodded. "I'm sure you'll do a great job. Your own division. I know it will be a success. You'll be the shining star of Conroy Corp."

He frowned. "I haven't accepted yet. I told my father I had to get some things sorted out before I could decide."

It took a moment for that to sink in. "You're not going to do it? What's stopping you?"

He grinned. "Waiting to find out if I'll be doing it with you by my side, silly."

She must have a concussion. She was obviously hallucinating.

His smiled faltered. "That is, of course, if you'll have me. I know I lied to you, and I'll spend the rest of my life making that up to you, I promise." His eyes burned into hers. "I know this doesn't change anything, but, Cassie, believe me, lying to you was one of the hardest things I've ever done in my life. So many times

I wanted to tell you, but I just didn't have the guts. I knew how hard it would be for you, and I didn't want to be the one to hurt you like that. I'm so sorry, Cassie."

"But…" Cassie's tangled thoughts didn't allow for coherent speech. What was he saying?

"I don't know what will happen in the future. The division may not work. There'll be a lot of uncertainty while I'm trying to set things up, but I'll do my best to be here for you as you figure out what you want to do. I know that uncertainty will be tough for you." He reached over and grabbed the hand that wasn't holding the ice pack to her forehead, clasping it between his. "But I promise I'll never let anything get in the way of us having a safe and stable home. I have enough money to support us—my shares in Conroy Corporation alone would keep us nicely even if neither of us ever worked again."

"Hang on." Cassie shook her hand free of his grasp and stood up, blinking against a moment of dizziness. "Ronan, I don't understand. We only had a weekend. That was all."

Cassie's stomach dipped and swerved. Wasn't this what she wanted? Ronan wanting to stay with her? Why, then, was she more afraid than she'd ever been before? Even years ago, that first night she'd slept on the street, alone and vulnerable, didn't match the terror she was feeling now.

She dropped the dish towel onto the coffee table and cubes of ice scattered across the surface and onto the floor.

"Ronan, I can't…" she began, backing away from

him. What about her carefully formulated four-part plan? It had been shredded to ribbons days ago, but she'd been sure she could resurrect it. Sit down and work out how to adapt it to changed circumstances. There'd be more time required on Part One now, since she'd need to find a new job, but it wasn't as if she didn't have plenty of that on her hands.

"Shh." Ronan stood and stepped toward her, his hands raised as if quieting a startled animal. "Cassie, listen to me. I love you."

Oh, God, she was going to throw up. Right now. Right in front of him.

"Just tell me one thing," he said. "Do you love me?"

Focus on breathing in and out. Her heart had joined in with her stomach in her body's rebellion. It squeezed hard, a physical ache that had her pressing her palm to her chest. "Yes, I love you." She hadn't meant to say it, but the words just wouldn't stay inside.

The relief on Ronan's face was undeniable.

"But, Ronan, I can't…" she repeated. *Can't what?* Cassie didn't know. "I'm scared…"

To her surprise, he smiled. "I know." He gave a careless shrug. "So am I. Cassie, I can't predict what will happen next. I can't promise that our life together will be a walk in the park. There are things we both have to work out." He reached out and tucked a lock of hair behind her ear. "It will be like that roller coaster, with hills and dips and unexpected curves. But we'll be together, holding hands. I promise I'll never let you face the world alone again."

Whoosh! Her vision blackened. The roller coaster

inside Cassie's belly teetered for a moment before rushing down the slope, taking her knees out from under her as it went.

"I've got you."

A moment later she was cradled in Ronan's lap on the sofa, her head tucked against his shoulder, his strong arms around her. "Cassie? Cassie?" His tone was becoming frantic.

"I'm okay," she mumbled, blinking up into his concerned gaze.

"I'm taking you to the hospital to get that head checked out. If you do that again, I'm calling an ambulance." But he didn't rise from the sofa or reach for the phone. Instead he held her closer.

Cassie knew her moment of faintness had nothing to do with the bump on her head, but there was no point protesting. She could feel his heart racing against her cheek, fast enough to match her own.

She'd fallen, and he'd caught her. Cassie knew what she was risking in opening her heart to someone. A flash of insight hit, almost blinding in intensity. The sorrow and life-changing grief of losing people she loved had kept her from ever taking that chance again. Even her carefully drawn up plan was merely a delay tactic. There was always something that had to happen before she got to anything remotely involving her emotions—whether it was gaining control of Country Style or something else.

But, she reminded herself, there were so many things she'd missed out on because of her fear. And as she'd learned over her weekend with Ronan, sometimes fear and excitement were two sides of the same coin.

Ronan had come back and apologized. Laid himself bare. Told her he loved her, that he wanted to be with her.

Could she really bring herself to push away the one man she'd ever loved just to stay safe?

It was terrifying as hell, but this time she'd focus on the thrill.

"Ronan?"

"Yes, sweetheart?"

"Can you please not start work on the new division until the deal with Country Style is complete and everything's handed over?"

He shifted against her and she could feel his puzzlement even though she couldn't see his face. "Why?"

"Because I want you to be the one to see it through to the end. You know the people. You'll make sure that they're treated well."

He hesitated but then she felt his chest relax as he heaved a long sigh. "I can do that."

"And, Ronan?"

"Yeah?"

"Can we go to San Francisco? I'd really like to meet your family."

"What about the plane trip?"

Cassie lifted her head to meet his eyes. "If you're with me, I can do anything."

EPILOGUE

"Hartman Designs, Mel speaking." Mel's cheery voice echoed through the small shop. "I'm sorry, Cassie isn't available right now. Can I make an appointment for you or have her return your call?"

Cassie smiled over at Mel. She was saying goodbye to Mrs. Johnston, a new client who'd just hired her to make over her formal dining room. Cassie was excited about the job, and planned to get straight on the phone to Brentons to see if they had any of their wonderful cabinets in stock.

Her smile broadened as a black Porsche pulled into the car space Mrs. Johnston had just vacated. The driver tipped the accelerator before killing the motor and Cassie shook her head in mock chastisement. Her husband's love of sports cars hadn't really come as much of a surprise.

Ronan emerged from the car, his mirrored sunglasses hiding his expression from her. But from the broad smile curving his mouth, it wasn't hard to guess that he was pleased to see her. He leaned over to grab a paper bag and a tray of cups from the backseat before walking over to where she stood in the shop's doorway and planting a solid kiss on her mouth.

"Good afternoon," he said, pulling back, but still standing far too close for Cassie's peace of mind.

"Come inside, it's freezing out there," she scolded, shaking her head at him. "You're letting all the warmth out."

"Yes, ma'am."

Cassie closed the door behind him, hiding her smile.

"Coffee and Danishes," he announced, placing the bounty down on the desk in front of Mel.

"Yummy!" Mel rubbed her hands together. "I was just about to do a coffee run. Thanks, you saved me a dash out into the cold."

Mel no longer used that flirty tone with Ronan, something Cassie was grateful for. But she was also glad that the two of them got along so well. Mel couldn't have been more thrilled when Cassie had broken the news about their relationship. The only thing that had topped it was Cassie's offer of a job after Mel had also become a casualty of the Country Style buyout. She was now Cassie's assistant at the newly established Hartman Designs interior decorating consultancy.

"What brings you here?" Cassie asked Ronan, leaning against her heavy oak desk. "Things a little quiet over at C-CAP?" She deliberately flicked her hair over one shoulder, delighting in the instant darkening of Ronan's eyes. She wore it loose all the time now. Mostly just to see that look in his eyes.

He pursed his lips at her joke. *Quiet* was the last word anyone could use to describe Conroy Corporation Asia Pacific, and Cassie well knew it. Ronan's workload as he hired a new team and set up a new business was matched only by her own.

Cassie had never been happier.

"Yeah, real quiet," Ronan echoed sarcastically. He held up a large FedEx envelope Cassie hadn't noticed he was holding. "Package from Mom."

"Photos?"

"Yep."

"Oh, Cassie," Mel broke in. "Pictures from the wedding?" She was so excited her voice was almost a squeak.

"Yes—she said she'd send them over as soon as the photographer got back to her."

Ronan handed her the envelope and she tipped it up, emptying the contents across her desk.

A small square of heavy cream card stock settled on top and Cassie picked it up first. A note from her new mother-in-law.

Beautiful photos of a beautiful day, it read. *Welcome to the family again, Cassie. Can't wait for our trip Down Under in September to see you again. Take care.*

Cassie hadn't been sure how she'd cope with joining Ronan's family—it had been so long since she'd experienced the complexity of being part of that dynamic. But they hadn't given her a choice. So loving and instantly welcoming, she'd never felt a moment of doubt that they embraced her as one of their own.

"You look gorgeous!" Mel reached for a photo of Ronan and Cassie surrounded by the Conroy family. His mother and father stood beside him, Siobhan had her arm linked through Cassie's. All of them were beaming. "It's just as you described it."

"It was a beautiful day," Cassie said, smiling at the memories. "Carmel is such a sweet place. And the weather was perfect."

Mel picked up another photo, this time of Cassie standing arm in arm with a grinning Graham Taylor. Cassie had sent him a last-minute invitation, a final salve on their mending relationship, even though she'd been sure he wouldn't be able to make it on such short notice. Her surprise and delight when he'd turned up had been genuine.

"Your dress is beautiful. It's just how I pictured it."

A purchase made with Siobhan at a little designer store in San Francisco, it had been done in a hurry— like everything about the whole wedding. When the impulse had struck when they were in California, Ronan's mother had put a halt to their registry-office plans. In a matter of days, she had organized an entire wedding at a gorgeous bed-and-breakfast in Carmel-by-the-Sea, just a few hours' drive south of San Francisco.

Cassie had never dreamed she'd have a day like it. A mother and sister to fuss over her as she got dressed, the man of her dreams waiting for her at the end of the aisle. And then the special surprise Ronan had arranged…

"Wait, is that…" Mel gasped as she flicked to the next photo. Cassie hadn't had a chance to fill Mel in on all the details of their whirlwind trip yet—since she'd got back a few days ago most of their talk had been about work. She hadn't told her about the arrangements Ronan had made.

"Is that *Pete?*"

Mel's jaw dropped in just the same way as Cassie imagined her own must have on her wedding day. She'd been about to walk down the grassy slope that served as her "aisle" with Graham, when a man caught her eye in the gathering.

As if the day wasn't emotional enough already, Cassie's heart had swelled even more as she looked at her brother for the first time in eleven years. She'd blinked hard, desperate to protect the makeup that Siobhan had taken almost an hour to perfect.

After the ceremony and the photos, Ronan had directed her and Pete into a gazebo, giving them time to themselves. Time to talk about their lives and catch up properly. Although they still had a long way to go, it had been an important beginning and it had made Cassie feel a little stronger to have two members of her own family among all of Ronan's, regardless of how welcoming they'd been.

A lump formed in her throat, but she smiled at Mel's wide eyes. "Yes, it's Pete."

"Oh!" Mel's eyes grew bright.

"Don't cry," Cassie warned. "Because if you do, I will."

Ronan threw up his hands at the display of female emotion. "Hope no one wanted the blueberry," he said, backing away to Mel's desk to rummage in the bag of Danishes he'd brought.

"Ronan arranged to fly him over from London,"

Cassie explained to Mel. "He's engaged and doing well. We might go to London in December for his wedding." Ronan shot her a look. Her husband understood how complicated the reunion with her brother was going to be. They'd made a start, but there were years of thorny issues to sort out.

"Oh, that's wonderful," Mel gushed.

It *was* wonderful. Difficult, but wonderful.

Cassie reached for a photo that was still partly hidden and pulled it out. The photographer had caught her and Ronan in a private moment, away from the clamor of family and friends.

Cassie's hair had been caught up on one side with a couple of tiny rosebuds, but otherwise her unruly curls had been tamed into glamorous waves that hung loose down her back.

In the photo, Ronan was pushing a stray curl behind her ear, as Cassie gazed up adoringly at him. Her bouquet was dangling from her hand, almost about to fall, unimportant.

"Can I have this one?" Cassie asked, hearing the thickness in her voice.

"Which one?" Ronan asked, stepping forward.

She held it up to show him.

He nodded. "That's my favorite, too."

They shared a smile, remembering their perfect day and all the other perfect days they'd had since.

Reluctant to break the mood, but aware of Mel's presence, Cassie gave Ronan a look that promised they'd be having yet another perfect evening, later. In return he gave her a slow smile that started up that now-familiar roller coaster inside her.

Cassie walked over to one of her display cabinets, filled with ornaments and trinkets that showed off her unique style for clients who visited the store. There was a silver frame that would fit the picture perfectly and she plucked it off the shelf. In a few deft movements, she had the photo properly displayed.

"There." She gave a satisfied sigh as she placed it on her desk. "Beautiful."

"Beautiful," her husband agreed. He'd stepped up right behind her and swept her curtain of hair back to plant a kiss on her neck.

Cassie could have sworn she heard Mel sigh.

"See you later," Ronan said, after nibbling one more kiss against the sensitive skin under her ear.

"Not too late tonight?" Cassie asked, turning to watch as he made his way to the door. "Someone has to walk Caesar." The elderly chocolate Labrador lying on a pillow behind Cassie's desk raised his head and thumped his tail on the floor at the sound of his name and the word *walk*. The loving, if creaky-kneed, old dog had come from the shelter almost as soon as Ronan had unpacked his cases.

"Not late." He grinned. "I've got an important ap-pointment with my decorator." He gave her a sly wink before he disappeared.

"Cassie, you are the luckiest woman in the world,"

Mel said, collecting up the photos scattered across Cassie's desk.

Cassie sighed. She had to agree.

* * * * *

HEART & HOME

Harlequin®
Super Romance

COMING NEXT MONTH
AVAILABLE APRIL 10, 2012

#1770 THE CALL OF BRAVERY
A Brother's Word
Janice Kay Johnson

#1771 THAT NEW YORK MINUTE
Abby Gaines

#1772 PROTECTING HER SON
Count on a Cop
Joan Kilby

#1773 THE WAY BACK
Stephanie Doyle

#1774 A RARE FIND
School Ties
Tracy Kelleher

#1775 ON HIS HONOR
The MacAllisters
Jean Brashear

HSRCNM0312

REQUEST YOUR FREE BOOKS!
2 FREE NOVELS PLUS 2 FREE GIFTS!

Harlequin®

Super Romance®

Exciting, emotional, unexpected!

YES! Please send me 2 FREE Harlequin® Superromance® novels and my 2 FREE gifts (gifts are worth about $10). After receiving them, if I don't wish to receive any more books, I can return the shipping statement marked "cancel." If I don't cancel, I will receive 6 brand-new novels every month and be billed just $4.69 per book in the U.S. or $5.24 per book in Canada. That's a saving of at least 15% off the cover price! It's quite a bargain! Shipping and handling is just 50¢ per book in the U.S. and 75¢ per book in Canada.* I understand that accepting the 2 free books and gifts places me under no obligation to buy anything. I can always return a shipment and cancel at any time. Even if I never buy another book, the two free books and gifts are mine to keep forever.

135/336 HDN FC6T

Name	(PLEASE PRINT)	

Address		Apt. #

City	State/Prov.	Zip/Postal Code

Signature (if under 18, a parent or guardian must sign)

Mail to the **Reader Service:**
IN U.S.A.: P.O. Box 1867, Buffalo, NY 14240-1867
IN CANADA: P.O. Box 609, Fort Erie, Ontario L2A 5X3

Not valid for current subscribers to Harlequin Superromance books.
**Are you a current subscriber to Harlequin Superromance books
and want to receive the larger-print edition?
Call 1-800-873-8635 or visit www.ReaderService.com.**

* Terms and prices subject to change without notice. Prices do not include applicable taxes. Sales tax applicable in N.Y. Canadian residents will be charged applicable taxes. Offer not valid in Quebec. This offer is limited to one order per household. All orders subject to credit approval. Credit or debit balances in a customer's account(s) may be offset by any other outstanding balance owed by or to the customer. Please allow 4 to 6 weeks for delivery. Offer available while quantities last.

Your Privacy—The Reader Service is committed to protecting your privacy. Our Privacy Policy is available online at www.ReaderService.com or upon request from the Reader Service.

We make a portion of our mailing list available to reputable third parties that offer products we believe may interest you. If you prefer that we not exchange your name with third parties, or if you wish to clarify or modify your communication preferences, please visit us at www.ReaderService.com/consumerschoice or write to us at Reader Service Preference Service, P.O. Box 9062, Buffalo, NY 14269. Include your complete name and address.

HSR11

*Taft Bowman knew he'd ruined any chance he'd had
for happiness with Laura Pendleton when he drove her
away years ago...and into the arms of another man,
thousands of miles away. Now she was back, a widow
with two small children...and despite himself, he was
starting to believe in second chances.*

*Harlequin Special® Edition® presents a new installment
in* USA TODAY *bestselling author
RaeAnne Thayne's miniseries,*
THE COWBOYS OF COLD CREEK.

*Enjoy a sneak peek of
A COLD CREEK REUNION*

Available April 2012 from Harlequin® Special Edition®

A younger woman stood there, and from this distance he
had only a strange impression, as though she was somehow standing on an island of calm amid the chaos of the
scene, the flashing lights of the emergency vehicles, shouts
between his crew members, the excited buzz of the crowd.

And then the woman turned and he just about tripped
over a snaking fire hose somebody shouldn't have left
there.

Laura.

He froze, and for the first time in fifteen years as a fire-
fighter, he forgot about the incident, his mission, just what
the hell he was doing here.

Laura.

Ten years. He hadn't seen her in all that time, since
the week before their wedding when she had given him
back his ring and left town. Not just town. She had left the
whole damn country, as if she couldn't run far enough to

get away from him.

Some part of him desperately wanted to think he had made some kind of mistake. It couldn't be her. That was just some other slender woman with a long sweep of honey-blond hair and big, blue, unforgettable eyes. But no. It was definitely Laura. Sweet and lovely.

Not his.

He was going to have to go over there and talk to her. He didn't want to. He wanted to stand there and pretend he hadn't seen her. But he was the fire chief. He couldn't hide out just because he had a painful history with the daughter of the property owner.

Sometimes he hated his job.

Will Taft and Laura be able to make the years recede...or is the gulf between them too broad to ever cross?

Find out in
A COLD CREEK REUNION
Available April 2012 from Harlequin® Special Edition®
wherever books are sold.

Celebrate the 30th anniversary
of Harlequin® Special Edition® with a bonus story
included in each Special Edition® book in April!